Memories

Miranda closed her eyes and bit her lower lip to keep from crying out. Her skin felt on fire.

"You take my breath away," Adam said. "I've never known a woman as beautiful as you."

They were extravagant words, stored away to be brought out and spoken during moments of passion, no more true than those uttered at the sight of a brand new baby. But she gloried in them. No one had bothered to tell her the tender lies that fed the soul in a long time.

She reached out to him, but pulled back at the last minute. He caught her hand. He was as ready for her as she was for him.

And then she remembered.

Books by Georgia Bockoven

A Marriage of Convenience

The Way It Should Have Been

Moments

Alone in a Crowd

Far From Home

Published by HarperPaperbacks

Far From Home

GEORGIA BOCKOVEN

HarperPaperbacks
A Division of HarperCollinsPublishers

HarperPaperbacks *A Division of* HarperCollins*Publishers*
10 East 53rd Street, New York, N.Y. 10022

Cover illustration by Danilo Ducak

First printing: May 1996

Printed in the United States of America

HarperPaperbacks and colophon are trademarks of HarperCollins*Publishers*

❖ 10 9 8 7 6 5 4 3 2 1

To Martha Sans.
Thank you, dear friend, for your encouragement, your
wisdom, and your love.

Acknowledgments

A big thank you goes to Ken Merrill for reliving a harrowing experience in his own life in order to give the ocean rescue scene in this book its authenticity.

And Janice Sutcliffe-Kaiser—I did what you suggested and you were right. Thanks for the nudge.

As always, Judy Myers came through when I needed answers to detail questions, and Amanda Scott and Deborah Gordon were there when I needed someone to talk to.

Marcy Posner—what a conference call. Thank you for your enthusiasm, your persistence, and your perseverance. I owe you, big time.

For fighting the good fight, providing perspective, and coping with writer's paranoia, I not only owe Mel Berger a great big thank you, but a cellar filled with the world's best Chardonnay.

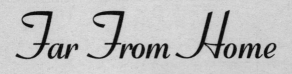

Far From Home

Prologue

—◆—

Suicidal or just plain stupid—Adam Kirkpatric couldn't decide which. Lacking another diversion as his boat rode the swells and he waited for a fish to show interest in his lure, he watched the woman in the bright red jacket. Periodically she inched closer to the edge of the cliff. When it seemed certain the next incoming wave would be the one to crawl up the sheer rock face and snatch her from her perch, she would take a quick step backward. It was almost as if she were challenging the ocean, playing some idiotic game of chance. Someone should have told her how rarely the sea lost such wagers.

When she wasn't tempting fate, she stood motionless, staring at the horizon, her hand raised to hold windswept hair from her face. He was too far away to see her clearly, but in his mind's eye he saw finely sculptured features and a reed-thin body.

She was undoubtedly a tourist, someone unfamiliar with the danger that accompanied the native beauty of the rock-strewn coastline. During the year Adam had lived in Mendocino, he'd learned it was rarely something as simple as a misstep that led to tragedy. It was almost always a case of someone being lulled into turning his or her back to the water by a deceptively calm day. It was at that moment that the ocean rose up to take them. The seventh wave, some called it, the surge of power that lurked unseen until it neared shore and erupted with a force that claimed the unwary.

The inns and hotels scattered along the Northern California shoreline did what they could with circum- spect cautions tucked in the back of vinyl-covered room-service menus or stuffed in a drawer with the stationery, but there was a fine line between giving the guests fair warning and scaring the hell out of them.

The woman in red turned to glance at something behind her. Seconds later she took several long strides parallel to the shore, paused, and returned to her original position. She reminded Adam of his neighbor's cat when it paced the edge of its owner's roof, trying to calculate the exact energy it would need to make the jump down to the deck.

The hair on the back of Adam's neck stood on end. His earlier, flippant thought that she was either stupid or suicidal had been judgmental of her actions, not her motivations. There were a hundred easier ways to end your life. Hell, he could come up with a dozen without even trying. What person in their right mind would—

A chill crawled up his spine. If she were in her right mind would she be standing on the edge of a cliff playing tag with waves powerful enough to knock a train off its tracks?

His imaginings had her near the point of dead

and buried when the real woman turned and walked back toward the highway. It wasn't often he indulged in mind games, but when he did, they took him for one hell of a ride. He dug in his jacket pocket for the apple he'd put there that morning. Seconds later the tip of his pole took a hard dip.

The halibut he brought up was inches short of the two foot limit. He removed the hook, returned the flatfish to the water, and dropped his line again. The weight hit bottom, he reeled in a couple feet of line and sat back to wait for the next strike.

Farther out to sea a commercial fishing boat rode the horizon headed north, its passage marked by a lone white cloud on a field of faded blue. Less than thirty yards away a string of gulls skimmed the water, lazily sharing the morning's gossip as they shopped for a mid-morning snack. There was no fog in sight, something to note in July. It was one of those mornings featured on coffee commercials, the kind that made a shot of caffeine seem redundant.

A large swell rolled under the boat, lifting it. From his new vantage, Adam could see over the cresting waves to the base of the cliffs. The boat had started its slide into the valley on the backside of the swell when something below the cliffs caught his eye—a flash of red in the field of white foam. His mind scrambled to apply logic to the aberration; his stomach did a slow, sickening roll.

"Son of a bitch," he muttered. She must have come back when he wasn't looking. Adam reached for his knife and cut the line.

Going for help was out of the question. If she was still alive now, she wouldn't be by the time he got back.

Not that he was any great bargain. Everything he knew about shoreline rescues he'd learned from tales told over drinks in the bars in Fort Bragg. His choices were limited—he could either make a high-speed run, grab her and hold on until they were clear of the breaking waves, or he could anchor the boat as close as possible and swim in. The run would be quicker, but if the engine sputtered or slowed or caught a piece of kelp and died, he'd never be able to turn the nose back into the waves before being swamped.

If he swam, there'd be no second attempt. Ice was slow melting in these waters; without a wet suit, one time out and back was the most he could hope for.

But if he lost the boat, it would be over for them both.

The choice was made for him.

Adam brought up the anchor, turned to the engine, and gave the rope an adrenaline assisted pull. The motor coughed puffs of blue smoke, caught, choked as if it were about to die, then picked up again. He waited until it settled into its normal dyspeptic rhythm before he removed his Giants baseball cap and shoved it into the tackle box.

As soon as he entered the kelp bed, Adam cut the motor and tied the anchor line to one of the swaying stalks, a trick he'd learned from an abalone diver. He was close enough he didn't have to strain to see the woman anymore.

Toeing off his tennis shoes, he slipped out of his jeans, trading weight and drag for increased exposure. Deciding the life jacket would be more hindrance than help, he took a bracing breath and entered the water. The cold hit with the subtlety of a cornerback going after a wide receiver.

He caught a wave and rode it in, diving under at the last minute to keep from being slammed into the cliffs. Surfacing, he sought his bearings and then the woman. She was less than thirty yards away.

A third of a football field.

His driveway was longer.

The cliffs were higher.

Then what was it about those ninety feet that made them seem more like three miles?

He tried calling to her but his voice was lost in an echoing roar of waves as they struck the cliffs and crashed down again. He was swimming in her direction when he saw her throw an arm in the air, open her mouth in a silent scream and disappear. It was as if an invisible, malevolent hand had risen from the depths to pull her under.

Adam knew it was useless to go after her. Still, it was everything he could do to stop himself. Instead, he waited where he was, fighting the swells and the airborne foam that caught in his throat and stung his eyes as he waited for her to surface again. Time became the enemy; he forced himself to count the seconds . . . one thousand and one . . . one thousand and two . . .

Finally he spotted her. She was behind him now, her eyes closed, blood covering the left side of her face. A spray of water cleared the streaked crimson, but it was no sooner gone than back again.

A wave rolled up to Adam. He cut through it, digging deep, pulling his weight with fear-driven strokes. His mind dictated the rhythm to legs and arms grown numb with cold . . . stroke . . . kick . . . faster . . . harder . . . His fuel was the gut feeling that the next time she went down, she wouldn't come up again.

His arms hit the water like pieces of driftwood; his legs seemed more hindrance than help. Over and over he repeated the cadence, stroke . . . kick . . . faster . . . harder . . .

He glanced up to gauge the distance he'd traveled. Damn it to hell, he wasn't moving—*or she was drifting away from him.*

With a desperate downward stroke of his arms he pulled himself up and half out of the water and turned to find the boat. It had grown soberingly small in the distance. He continued to tread water while an inner voice insisted it was futile to go on. There was no way he could reach her in time. It would be insane to keep trying.

But he couldn't go back without her. It wasn't that he was some kind of hero anxious to march at the head of the parade, it was more that he simply didn't know how to quit. Even when he'd been in Africa working the refugee camps and the food ran out, he'd stayed until the new supplies arrived, held by the belief no one should have to die alone.

A wave crested several yards in front of Adam. Without further conscious thought, he dove and came up swimming—away from the boat.

Adam sat forward on the brown leather sofa listening to unidentifiable sounds coming from the next room. He couldn't remember ever being so tired. In his mind, he paced the long narrow room, stopping to glance out the window, to straighten the Norman Rockwell print he'd hit with his shoulder on the way in, and to clean the sand out of his shorts. But his legs and arms felt weighted, refusing even simple commands.

He leaned farther forward, bracing his elbows on his knees. With impatient, clumsy strokes he tried to wipe fatigue from his eyes. Failing that, he combed his hand through his still damp hair.

The door opened and Vern Lansky came through, without his usual smile. Normally Vern's medical practice ran more to sprained ankles and removing fish hooks than resuscitating half-drowned women. Without saying anything, he closed the door, leaned against it and stuffed his hands into the pockets of his starched smock. His bushy brows drew together in a frown.

"Is she all right?" Adam asked. He'd checked her pulse after he got her in the boat. It had been slow, but steady—not bad for someone who'd been through what she'd been through, or so he'd thought. She was unconscious, but he'd put that off to the bump on her head. There was blood, of course. She had that cut on her scalp and growing up he'd learned from personal experience that head wounds always bled a lot.

"She has a concussion, but as far as I can tell, nothing's ruptured or broken. We won't know for sure, of course, until they get through with her at the hospital."

"You called the ambulance?"

"It's on the way." Vern moved across the room and put his hand on Adam's shoulder. "You okay?"

"Yeah . . . sure. Why wouldn't I be?"

"Oh, no reason, other than you having been the same place she was."

"Big difference—I didn't get there the way she did."

Vern massaged the top of his ear with his thumb and forefinger, a sign Adam had discovered in the year they'd known each other meant something was bothering him. "How much do you know about this woman?"

"Nothing," Adam replied. "I never saw her before today."

"I'm sure you have. You just don't recognize her looking the way she does. Her name's Miranda Dolan. She's been renting that house of mine up in Caspar for about six months now."

Adam tried to place her. He shook his head. Caspar was only six miles or so north of Mendocino, not a town so much as a collection of houses. Most shopping and recreation would have taken her into Fort Bragg. It didn't surprise him their paths hadn't crossed. "I remember a while back you said you had some work you wanted me to do over there. You were going to make a list, but never got back to me." His eyes narrowed in thought. "What's happening here, Vern? What difference does it make whether I know her or not?"

"I was just curious, that's all." As if realizing how ominous his evasion must sound, Vern quickly added, "It's not what you think. She isn't infected with anything contagious, at least nothing I know about."

"So what's eating you?"

"She has these scars . . . on her arm and shoulder and one on her stomach." He cast a hopeful look at Adam. "Did you happen to notice them?"

It was a reasonable question. Fearing hypothermia, Adam had taken her wet clothes off as soon as he got her to the truck. He'd wrapped the blanket he used to cover the seat around her and aimed all the heating vents to her side of the cab. Still, she seemed as cold when he got to Vern's office as she had when he first pulled her out of the water. "All I noticed was how beaten up she looked from hitting the rocks . . . and how skinny she is."

"I could be wrong, but I'd swear the scars are bullet wounds. Someone shot her, Adam, three times, and not all that long ago."

One

Miranda Dolan left her car on Main Street, across from Vern Lansky's office, then cut across Lansing to Little Lake Road. When she'd first arrived in the Mendocino area, determined to start her life again, she'd bought a book on the old mill town with the intention of learning the history and exploring the streets and old Victorian houses. Since then she'd hardly skimmed the book but she'd walked the town late at night after everything was closed and everyone had gone home. In six months she'd come to know the roads and byways of her adopted community; the people were still strangers.

The town itself sat on a high, flat promontory that jutted into the ocean like a fat thumb. A river flowed along the south side depositing sand on the bay where the original settlers had loaded redwood lumber onto ships headed for San Francisco. Here and there were occasional reminders of the town's rowdy beginnings, but, for the most part, it was an artist's community still paying homage to the sixties and specializing in quaint.

Every weekend in the off-season hundreds of tourists braved a treacherous, narrow, two-lane road that hugged the cliffs and mountains of California's north coast to spend two days absorbing what travel writers liked to claim was one of the most beautiful coastlines on earth. In the summer, during peak season, thousands made their way north, the less adventurous taking the faster inland highway, 101.

Forested mountains sat across the two-lane highway from Mendocino. So did Adam Kirkpatric's house. Miranda brushed wheat colored bangs off her forehead as she waited for a string of cars to pass. The highway was busier than usual this time of morning. The road no sooner cleared in one direction and something was coming from the other. She considered going back for her car, but after being cooped up in a hospital for two weeks, it felt too good to be out in the open again.

Instead, she took advantage of the delay to go over her prepared speech. It was important that she sound properly grateful and absolutely sincere, which, considering the circumstances, shouldn't be all that difficult. She was well-practiced at hiding her true feelings. All successful lawyers were.

Why then had she been struggling for the past week to put together the right words for today? Maybe it was that she couldn't comprehend someone purposely risking his life for a stranger, and it was in her nature to question what she didn't understand. Mixed with her admiration for this Adam Kirkpatric, was a strong dose of suspicion.

A motor home crested the small rise to Miranda's left and slowed, creating a break in the traffic. She sprinted across the road, pulling up at the other side with a soft groan when her still-stiff knee threatened to buckle in protest. According to the hospital staff, she was weeks ahead of herself in the recovery process. With the beating she'd taken against the rocks it was amazing she'd escaped with only bruises, a minor concussion, and no broken bones.

Funny how easy it all became when you stopped caring.

After testing her knee, Miranda started walking again, following the directions Vern had given her. Adam Kirkpatric's place was on the third cross street, off Station Lane. Vern had warned her the house sat back in the trees and was hard to see from the road. She was to look for a bright yellow mailbox with Adam's name on it. Somewhere nearby was an over-grown, packed-earth driveway.

She spotted a flash of yellow as soon as she rounded the corner. The ground had been cleared recently, almost as if he'd been expecting her. Peering through the trees, she spotted a corner of the house. It looked normal enough for the area, wood siding, a pipe chimney for a free-standing stove, several stained glass windows and the obligatory deck. The architectural style was one she'd come to think of as retro-California hippie.

Vern had told her she was likely to find Adam this early in the morning in the shop behind the house. She took a shortcut through a tangle of vege-tation and caught the leg of her sweatpants on a rhododendron branch. When she stopped to free her-self she heard the high whine of an electrical saw. At least he was home and she could get the ordeal out of the way.

After checking to see no damage had been done

to her pants and plucking a leaf from her sleeve, she went on. A few seconds later she caught sight of a dark blue pickup truck and then the shop itself. Here the yard was not only cleared of undergrowth, but free of the usual assortment of pine needles, broken branches, and pinecones that littered the nearby forest floor. Giant fuchsias hung from hooks set high on the eaves. The flowers gave her pause. They were an unexpected detail, something that didn't fit the description Vern had given her of Adam Kirkpatric.

Or was it her own idea of what a twenty-nine-year-old handyman would be like that made the flowers seem out of place?

Her gaze shifted to the shop as a man stepped through the door. He was wearing jeans and tennis shoes, but was bare from the waist up. Dappled sunlight accentuated his powerfully muscled chest and arms. His hair was straight and somewhere between dark brown and black; his skin, a Mediterranean bronze. Stepping farther into the yard, he gave several hard shakes to what appeared to be a red T-shirt.

Until now she hadn't understood how he had managed to pull her from the surf single-handedly. But then she'd pictured an average man.

There was nothing average about Adam Kirkpatric.

He was one of those rare male specimens held up by society as the standard by which all other men were judged. In reality, he was as much a genetic anomaly as were fine-boned, six-foot-tall, one-hundred-twenty-pound women. He moved with an athlete's grace and the objective confidence that his body would do whatever was asked of it.

Across the yard Adam held his shirt up and checked to see if any sawdust remained. Satisfied, he pulled it over his head and tucked the tail in his jeans. He reached up to comb his hands through his hair and noticed a woman standing at the edge of the forest. "Can I help you?" he called to her.

She seemed embarrassed at having been discovered. Several seconds passed before she answered. "I'm looking for Adam Kirkpatric."

"You found him," he said and smiled. "What can I do for you?"

"I'm Miranda Dolan."

He looked a little harder, but found nothing familiar. The dry version was decidedly different from the wet. He started toward her. "I thought you weren't due to get out of the hospital for another week."

"I'm a fast healer." Miranda braced her hand against a tree for support and stepped over a fallen branch.

Adam waited, letting her come the rest of the way to him. He detected a slight limp, and as she drew closer, he was able to see traces of green and yellow bruises on her face that she hadn't been able to hide with makeup.

"You look terrific." Nothing like he remembered.

"Thank you. I feel that way, too." She extended her hand.

The formality seemed strangely out of place considering all they'd been through together, but he took her hand, enfolding it between both of his own. "I'm sorry I didn't get in to see you at the hospital. The nurse was a real hardnose about the no visitor thing."

"I'm afraid that was my fault. I didn't feel up to seeing anyone in the beginning and then I guess I just forgot to change the order." She extracted her hand

and slipped it into her pants pocket. "Besides, it wasn't as if you weren't getting daily updates on my progress."

"Who told you that?"

"The nurses. They said there was a mysterious man who called every shift to see how I was doing."

"I don't know about the mysterious part," he said.

"And am I to assume the flowers were from you, too?"

"Guilty."

She didn't smile. "It seems my list of things to thank you for just keeps growing."

Her reaction threw him. "And that upsets you?"

"What?" She seemed honestly confused. "No . . . that's not what I meant at all. I'm sorry if it seemed that way." She offered a tentative smile and hugged herself. "You must think I'm awful. Especially after everything you've done for me."

"Maybe that's what's wrong here. You seem to think you're indebted to me."

"Of course I am," she insisted. "You saved my life."

"Look, there's something we need to get straight between us. I'm no hero. I just happened to be at the right place at the right time. I didn't do anything anyone else wouldn't have done."

"I doubt there's anyone else around here who could have done what you did. Vern told me—"

"There's where you went wrong. Vern loves to tell stories. Trouble is, the more he repeats them, the better they get. He's had a couple of weeks to work on this one. I doubt it's still kissing cousin to the truth."

"So what am I supposed to do, act as though what happened wasn't anything out of the ordinary?" Clearly frustrated she shifted her weight from one foot to the other and then back again. "What's so wrong with me thanking you for saving my life?"

Adam wondered why he didn't believe she was all that grateful. "You're welcome. Now that we're through—"

"That's it?"

"All right, that's obviously not what you wanted to hear, so why don't you tell me what you had in mind?"

"I want . . . I feel I should do something to show my gratitude."

Adam studied her, taking in the nondescript gray sweatpants and jacket and the lack of jewelry even though her ears were pierced. She had a detached look about her that she tried, but failed, to disguise with an egalitarian air. Despite her present appearance, Miranda Dolan was obviously a woman accustomed to a privileged lifestyle. Adam was familiar with the breed; he'd grown up in the herd. A provocative, perverse thought struck. "You could take me out to dinner."

She hesitated just long enough for Adam to see he'd struck a cord. He almost laughed out loud. There was no way in hell she wanted to go out with him. "Well?" he prodded.

"Where would you like to go?"

"I hear they serve great food at the Heritage House." He dropped his gaze in what he hoped was a properly humble fashion. "At least that's what a lot of the people I work for tell me." Actually, the inn and restaurant were old favorites of his family's, introduced to him as a child long before he had sense enough to appreciate either the accommodations or the food.

"Then the Heritage House it is," she said. "Is Friday okay?"

Either she liked challenges, or wasn't the complete social snob he believed. "Yeah, Friday's fine."

"Shall I pick you up?"

"You don't have to do that, I—"

Miranda smiled. It wasn't an expansive smile or the kind that reached her eyes, but it transformed her face. Adam was intrigued at the change.

"Sure, why not?" he said, changing his mind. "Whatever you drive is probably a better ride than my truck."

"I'll see you Friday then." She turned and started back the way she'd come.

"Actually, you'll see me later this morning," he called after her. "I'm scheduled to do some repairs at your place."

She whipped back around. "Since when? I just saw Vern and he didn't say anything about any repairs."

He was caught off guard by her strong, almost panicked reaction. "He probably forgot. If there's a problem with me being there today, I could switch some things around and make it tomorrow."

"It isn't just today, it's any day. I sleep late most mornings."

Vern had warned him this might happen. He'd said Miranda had an almost fanatic insistence on privacy and was something of a recluse. In the six months she'd been renting from him, he'd never driven by the house that her car wasn't in the driveway. The only time he saw her was when she brought the rent check by the office. Even more telling had been the locals' reaction when they heard of her near drowning; not one of them could remember ever seeing her. "I was going to try to get the work done before you came home from the hospital. I figured I had another week."

"So that's why you were always calling to check on me."

She was good at hiding her feelings but not so good he hadn't seen a flicker of disappointment. "I didn't need to call every day to find out when you were coming home. I did that because I was interested."

Miranda tilted her head back and stared up at the sky. "How long will these repairs take?"

"Most of it's small stuff. Shouldn't be more than a day or two, unless I discover there's more than that one patch of shakes that need to be replaced. But I won't know for sure until I get up there and take a look."

"I did have a leak in the kitchen the last time it rained," she admitted.

"And that's not even near where I was going to be working." He was tempted to close the distance between them, but she seemed more comfortable the way they were.

She didn't say anything right away. "What time this morning?"

"Ten thirty? Eleven o'clock?"

Before she could answer, she was distracted by sounds coming from the front of the house. Seconds later, a young woman appeared riding a mountain bike.

"Damn it, Adam—you swore you'd be ready when I got here." She braked to a dusty stop only inches from Adam's feet, leaned over and planted a friendly punch on his arm.

Adam put his hand on the top of her helmet and turned her toward Miranda. "Susan Lansky . . . Miranda Dolan."

Susan shot a look at Miranda, taking her measure. The whole thing happened so fast Miranda wondered if she hadn't imagined it. As it was, she didn't know whether to feel flattered Susan considered her a potential rival for Adam's attention, or depressed she'd been so casually and easily dismissed.

"Gosh, I'm sorry," she said to Miranda. "I didn't know Adam had company. I must've missed your car."

"I walked over from your father's office."

It was as if a lightbulb went off in Susan's head. "Oh, I know who you are. You must be here to thank Adam for saving your life."

"*Susan*," Adam groaned.

Miranda hadn't even known Vern Lansky had a daughter. But then she'd stopped asking people about their children. "Well, that's why I came, but Adam doesn't seem to think what he did was important enough to warrant any special thanks."

"He's like that," Susan said. "You can't let it bother you or you'll go crazy."

"I thought you were going to pick up Jason on your way over here this morning," Adam said to Susan. If he didn't do something to shut her up, she'd be telling Miranda he'd walked on top of the water to rescue her.

"He said he didn't feel like riding today."

"How did he look?" He tried to make the question sound casual, but there was no fooling Susan when it came to his concern about Jason.

Susan leaned back on her seat. "Tired."

"I think I'll go over there before we take off. You can stay here if you want. There's coffee and bagels."

"Yuck—not more of those doughy things you bought in Fort Bragg last week."

Miranda felt as if the circle that had enclosed the three of them had contracted, leaving her on the outside. It wasn't that Adam and Susan had purposely excluded her, more that the subject, this Jason, had taken them another place. Clearly Adam was worried about his friend. Miranda wanted to leave, but was reluctant to break into their conversation to say good-bye.

As if he could sense her discomfort, Adam turned to Miranda. "I'm sorry. I should have offered you coffee, too. You're even welcome to try a bagel, if you're brave enough after Susan's slam."

"Thanks, but I've had breakfast. I should get going anyway. I've been away a long time and have a lot to do this morning." It was a lie, but it sounded convincing, even to her.

"I'll see you later then," he said.

"Nice meeting you," Susan piped in.

"It was nice meeting you, too," Miranda replied automatically and headed down the driveway to the road.

That was the comforting thing about manners, they filled in awkward spaces with empty, socially acceptable words. But manners could only take you so far. It had been a mistake to agree to go to dinner with Adam. After the polite banalities, what would they use to sustain conversation? Instead of a proper thank you, the evening could very well turn into one Adam would be eager to forget.

*   *   *

Miranda leaned over the kitchen sink and nudged the curtains apart with her finger. It was almost a quarter after twelve and no sign of Adam. She wasn't surprised. In the almost eleven months it had taken to build the house in Denver, not one contractor had arrived for an appointment on time. Keith had handled the delays and missed meetings the way he handled everything else, with an annoying forbearance and tolerance.

At times, Keith's seeming indifference to what she considered unprofessional behavior was as frustrating as the contractors themselves. She'd learned her intolerance at her father's knee. She was his favored child, the malleable one, the one who would practice the piano for hours or study into the night to bring home perfect grades because, once in a while, when she worked very hard and he was in just the right mood, he would smile and tell her she'd done a good job—something he never did with any of his other children.

She'd been too young to foresee that the favored state she worked so hard to achieve would leave her the outsider. While her siblings formed what would be lifetime bonds, in her instinct for survival, she chose the wrong side.

Her father wasn't a hard man to please, not when she did what was expected of her. He hadn't smiled at her wedding or when she'd had her daughter, but he'd actually beamed when she graduated law school.

In the beginning Keith's decision to stay home and raise their daughter while Miranda concentrated on her career seemed the perfect solution. Only they'd failed to take into consideration how the unorthodox arrangement would look to others. Over time Keith became an alien being to her law partners, men and women alike, and an outcast in her father's eyes. Their negative attitudes toward him were subtle, but pervasive, and to Miranda's lingering shame, contagious. The gratitude she'd felt in the beginning when Keith moved his office into their home had, over time, insidiously turned into a barely repressed scorn.

She picked up the coffeepot and topped off her cup before wandering back into the living room. On the table was a neatly arranged fan of magazines that she'd been meaning to throw away. Most of them were women's with an assortment of *People* and *Us* thrown in, all were over a year old. They'd come with the house, left behind by previous renters. Some had missing pages, always, it seemed, containing the end of something she was reading, making her wonder if the people who worked in layout departments at the publishers took secret, perverse pleasure in putting recipes and coupons on the backsides of feature articles.

Since living in Mendocino she'd caught up on the lives and loves of everyone from Supreme Court justices to rock stars. She'd learned how to hang wallpaper, fix a leaking toilet and make thirty Christmas presents, each for under ten dollars.

Only there weren't thirty people she wanted to give gifts to anymore. There had been once, but none had been the type to welcome handmade place mats or holiday slippers. Her friends and associates were the small, but tasteful gift types, something along the lines of a Lalique ashtray or a Baccarat paperweight.

This past year Christmas had come and gone without Miranda going near a store. She'd even skipped grocery shopping, emptying the already poorly stocked cupboards in her kitchen, making meals out of popcorn or spoonfuls of peanut butter until all that was left was a can of the anchovies Keith had once used to make Caesar salad.

It wasn't the decorations or the gift baskets or the ends of aisles stacked with cranberry sauce, cans of pumpkin and stuffing that had kept her away from the stores, it was the pervasive good cheer. She couldn't summon responding smiles for the clerks. Even pleasant nods to the people she passed on the streets were beyond her. How could their worlds be so right when hers was so wrong? She didn't want to take their happiness; she would have settled for a feeling of detachment or even a return to the numbness that had gotten her through the first six months. Anything but the unrelenting emptiness.

Not until late at night, long past an hour when the phone might summon her and require she answer in a voice and demeanor that bespoke healing, would she sit in the corner of the green and white sofa where Jenny had loved to curl up and read. Alone in the dark she would listen to the tick of the grandfather clock in the hallway as it echoed her heartbeat. They were the only sounds in a house she'd once complained was too noisy to concentrate on the work she inevitably brought home from the office. The deafening silence exposed the fear that had imprisoned her in a house that guilt would not let her escape.

The memories that haunted her as she moved from room to room were painful, but known quantities. It was fear that had kept her a prisoner in her own house through the holidays. What would she do if she went out into the world again, turned at the end of a store aisle or stepped onto a sidewalk, and caught sight of an eight-year-old girl with golden hair and freckles?

She'd left Denver two days after Christmas. Actually, she hadn't simply left; she'd run away. Before the sun could set one more time with her in the house, she'd gone into the bedroom, grabbed clothes without regard to season or style, stuffed them into a nylon gym bag that had belonged to Keith, and walked out the door.

She could remember little of the trip—a two day layover in Salt Lake City while a blizzard moved through and she waited for the roads to be opened again, a town in Nevada with slot machines in the grocery store, a billboard somewhere in Oregon advertising pre-need funerals. When she arrived in Mendocino mid-January it wasn't a destination, more the end of the road. She'd run out of fuel and the energy to go on at the same time she saw Vern's FOR RENT sign.

The sound of footsteps on the wooden deck snapped her out of her trance. She glanced at the clock before she looked outside. It was twelve-thirty. She was instantly, unreasonably angry. Adam Kirkpatric was either an hour and a half, or two hours, late depending on which arrival estimate she went by. Maybe if she said something, the next person on his list wouldn't have to put up with the—

Good God, what was happening to her? What possible difference did it make what time he arrived? It wasn't as if she had someplace else she had to be or something else she had to do. And why should she care about the other people on his list?

Carrying her coffee with her, she went to the sliding glass door and looked outside. Although he'd changed into a long-sleeved plaid shirt and had his back turned to her, she recognized Adam by his size and thick thatch of dark brown hair. His hands were raised over his head and he was doing something to the beam that supported the deck cover. She looked closer and saw that he was installing a large hook. When he finished, he left and returned a minute later with an enormous fuchsia, covered in red and white flowers. He looped a triangle of wires over the hook, made a couple of adjustments to the loose, flowing branches, and stood back to study his handiwork. Apparently satisfied, he started to walk away.

Miranda slid the door open and called to him. "Hey, wait a minute." She couldn't believe Vern Lansky had included gardening in Adam's work order and was damned if she would pay for something she hadn't requested or approved.

Adam caught himself just as he was about to step onto the gravel path that led around the side of the house. He looked surprised to see her. "I thought you were gone."

"I parked the car around the corner so you could use the driveway."

"Thanks. That'll make it a lot easier to unload the shingles."

"About the plant . . ."

"You like it?"

"That's not the point. What is it doing here?"

"With any luck, feeding some of Anna's hummingbirds. It might take a while to attract them, it's been a while since there was anything around here for them to eat. Don't give up if you don't see any right away."

Now she understood the reasoning behind the flowers around his place. Bird watching didn't fit him somehow. She leaned her shoulder into the door frame and took a sip of coffee. "I take it this wasn't Vern's idea?"

"Does it matter?"

"I didn't think so. Vern strikes me as too pragmatic for something like this."

"Look, it's just a plant. I thought that after all you'd been through lately, you might like the distraction." He hiked his tool belt higher on his hips, took out his hammer and held it suspended in his hand as if anxious to get to the real reason he'd come.

"It was a nice gesture, but—" Why was she making such a big deal out of a plant?

"But?" he prompted.

"Nothing. It was a nice thing to do, that's all. I've never paid much attention to things like hummingbirds. Who knows, it might be kind of fun. Thank you for thinking of it."

"You're welcome."

She straightened. "Well, I suppose I should go inside and let you get to work."

"When you went back to get your car this morning did Vern happen to say anything about replacing those sprinkler heads out front?"

"He said there were some things he wanted to go over with me, but before he had a chance a woman came in to get her hand stitched. I waited around for a while but then another patient arrived so I left a message with his nurse that I'd see him later." Why had she rattled on like that when a simple, no, would have done?

"He was also supposed to ask you if you had anything else around here you wanted to add to the list."

"You mean besides the leak in the kitchen?" There was a window that wouldn't lock in the bathroom and the fireplace didn't always draw properly, but she'd rather put up with the inconvenience than the disruption of having Adam around.

"When you first took this place Vern must have explained that he doesn't usually rent by the month. Mostly it's a Friday, Saturday, Sunday kind of thing— which gives me plenty of time to get in and out to take care of whatever needs to be done without disturbing anyone."

She didn't want him to see how much the thought of having him around bothered her. He wouldn't understand that her normal routine was to walk half the night and sleep through the day and she wasn't about to explain. "I've only been here six months. If you kept up with everything before then, I can't see how there can be all that much to do now."

"Why don't I get the list Vern gave me so you can see what's on there for yourself? If there's something that can be put off, then I'll wait until—"

"I've moved on?" She resented the natural conclusion even if it did make sense. She was paying an exorbitant rent for a vacation house and should be able to find something a lot cheaper if she intended to stay in the area.

"Until you plan to be out for the day."

Miranda walked to the edge of the deck and tossed her now-cold coffee onto the lawn. She put her cup on the railing and fixed her gaze on the bank of fog sitting offshore. To continue fighting him would be too obvious. "Do what you have to do."

Two

A clanking noise broke the stillness as Jason Delponte wheeled a gas barbecue across a flagstone patio. He stopped, checked overhead for low branches and then pushed the cart forward another three feet. With the flat of his hand, he wiped a thin, nearly invisible layer of dust from the shiny black enamel dome.

"Are you sure you're up to having a dozen people over here tonight?" Adam asked. It wasn't the work involved that concerned Adam as much as the possibility one of those twelve people had some germ they would pass on to Jason.

"You promised you wouldn't do that," Jason said with barely suppressed annoyance. "I told you I only begged off the bike ride with you and Susan this morning because I wanted to work on the new painting."

Adam would have liked to remind Jason that he, too, had made a promise—to keep up with his exercise. But he refrained, knowing it would take a little of the glow off an evening Jason had been looking forward to for weeks. He opened the ice chest and took out a beer. "You want one?" he asked Jason.

"I'm sticking to Pelligrino tonight. The best and the brightest are going to be here,"—he stopped to glance at his watch— "in less than an hour and I don't want to miss anything."

"Did you ever hear from Rhonda?" Rhonda Underkoffler was the grande dame of the art world in their extended coastal community, invited to every party but showing up at so few it was not only considered a personal coup, but a social triumph to have her in attendance. Having Adam as a guest at a gathering of artists was at the other end of the social triumph scale. He wasn't exactly a liability for Jason, but he was a long way from being an asset.

Through loyalty, or simple stubbornness, when he'd arrived in Mendocino, Jason had insisted his artist friends treat Adam with the same deference they treated everyone in their inner circle, even though Adam lacked the most basic credential for such acceptance.

Jason tried, but couldn't contain an exultant smile at Adam's question. "She called yesterday."

"And?"

"She's coming." The smile grew until it lit up his face. "And she's bringing John Sidney."

The gleeful way Jason had told him let Adam know he was supposed to be impressed. "That's great," he said with what he hoped was a proper show of enthusiasm.

Jason laughed. "Are you attempting to convince me you actually know who he is?"

"He's an artist," Adam ventured.

"He's a critic," Jason corrected.

"I'm not even going to try to understand you people anymore. Isn't asking a critic to show up at a party with a bunch of artists a little like throwing the lion in with the lambs?"

Jason considered Adam's question. "I guess each of us is convinced it'll be some other lamb on his menu."

"Do you know how sick that sounds?"

"Yes, I suppose I do," Jason admitted with a laugh.

"Then why would you—"

"I thought you said you were going to give up trying to understand people like us."

"Indulge me this one last time."

"I can only speak for myself, of course, but I suppose it's as much the stimulation of being around power as it is knowing how dangerous that power can be. Let's face it, most artists lead incredibly boring lives. You can hardly blame us for wanting to take an occasional walk on the wild side."

One of the things Adam liked best about Jason was his willingness to cut through the bullshit. Which, Adam supposed, was one of the reasons Jason was so adamant about accepting responsibility for what was happening to him now.

Jason bent, picked up a pinecone and tossed it into the trees. As if he'd been tuned into Adam's thoughts, he followed their path, only out loud. "Isn't it amazing how we're all born knowing there are only so many minutes in the hourglass we're given and yet we go through life acting as if we'll find a way to beat the system, that somehow at the last minute some mystical being is going to come along and give us one more scoop of sand."

At night, when Adam couldn't sleep, he would try, but had never been able to imagine with any real understanding what it must be like to know that instead of the forty or fifty years Jason should have ahead of him, there could be as few as two or three. Not even the seemingly casual attitude toward life Adam had witnessed in the third world countries where he'd lived and traveled had prepared him for the witnessing of the certain, inescapable death of his best friend.

"God, what I wouldn't give to have just one week of that kind of naiveté again," Jason went on. "Now it seems I'm either scared shitless or just plain weary of thinking about it. There's nothing in between, there isn't a minute where I can hear about someone working on a book and not wonder whether I'll be around to read it, or see something I want to paint and not wonder if I'll have enough time."

"Jason—where are you?" came a shout from inside the house.

"Ah, the ever-punctual Susan," Jason said with instant good humor. "We're out here."

"You invited Susan?" Adam made no attempt to hide his surprise.

"Not invited, hired."

Before Adam could say anything more, Susan came to the back door, slid open the screen, and threw her arms wide. "So, what do you think?" she asked. "Pretty outstanding, huh?"

Her black, mid-thigh dress hugged her breasts and buttocks with the enthusiasm of an adolescent lover. There was a small ruffled apron around her waist, worn more for show than function. Black stockings, and heels so high they made her look as if she were standing on point, completed the outfit.

"That's quite a rig," Adam acknowledged.

The comment brought an abbreviated bow and flirtatious wink. "It's your turn, Jason."

He took his time answering. "I can honestly say I've never been to a party where the help outshone the guests, but then I admit I run with a pretty staid crowd."

With hands propped on her narrow hips, she glanced down at herself. "You think it's too much? Should I trash the apron?"

"No," Jason answered, almost too quickly. "The apron's perfect. Leave it."

She grinned. "I thought it added something. Besides, I don't want anyone mistaking me for one of the guests." An exaggerated shudder accompanied the statement.

"Where did you come up with the idea?" Jason asked.

"I saw it on an old movie, only the skirt was shorter and real full. It had tons of starchy white stuff underneath."

Adam took a swig of beer to drown the laugh he felt building. "Are you sure your feet are going to make it in those shoes?"

"You don't wear heels like these because they're comfortable." After making a slow, pivoting turn, she stopped and looked at him over her shoulder. "Any more questions?"

Adam put his hands up in surrender. "Not from me."

"I came early so you could show me what to do," she said to Jason.

"Come with me." Jason led her into the house, casting a beleaguered look at Adam before he closed the screen. "About ten minutes before the guests

arrive, I want you to take the hot hors d'oeuvres out
of the refrigerator and put them in the oven . . . "
His voice was lost as they moved deeper into the
kitchen.

Adam got up and moved to the edge of the patio,
attracted by a gray squirrel's contortionist attempt to
gain access to a bird feeder. This was going to be a
night to remember, but not entirely for the reason
Jason had planned. A Steller's Jay sat on a nearby
limb, screeching its disapproval. The squirrel went
about its business, oblivious to the jay's protest.

He understood what it felt like to be ignored.
He'd suffered the same treatment from Miranda
Dolan that day. After her brief appearance and peculiar reaction to the fuchsia, she'd gone into the house
and hadn't come back out again during the four
hours he'd been there.

She wasn't like anyone Adam had ever known,
and he'd known a lot of people. He was curious to see
if she would show up for their date on Friday. For
someone obviously determined to keep her own
company, going somewhere as public as a restaurant
would be a dramatic departure, especially with the
local handyman in tow. But then she believed she
owed him something, and despite the superficial way
he'd chosen to let her pay her supposed debt, he had
a feeling she would do whatever necessary to clear
the slate.

For all her mystery, there was a part of Miranda
that Adam knew as well as he knew himself. From
the clues he'd gathered so far, he was already sure of
one thing. He'd been raised in a world much like the
one she'd left, an environment where unspoken but
implicit rules provided the structure, a society where

everyone recognized and accepted their place. To do otherwise was to risk ostracism.

Somehow, something in that world had gone wrong for Miranda. Terribly wrong if Vern had it right and the scars marring that otherwise unblemished ivory skin were, indeed, from bullet wounds.

"Tell me what made me think hiring Susan to help out tonight was a good idea," Jason said, coming up behind Adam.

He knew Jason didn't expect an answer but Adam gave him one anyway. "Maybe you thought she could use the money for school."

"Yeah, right—with her father owning half the property between here and Fort Bragg. He could put her on the ten-year plan through Vassar and it wouldn't make a dent in his bank account."

Adam put his hand on Jason's shoulder and guided him to a chair. "All you have to do is keep her out of the way until everyone arrives. Get a couple of drinks down them and then casually ask if anyone knows anything about the report that Picasso faked his own death and is still painting somewhere in the South Pacific. After that you could have a gorilla serving drinks and no one would notice."

"You missed your calling, Adam. You should be working for the tabloids."

"Just trying to help out."

Jason waved his hand. "I'm already past how she looks, anyway."

Adam was sure he didn't want to hear the answer, but couldn't resist asking, "Now what's she done?"

"She insisted I take the grapes off the fruit tray. According to our newly-spawned little activist, they remain politically incorrect."

Adam smiled. He liked Susan. She was bright and articulate and had a wonderful, off-center, eighteen-year-old way of looking at things. She gave a touch of whimsy to Jason's world, something he desperately needed and that Adam was incapable of providing.

"She's right, you know. The pesticides the growers—"

"Please, I've already heard all about it. The grapes are history and the tray looks like hell, but who cares? I'll just keep reminding myself no one comes to these things for the food."

"I do," Adam said.

"Since you aren't remotely like any other human being on this planet, you don't count." Jason stood up, shoved his hand in his pocket, pulled out a box of matches and began lighting the citronella candles.

Jason's statement wasn't an insult, it was one of his ass-backward, off-the-wall compliments. "What can I do to help?" Adam asked.

"Nothing, you're a guest."

Adam laughed. "Since when?"

"Ouch, damn it." Jason dropped the match he'd been holding. "I *always* burn myself when I light these things. It's as if I had it in my head that matches were rare or something." He stepped on the still burning sliver of wood.

"Here," Adam said, "let me." He reached for the box. "I don't have that problem."

Jason closed his hand around the box. "You already do too much for me—none of it necessary. At least not yet."

"Lighting a couple of candles is not that big a deal, Jason." But Adam backed off. They had an agreement that as long as possible, Jason was on his own. There were times, like now, when simple courtesy was misinterpreted as interference, and it would probably stay that way until Jason stopped being so damned grateful Adam had moved to Mendocino to be with him.

Adam picked up his beer and wandered over to the totem pole he'd given Jason as a gift when he graduated from art school. He'd brought the fierce looking piece with him on his way home from a year working the ships and canneries in Alaska, presenting it and himself at Jason's parents' home in Hillsborough, crashing Jason's mother's annual charity lawn party.

He and Jason only saw each other a half dozen times after that, always when Adam was on the move again and had stopped in San Francisco to visit his mother. His constant traveling was a source of frustration for his mother and a puzzle to his friends. He never bothered to explain the reason he'd become a roamer, believing it too personal to share and chance someone not understanding. It was simply the way he lived, or at least the way he'd lived until he moved to Mendocino.

Adam stretched his arms overhead, dropped them to his sides and rolled his shoulders. "Would you mind if I cut out early tonight?"

Jason looked surprised. "Something wrong?"

"It's been a long day."

"Long or frustrating?"

Adam cocked an eyebrow in question. "What makes you ask that?"

"I understand the inscrutable Ms. Dolan isn't what you expected."

"Who told you—never mind, I can guess." Susan

had been at it again. He wouldn't be surprised if the entire town knew Miranda had dropped by his house that morning. There were times he regretted letting her join him and Jason on their morning ride, but most of the time she was good company for the two of them. And, as she frequently pointed out, they were lucky to have an athlete of her caliber to train with.

Jason pulled a chair from under the table, straddled it and leaned his arms across the back. "So, give. What's she like?"

"Different," Adam said.

"Obviously, but how so?"

"I haven't figured it out yet."

"What does she look like? Would you have recognized her if she hadn't told you who she was?"

"Not in a million years. Her hair's a lot lighter than I thought, kind of halfway between blond and brown. She still has a few bruises, but her face isn't swollen anymore, or at least not as bad as it was." He stopped and thought how wary she'd been of him and how that had made him feel. It was something he didn't understand and couldn't explain. "She's pretty in a tight-ass kind of way, but much too skinny. The sweats she had on this morning actually hung on her."

"Remember, she's been living on hospital food for the last two weeks."

"She's not just skinny, Jason, she's emaciated."

"Interesting. Self induced, you think?"

"God, I don't know. That never even occurred to me."

"Well, bring her by some time and I'll do what I can to fatten her up."

"We're going out to dinner Friday but I have a feeling it'll be the first and last time."

"I take it you're not her type?"

Adam walked over to the plastic garbage can and tossed his empty bottle inside. "Not even close. Actually, right now I don't think anyone is her type."

"I admit I'm particular," Susan said from behind the screen door, "but I'm not about to sit at home waiting for the perfect guy to come along. Life's short. You gotta grab a little lovin' while the grabbin's good."

"My sentiments exactly," Jason said.

Susan came outside. "So if it wasn't me you were talking about, who was it?"

"It's not polite to eavesdrop," Adam told her.

"If I'd been eavesdropping, I wouldn't have to ask who you were talking about," she said.

Jason stood, swung the chair back around and slid it under the table. "Did you finish the trays?"

Susan came outside. "You're changing the subject."

"Which should give you a pretty strong clue that I'm not going to tell you what you want to know," Jason said.

"Yes, I finished the trays. And I put the salmon in the marinade. I even unloaded the dishwasher."

"Then you've done all there is to do for now," Jason said. "You might as well stay out here with us until people start coming."

"Is that kind of thing allowed?" She adjusted her apron and patted her close-cropped hair. "I mean isn't there some unwritten rule somewhere about the help fraternizing with the boss?"

"You're right," Jason said and slapped his hand to his forehead. "How could I have forgotten something so basic?"

"You're really good at this," Adam told her. "Maybe you should rethink college."

She gave him a dirty look. "You have something against college-educated domestic help?"

"She got you," Jason said.

"Come here and sit down next to me for a minute." Adam moved to give her room. "I promised Matt I would talk to you about—"

"I don't want to hear anything Matt has to say." She crossed her arms over her chest.

"Not even that he's sorry about the other night?"

Her eyes widened. "He told you what happened?"

"He didn't tell me any of the details, only that you'd had a fight and that you wouldn't let him apologize."

"He can apologize all he wants, it's not going to do him a damn bit of good. I'm never going to forgive him. Not this time."

"Not ever?" Jason asked, clearly startled at the force of her declaration.

"You don't know what he did."

Adam had been privy to the volatile relationship between Susan and Matt from the first day he'd arrived in Mendocino. He'd stopped by Jason's studio to pick up the keys to the house he'd rented and overheard Susan using her private lesson time to relate the latest battle between her and Matt. She'd stopped the telling long enough for Jason to introduce them, then went on with her story as if Adam were an old friend. Since then Adam had been included in every up and down of the roller-coaster relationship. He'd heard Susan express volumes of anger, but never the sharp edge of pain the way she did now.

"Do you want to talk about it?" Adam asked.

She shook her head. "Huh uh."

Jason and Adam exchanged glances. "We're here when you're ready," Jason said.

"I know." She shifted her weight onto one foot and brought the other back until her heel rested on the tip of the spiked heel. "I can always count on you two."

"What do you want me to tell Matt?" Adam asked. "He said he would call tomorrow after work."

"Tell him I said to leave you alone. This is between him and me and I don't want you guys involved."

The doorbell rang. "I'll get it," Susan said when Jason started across the patio. She gave her skirt a hard tug, lowering it all of a quarter inch. Before she left, she flashed an impish grin and it was as if all was right in her world again.

"Did you see that?" Jason asked Adam when she was gone.

"Amazing, huh?"

Jason continued to stare at the door Susan had gone through. "If you had asked me ten minutes ago, I would have told you Susan could no more hide what she was feeling than she could actually break up with Matt."

"What do you suppose he did?"

Before Jason could answer, Susan was back with Bob Terrill, the owner of a local art gallery. She asked Bob what he would like to drink and turned the job of bartending over to Adam when she heard the doorbell ring again.

Adam stepped behind the portable bar to fix Bob a gin and tonic and get another beer for himself out of the cooler. There was no way he could just disappear from the party now without being obvious. If he stuck around until after dinner and tried to leave then, he took the chance of starting an exodus.

Staying there was probably for the best anyway. He had no business driving by Miranda's house to check on her. She'd made it clear she wasn't interested in having anything to do with him.

Nice lecture. Too bad he wasn't the type to listen to lectures.

Miranda grabbed her jacket off the back of the tweed-covered recliner. Even though the sun wouldn't be down for another half hour, she could no longer fight a gnawing restlessness that made it impossible for her to stay inside.

After looking out the window to see that no one was on the path that ran behind the house, she opened the sliding glass door and stepped out onto the deck.

Fog sat in the distance, covering the ocean like a thick feather comforter. It would be cold and damp in an hour or two; not even the heartiest of tourists would be on the trails. She would have the night to herself.

As if verifying her prediction, a sudden gust of wind swept in, sending the neighbor's outdoor chimes into melodious discord. Since coming west she'd discovered certain items were de rigueur on the outside of homes in coastal communities. At least one set of chimes, a few pieces of twisted and bleached driftwood and an assortment of abalone shells. The shells could be nailed to fence posts or garage doors or arranged in baskets by the front door, the method of display was left to the discretion of the homeowner. Her lack of participation in the code marked her an outsider as clearly as the Colorado plates on her car.

The wind picked up, tugging strands of hair from her ponytail. She shivered and brought her jacket up to slip it on but then let it drop back to her side. It wasn't often things penetrated anymore, not even simple things like hot and cold.

She knew what she was doing was dangerous. It wasn't possible for her to pick and choose what she felt. If she allowed one emotion or sensation to slip in, how would she keep others from following?

But it was so good to feel something, anything besides the constant, aching emptiness, that she couldn't resist. She closed her eyes, stayed very still and let the crisp, damp air swirl around her. Time passed. The sun disappeared. The fog crept toward shore.

She moved onto the grass.

The mist on her face reminded her of snow.

How Jennifer had loved the snow . . . she would stand at the front room window for hours, her gaze lifted to the sky. By the time the storm had moved on, the glass would be covered with finger and nose and cheek prints.

The jacket slipped from Miranda's grasp as she brought her hand up to touch her mind's image of the glass; to run her fingers across the simple houses and stick figures and boxes Jennifer had drawn in the fog created by her breath. She traced the flowers and hearts and felt her heart break with regret as she heard her own voice chastising a little girl whose only crime was being a child.

To keep her teeth from chattering, she clamped her jaw. To keep tears from escaping, she held her eyes tightly closed.

She couldn't remember ever being so cold. Not even when she'd been in the water. But it wasn't the cold she'd been thinking of then.

It must be possible to be colder yet. She was still standing; her mind still functioned. A long time ago she remembered reading that just before someone froze to death they experienced a sense of peace. She'd always wondered about stories like that. Who told them?

"Are you all right?" a male voice asked.

The question shattered Miranda's emotional cocoon. She reacted instinctively, jumping backward in alarm. Her foot caught in a tuft of grass and she lost her balance.

"It's me—Adam." He caught one arm and then the other. Instead of letting go when she was steady again, he held her hands close to his chest. "I'm sorry I scared you."

Miranda reared back and tried to free herself but his grip was too sure. "What are you doing here?"

"I was driving by, and saw you standing outside all alone, and I thought . . . " He relaxed his hands and then released her. "I don't know what I thought."

"You're trespassing. You have no right to be here."

"I got home and realized I didn't have my drill. I thought maybe I'd left it on the deck after I put up the fuchsia." Before she could respond, he asked again, "Are you all right?"

There was concern and confusion in his eyes. He

was only trying to help her. It was the last thing she wanted from him. "How I am is none of your business."

"True." He picked up her jacket and put it around her shoulders. "But I'm not the kind of person who lets something like that get in his way."

The cold had finally penetrated, and to her frustration, she began to shake. She pulled the jacket closer. "I'm going inside." She meant it to be a dismissal.

He nodded. "I'll see you in the morning, then."

"The morning?"

"I still have a couple days work to finish around here."

With sudden clarity she understood something about Adam Kirkpatric. He wasn't the occasional salesman she could turn away or the meter reader who walked into her sphere and out again without a backward glance. He wanted something from her.

He seemed such a clever young man. Why couldn't he see she had nothing to give?

Three

"I didn't think you'd come," Adam said.

"A deal's a deal." Miranda opened the napkin and laid it across her lap. She glanced out the window at a seagull making a slow, swooping landing on the broad expanse of lawn. Two hundred yards in the distance she could see waves silently hitting the cliffs in the small cove. Inside, there was the occasional clink of cutlery and an unobtrusive recording of a string quartet. The restaurant was old and meticulously maintained with a view that belonged on the cover of a chamber of commerce brochure.

"You know, if you bend just a little, you might actually have a good time."

He was trying, she had to give him that much. "I'm here to pay a debt, not have a good time."

Adam stared at her long and hard. "I absolve you of your debt. Now, would you like to leave?"

It wasn't anger she heard so much as defeat. The realization stung. She'd been behaving abominably since picking him up. "No," she said contritely.

Adam dropped his gaze to the menu. "If you like seafood, the scallops in white wine are the best I've had anywhere."

He was quick to forgive. She liked that. "You've eaten here before, I take it."

"I've been here a few times," he admitted.

"Somehow I got the impression—never mind, it's not important." He certainly fit in, something she realized she hadn't expected until she picked him up and saw how he was dressed. The tailored blue sport coat, Ralph Lauren shirt, khaki slacks and loafers hid all signs of the rough-around-the-edges, hammer-wielding handyman. He could have passed for one of the law clerks in her office. She picked up her own menu and gave it a quick perusal looking for something she could get down without too much effort.

"What would you suggest for someone who prefers beef?"

"Sorry, you're on your own."

"One of those, huh?" She came from cattle country and was always a little bemused by people who lived by the latest medical bulletin.

"If by 'one of those' you mean I'm someone who likes seafood, you're right." The sommelier approached and handed Adam a leather-bound wine list.

"Would you like me to make the selection?" Miranda asked. Sommeliers had a tendency to treat the uneducated like philistines. While she wasn't a connoisseur, she knew enough not to be intimidated.

Adam handed her the list. "Please. I know what I like, but the selection here is—"

"Do you have a preference?" When he didn't immediately answer, she added, "Red or white?"

The corner of his mouth drew up in an indulgent smile. "Oh, it doesn't matter. One goes down as easy as the other."

The sommelier give Adam a puzzled look.

"Caymus Vineyards produces some outstanding Cabernet Sauvignons," she said spotting a familiar name. "And there are a couple of Clos du Bois Chardonnays that are truly wonderful." She set the list aside. Clifford would be proud of her, she'd remembered his lesson on the best of California wines, something he frequently stressed that all the partners should know. "So I guess it comes down to which would go better with our choices for dinner."

"And that would be?" the sommelier questioned.

"I'll be having the pork tenderloin," Miranda said.

He turned to Adam. "And you, Mr. Kirkpatric?"

"I was thinking about going with the calamari . . ." It was as much a question as a statement.

After a slight hesitation, the sommelier said, "May I suggest the sea bass, or perhaps the salmon?"

"The salmon it is."

He nodded and turned his attention to Miranda. "Will you be going with the Chardonnay then?"

"Yes," Miranda told him.

"And may I be allowed to make the selection for you?"

"That would be fine."

When he was gone, she questioned Adam. "A friend of yours?"

"More my father's actually. They were in business together several years ago."

"You're from around here then?"

"San Francisco. At least originally."

"And since?"

"No place in particular." He took a drink of water. "I move around a lot. What about you?"

"What about me?"

"Where did you live before you came here?"

She didn't want to talk about herself, but sometimes it was easier to give answers than sidestep the questions. "My home is in Denver."

"A beautiful city, or so I hear. I haven't made it there yet, but it's on my list."

The sommelier returned, showed the bottle to Miranda, uncorked it and laid the cork on the table. This was the part she hated. She brought the cork to her nose and inhaled. According to Clifford, as long as there was no sour smell, it wasn't necessary for her to say anything, she just returned the cork to the table. As soon as she did so, the sommelier poured a small amount of wine into the glass with the smaller bowl. She lifted the glass, swirled the light gold liquid, sniffed and tasted.

"It's fine," she said.

He filled her glass halfway and then Adam's. Instead of leaving right away, he waited until Adam had also tasted the wine and given a far more enthusiastic approval.

"I guess he wanted a second opinion," she said.

"I think it was more a matter of showing off a little," Adam told her. "The wine is from the restaurant's private reserve."

She felt as if she'd been chastised, gently to be sure, but he'd made his point. "You said he was in business with your father—what kind of business?"

"They owned a winery."

The waiter came and took their order. When they

were alone again, Miranda asked, "I take it the venture into winemaking wasn't successful?" She wasn't really interested, but it would keep the conversation going for a while.

"I don't know if he made any money, but my father always claimed it was the best investment he ever made. I believe David feels the same."

"Then what is he doing working here?" None of what he was telling her made sense.

"I've never asked him, but if I were to hazard a guess, I'd say it's because he likes being around people."

"But as a waiter?"

"A sommelier," Adam corrected. "You live by some pretty rigid guidelines. You need to loosen up a bit."

The criticism instantly put her on the defensive. "I've done all right for myself."

"Have you?"

"Why is it you have this compelling need to pry into my life?"

He considered her statement. "I suppose with all that's happened, I can understand how you might think that."

"Are you telling me I'm wrong?"

"I admit I'm curious how you came to be in Mendocino."

"By car."

Their salads arrived. The waiter lingered to offer fresh-ground pepper. As soon as they were alone again, Adam picked up where he'd left off. "You said your home was Denver, but you've been in California several months."

"Have I?" She nudged a piece of endive to the side.

Adam sat back in his chair. "All right. You win."

"Meaning?"

"No more questions."

"Then I have one for you. What were you really doing at my house the night before last? And don't give me that crap about looking for your drill."

"I was on my way home from a party and happened by."

"No one happens by Royce Circle, it's one of the reasons I rented there."

He took a slice of the thick sourdough bread and broke off a piece. "I was concerned about you."

"I don't want your concern. What do I have to do to convince you of that?" She didn't wait for an answer. "In a day or two you'll be finished working on the house. After that I don't want to see you there again." The statement sounded colder than she'd intended.

"Why is it so hard for you to accept someone caring about you?"

She gave up pretending to eat. "You don't care about me. I'm a curiosity. As soon as you find out whatever it is you want to know, you'll move on to something or someone else."

"If that's true, it seems you've come up with the perfect way to get rid of me."

A busboy came to clear their salad plates.

"My privacy isn't a bargaining chip," she said.

"Then what about a trade? I'll tell you something about me, and—"

"There isn't anything I want to know about you."

"What if I tell you anyway?"

At the rate they were being served, they still had a half hour before dinner would be over, an hour if they had dessert. Passed in silence it would seem twice as long. "Go ahead. But I won't change my mind."

"I'm twenty-nine."

"I already know that."

"Oh?"

He'd caught her. "Vern told me."

"Because you asked?" Adam wasn't going to let her off that easily.

"He likes to talk."

"You didn't answer my question."

"I thought it might be helpful to know something about you before I went to your house." She wasn't used to being the one interrogated and didn't care for the feeling. "I thought this was your show."

He pushed his chair back a little to give himself more room. "I left Stanford my sophomore year."

The caliber of the school surprised her more than his leaving. "Why?"

There must have been something in the way she looked or the tone of her voice, because he smiled knowingly at her response. "I was in the middle of a lecture on the manipulation of middle management and couldn't figure out a reason I should give a damn."

"I take it you've never gone back?"

"I've thought about it," he admitted, "but can't come up with a reason that makes the effort worth the degree."

"Surely you don't want to be a handyman all your life." It wasn't until she spoke the words out loud that she realized how demeaning they sounded. But that didn't mean they were any less true.

"Why not?" he asked. "It fits my lifestyle perfectly. I can get a job wherever I go and know that what I do is necessary and appreciated."

"It's a dead-end job. You'll never go anywhere."
She'd met men like Adam, had even married one, but
she'd never understood them. Anyone who could get
into Stanford could have a career. "Don't you have
any ambition to better yourself?"

He laughed. "What could be better than freedom?"

"Freedom from what?"

"From dying of a heart attack at fifty-two without
ever having seen a sunset in the Himalayas or a black
sand beach."

"It's a hell of a lot better than living a day-to-
day life without challenge all those years. There
are videos of sunsets and travel magazines with
beautiful glossy pictures of both black and white
beaches."

"What about the people you'd miss meeting?"

"People are the same everywhere." But that
wasn't true. Adam Kirkpatric was different. There
were things about him she recognized, but not many.
But then he wasn't the kind of person she would
have had any reason to be around before she'd come
to California. Her social scale hadn't been that broad
or egalitarian. "It just seems that ten years is a long
time to put your life on hold. When you finally do get
around to settling down you're going to find it's too
late to get anywhere."

"That isn't something I have to worry about."

Normally she liked confident attitudes; Adam's
she found irritating. It was as if he were dismissing
everything she'd worked so hard to achieve by making it seem something he could do at will. She picked
up her wine and was startled to realize she could
actually taste it and that it was truly wonderful.

He went back to eating, filling his fork with the

rice pilaf. Before taking another bite, he looked over to her plate. "The tenderloin isn't what you expected?"

"What?"

"You're not eating."

He'd obviously decided to stage a retreat. "I guess I wasn't very hungry."

"Too bad. The desserts here are the best I've had anywhere."

"That's what you said about the scallops." Was this really her, teasing him? She didn't recognize herself. But which self? Hadn't she been this way once, a long time ago?

"But not the pork," he reminded her.

"The pork is wonderful." What was it about him that made her so defensive? Miranda looked up and saw a young man in an athletic jacket headed toward them. He stopped beside Adam and stood quietly, waiting to be noticed. "I think someone wants to talk to you," she said.

Adam turned in his seat. "Matt—I didn't see you come in. Are you here with Susan?"

He came closer, nodding to Miranda, but focusing on Adam. "I'm sorry for butting in on you like this, Adam, but it's kind of important. I'm afraid if I don't find some way to stop her, Susan is gonna do something really stupid."

"Sit down, Matt." Adam indicated the chair beside him.

He dropped into the seat. "I've tried every way I know but she won't listen to me. I'm goin' outta my mind."

Adam looked over to Miranda. "Miranda, I'd like you to meet Matt Foster. Matt, this is Miranda Dolan."

Matt sat up straighter and offered his hand over the table, suddenly interested in something besides his own problem. "You're the one Adam pulled out of the surf."

"That's me," Miranda said.

"Man, were you lucky it was him and not one of the weekenders out there fishing."

"You said you were afraid Susan was going to do something stupid," Adam said impatiently. "What did you mean by that?"

"I heard her and a bunch of girls were going over to Ukiah tonight. You know what kind of trouble they got into last time they went over there."

"What did you want me to do about it?" Adam asked.

"Talk to her. Tell her she's acting really dumb going off the way she is and that she should give me another chance."

Adam laid his napkin beside his half-eaten dinner. "It's almost eight, Matt. If they were going, they'd be long gone by now."

Matt let out a groan. "I didn't know what else to do. I had to talk to someone or I was going to go out of my mind thinking about it."

"Come over to my place tomorrow and we'll talk then," Adam said. "By the way, how did you find me?"

"Jason told me." His mouth turned up in a guilty smile. "I said it was an emergency."

Miranda watched Adam's reaction. She couldn't see any sign of anger at the obvious deception. Had their positions been reversed, she would have been furious at the interruption, especially for something as inconsequential as a case of teenage angst.

"I don't want you to involve Jason in something like this again," Adam said. "He has enough going on in his life without you adding to it."

"I just thought—"

"It's okay this time."

There'd been no shouting, no threats, but there was also no doubt in Miranda's mind that, from then on, Matt would do exactly what Adam told him.

Matt leaned heavily back in his chair. "I knew I could count on you. This really means a lot to me, man."

"I'm not making any promises." Adam rolled Matt's chair back with his foot. "Now get out of here so Miranda and I can finish what's left of our meal."

Matt turned to her. "Hey, nice meeting you. I owe you one."

Taking her clue from Adam, Miranda said, "No you don't. I know what it's like when you think your world's falling apart."

As soon as Matt was gone, the waiter approached. "Would you like me to have the chef warm this for you?" he asked.

"Miranda?" Adam questioned.

"No thank you. But I would like some coffee."

The waiter turned to Adam. "And you, sir?"

"No on the warm up, yes on coffee, and if you have it tonight, the chocolate spoon cake. And bring two forks."

"I appreciate the gesture, but I don't eat desserts," Miranda said when the waiter had gone.

"Because you don't like them?"

Her answer had been automatic, developed over years of salads, aerobics and self denial. It had nothing to do with the way she looked now. She knew she needed to put on a few pounds; her clothes fit the hanger better than they did her. The hospital had even sent a dietician to talk to her.

It wasn't that she didn't eat on purpose, it was more that she forgot. When she did remember, it was everything she could do to choke down a sandwich.

Their coffee arrived, quickly followed by Adam's cake. "It looks wonderful," she said.

Adam cut through the custard-filled center, lifted his fork and waited to see if any of the cherry topping was going to drip before he held the offering across the table for her to take the first bite.

Miranda's stomach convulsed. "No, thank you."

"One taste and I'll leave you alone. Remember, my culinary reputation is on the line here. I told you there were no better desserts anywhere."

To refuse would make the moment too important. She leaned forward and let him place the fork in her mouth. The instant the confection hit her tongue there was an explosion of taste. The sweet chocolate cake, the custard, the dark chocolate decorative curls and whatever had been added to the cherries, came together to make something unbelievably wonderful.

"Well?" Adam prompted.

She felt a crumb at the corner of her mouth and retrieved it with her tongue before answering. "It's all right."

He laughed. "The look on your face said it was a hell of a lot more than all right."

"Okay," she admitted reluctantly, "it was everything you said."

He cut another bite. "More?"

"No, go ahead." She watched as he took the second bite. When he cut the third piece and had the fork raised she put her hand on his arm. "My turn."

"When we come again we'll try the golden raspberry tart."

She was about to tell him that wasn't going to happen but didn't want to put a damper on what had turned out to be a unexpectedly pleasant evening. There would be time enough later when she took him home. Until then, she would enjoy the hour or so they had left.

Miranda pulled her crimson BMW onto the two-lane highway and headed north, back toward Mendocino and Adam's house. The road was relatively empty for a weekend, allowing her to drive at a leisurely pace without worrying about backing up traffic.

When she'd first started walking at night she would climb a hillside and sit with her back to a tree watching the cars below as they raced from one curve to the next only to slam on their brakes at the last minute. They were all in such a hurry, the way she had once lived her life. She started making up stories for them, creating people they'd left and those they were rushing to meet. She gave them friends and lovers and children and imagined their homes warmed by crackling fires, music and laughter.

And then one day she grew tired of the game and never went back to her tree on the side of the mountain.

Instead, she traded sides of the road and walked the edge of the world, traveling the cliffs with the surf pounding below, her existence confined to a narrow dirt path.

When the sky changed from black to deep purple, she would go back to her rented house and read old magazines filled with articles about people she would never meet, or historical novels about people leading lives far removed from her own, and wait for the moment exhaustion would finally let her fall into a deep, dreamless sleep.

The lights of town flashed between trees as Miranda neared the headland. Adam turned to her. "Would you mind dropping me off at Jason's? I want to let him know Matt found me and see if Susan ended up there instead of in Ukiah with her friends."

"I don't have to drop you off. I can wait."

"Thanks, but that's not necessary."

"How will you get home?"

"Be careful," he gently teased. "I might start thinking you care."

She let the comment slide. "What was this terrible thing that happened the last time Susan took off with her girlfriends?"

"They went partying, got drunk and slept it off at some friend's house."

"That's it?"

"Not quite. Their folks had everyone from the county sheriff to the Coast Guard out looking for them the next morning. They were convinced the car was at the bottom of a ditch or under water somewhere."

"None of the girls called home, I take it."

"They said they all thought one of the others had."

"Those parents must have gone through hell. I'm surprised they ever let their kids out again."

"Is that what you would have done if it had been your daughter?" Adam asked. "Locked her up?"

She tensed. Did he know something? He couldn't. "I don't know." But she did. "I probably would have been so glad to know she was safe, I would have held her in my arms until she demanded to be let go and forgiven her anything."

"It's the next turn," Adam said, indicating an upcoming road. "Three blocks and then take a right."

Several minutes later Miranda pulled into Jason's driveway. There were lights strategically placed around the front of the weathered-wood house, some hidden in foliage, others suspended from ornate poles. The yard was terraced and planted English-garden fashion with a profusion of flowers seemingly set at random and allowed to flourish.

"It's beautiful," Miranda said.

"Jason is like this with everything he does," Adam told her.

"What kind of work does he do?"

"He's a painter—pictures, not houses."

A wisp of a smile crossed Miranda's lips. "Am I really so obvious?"

Adam shrugged. "Yeah, I'm afraid you are." He moved to get out, stopped and said, "Why don't you come inside? I have a feeling you and Jason would like each other."

"Not tonight. I have some things to do back—" Her answer had been automatic, the lie coming as easy as breathing. "That's not true. I don't have anything that needs doing. I just don't want to meet anyone else tonight."

"What if I told you I would consider it a personal favor if you came inside with me?"

"You said dinner would take care of things like personal favors, that you didn't want anything more."

"So, sometimes I lie, too."

"First tell me why this is important to you." Could she really be considering going in with him?

"Jason loves to meet new people," he said simply.

"He must be a really good friend for you to go to so much trouble."

"What trouble?" Adam said. "I just know you two would hit it off." When she didn't answer right away, he went on, "I was right about the cake, wasn't I?"

There was more than he was telling her. She'd questioned too many witnesses not to recognize when someone was holding back. "All right, but I really don't want to stay long."

Adam went to the front of the car and waited for her. They walked up the steps together. Miranda was acutely aware of his hand touching the small of her back. She wasn't sure how she felt about him making the familiar gesture, only that it made her aware how long it had been since she'd led anything approaching a normal life.

Jason must have heard them drive up because he was at the door to greet them. "Miranda Dolan, I presume," he said, coming forward, his hand extended.

He was tall and lean, had blond curly hair cut short, and a boyish smile. At first glance she thought he was younger than Adam, but when she looked into his eyes, she changed her mind. She dug into her memory for one of her cheerful, so-glad-to-meet-you smiles. "I hope we're not intruding."

"Not at all. Drop-by company is the best kind. Lets me know someone's thinking about me." He stepped out of the doorway. "Please, come in."

Miranda glanced around as she moved from the

entrance to the living room. There was an instant sense of belonging, as if she'd been there a hundred times before. The furniture was big and overstuffed, the kind you curled up in with your feet tucked under you and a cup of mulled wine or hot chocolate clasped between your hands.

The floor was wood and polished to a deep, hand-rubbed shine. A large, Faraghan Sarouk carpet, its fringe worn with age, sat in the middle. There were floor to ceiling bookshelves at one end of the room, a stone and brick fireplace at the other.

Miranda moved to get a closer look at a watercolor that hung behind the sofa. It was a picture of a lone man walking a grass and dune covered beach, his shoulders hunched against the wind, the sea more implied than detailed. Considering the components, there should have been a sad or lonely feeling, instead Miranda was overcome by a sense of peace. "This is breathtaking," she said. "Who's the artist?"

"It's one of mine," he told her.

"I'm obviously not needed in here," Adam said. "How about if I go in the kitchen and make us some coffee?"

"Tea for me," Jason said.

"Me, too," Miranda added. When Adam was gone, she turned her attention back to the picture.

"Adam said you painted, but I never expected anything like this. Jason—" She was at a loss for words. "It's wonderful." She wasn't an expert. Her ability to spot talent was more intuitive than educated. It just happened that when she saw something she liked, invariably it turned out to be the most expensive piece in the gallery, or something by someone who was on his way up. When she stumbled on an unknown whose work was still affordable, she always bought at least one painting. At last appraisal her collection had been valued at over a million dollars. She hadn't thought about the pictures that still hung on the walls at her home for months. Now that she had, she realized how much she missed the pleasure they'd once brought.

Jason came up beside her. "I like it, too. But I'm afraid we're in the minority."

"You're kidding." She turned to look at him.

"Most people think it's depressing."

"Oh, no, that's not what I see at all." She studied the picture with a new intensity.

"Tell me what you see," Jason prompted.

To do so could reveal a part of herself she wasn't sure she wanted exposed. But there was such poignant need in his voice she couldn't not respond. "What I see is a man at peace with himself—someone who has battled being alone and doesn't fear it anymore. The wind you've drawn is going to bring rain, but it won't drive him away, it will make him feel even more alive."

"That's amazing," Jason said softly. "You're the only one who's ever understood."

Miranda glanced up and saw that Jason was studying her as intently as she had studied the painting. They made eye contact and she felt as if he were only a second away from seeing everything she'd worked so hard to keep hidden all these months. And then there was a change in his expression. Compassion replaced curiosity.

He'd discovered her secret, not the details, only the pain. Her hiding place had been exposed.

He knew.

But more important—he understood.

How was that possible?

Four

Miranda rolled to her side in the middle of the queen-size bed and tugged the pillow over her top ear. She could still hear the pounding. Slowly, reluctantly she came up from the depths of sleep.

Why was there pounding? Adam had finished his work two days ago. She sat up and listened, trying to convince herself the noise had been part of a dream. A blessed silence greeted her; she settled back into the warm spot, stretched her legs and then brought them up tight against her body.

Her eyes were closed and she was beginning to drift again when something hit the window.

"What the hell?" She got out of bed and threw open the curtain. It was Adam. A thick blanket of fog surrounded him. She flipped the latch and shoved the window open. "What are you doing here?" she demanded.

He responded to her ill humor with an enticing grin. "Let me in and I'll tell you."

"I'm not in the mood for this, Adam." She hugged herself against the cold and glanced at the clock. She'd been in bed less than three hours. "I was up late last night. I'm tired."

"I promise you, this is better than sleep." He had his hands tucked in the back pockets of his jeans, his head cocked at a confident angle. "Come on, Miranda, time's a wastin'."

"Go away, Adam."

"Not until you see what I've brought."

"Then will you go away?" Why was she bargaining with him? She should just close the window and be done with it.

"I'll meet you at the back door."

"All right," she said as disagreeably as possible. She reached for her slacks and had them half on when she realized greeting Adam dressed would only encourage him to stay. Her other choice was the emerald green satin robe Keith had given her for Christmas. A floodgate of memories opened as she slid the robe from its hanger. Even with the collar poised over her shoulders, even knowing Adam was waiting for her, she hesitated.

She couldn't do it. Her hands shook as she hung the robe back on the hanger. Seconds later she had her slacks on again. Checking herself in the mirror, she decided the nightshirt was as good as a blouse. She stepped into her slippers and headed for the kitchen.

Tired and irritated and acutely aware of the personal test she had just failed, Miranda flung open the door. "This had better be good."

Adam stepped inside. "If I didn't know you better, I'd think you weren't happy to see me."

"You don't know me at all."

He put his hand on the wall over her shoulder and leaned close. "Which is something I intend to remedy."

Good God, he was coming on to her. She was too stunned to do anything but stare.

"Now, where do you keep your coffee?" Adam asked. "Something tells me you're the type who can't get moving in the morning without it."

How had this happened? What had given him the impression he could pursue her? He was a kid, for Christ's sake. She watched him opening cupboards as he looked for the coffee, saw the way his plaid shirt stretched across his back and shoulders, noted the way his jeans hugged his buttocks and legs. Maybe he wasn't a kid, but he sure as hell wasn't a man. At least not the kind of man she would be interested in.

Adam opened the refrigerator and found the can of coffee. "Ah, success at last. I knew it had to be somewhere." He went to the sink and turned on the water, letting it run for several seconds before filling the pot.

"You said you were going to show me something," Miranda reminded him. She would let him do what he'd come for and then send him on his way.

He pressed the button on the coffeemaker and turned to look at her. "It's in the truck."

A sudden feeling of being underdressed hit; Miranda folded her arms across her chest in a protective gesture. "Well, I guess you'd better go get it then."

He showed no inclination to move. "I like your hair that way."

Her hand came up. She gathered a thick strand and shoved it behind her ear. "It needs cutting."

"Is that why you always wear it up?"

He was after something and it had nothing to do with how she wore her hair. "I look better with it up."

"Better or older?"

It was a strange question, but maybe if he knew how old she really was he would leave her alone. "How old do you think I am?"

"Thirty-eight."

She felt spied on. There was no way he should know so much about her. "How did you gather that piece of information?"

"It was on your driver's license."

"What were you doing looking at my—" But then she knew. She'd had her ID with her the morning he pulled her out of the water. The nurses had told her that he was the one who'd brought her jacket to the hospital. Of course he would have checked the pockets first. "What else has your snooping told you about me?"

"That you're five-foot-eight and at one time you weighed a hundred and thirty-five pounds." He pointedly let his gaze sweep the length of her. "I've heard of people lying about their weight on their driver's license, but never one who added to it. I'd say that's a pretty good indication you've lost a few pounds since then."

"Could we please get this over with? I told you I'm tired. I want to go back to bed."

Adam sauntered over to where she stood, not stopping until only inches separated them. He seemed to be purposely testing her to see how she would react. She didn't move. "We're heading some-where, Miranda." His voice was low, his words a caress. "I don't know where yet, but I do know it's going to be a hell of a ride."

She could feel his heat; it insinuated itself into her senses and awakened feelings she thought long dead. She didn't like what was happening and feared if she didn't escape, she would do something stupid, like give in to her impulse to touch him, something she wouldn't be able to explain or take back. "Do you want a cup of coffee?"

He reached up and swept a strand of hair behind her ear, the same strand she'd put there earlier. "Milk, no sugar."

With summoned determination, she shouldered her way past him and went over to the counter. "This surprise you keep talking about?" she asked pointed-ly, keeping her back to him.

"I'll get it."

She heard the door open and close and felt cold air against her bare arms. He was gone, at least for the moment. She pressed her hands against the tile, seeking outside support for an inside turned to dis-jointed, uncooperative pieces.

Keep busy.

Focus.

If she could control her thoughts, her actions would fall in line. She opened the cupboard and took out two cups, adding milk to one, nothing to the other. When she'd poured the coffee and Adam still hadn't returned, she reached across the sink and pulled the blind.

A blurred motion caught her eye just as she began to look away. She turned back and peered outside. The air was still and laden with fog. She waited. Nothing. And then she saw what had attracted her. There was something near one of the fuchsias—a hummingbird.

Her breath caught in her throat as she watched the flash of iridescent green pause to dip its long beak into one red and white flower after another. The sight transfixed her. She willed the tiny bird to stay, knowing all the while it would not.

Abruptly the bird pulled back, hovered beside the plant, circled, and started to fly away. Then as if drawn by Miranda's silent message, it made a quick turn, came to the window, and looked inside. It was a moment of pure, elemental beauty, the first that had touched Miranda since all things beautiful had died on that sun-filled Friday afternoon.

The hummingbird stayed but a heartbeat and was gone. It was enough to make her note the loss with a sigh.

Behind her a light tap sounded on the door. She turned as it opened and Adam came inside. He was carrying a wicker basket that he put on the table before he looked at her.

Concern crossed his face. "Did something happen while I was gone?"

She shook her head, afraid if she told him about the hummingbird, the special feeling would disappear. She didn't want that to happen. "What's in there?"

"An apology from Matt for disrupting our dinner." He folded the handles down and opened the lid. "Come see."

Inside was an elegantly appointed picnic, complete with china, crystal, and linen. Her eyes widened in astonishment. "This must have cost a small fortune."

"It came from his grandparents' deli in San Francisco so I'm sure they gave him a good price. I'm impressed that he thought of it at all." Adam shifted the contents to let Miranda see the assortment of food. "He wanted you to know he kept everything on ice and even included some of those reusable frozen things in case we got sun or a late start this morning."

"Someone had to have put the idea in his head. Kids today don't do things like this on their own."

"Shame on you, Miranda," Adam gently scolded. "Besides, what possible difference does it make whose idea it was? Matt was the one who saw it through."

"You're right." And he was. When had she become such a curmudgeon? She glanced back inside and was drawn to the picture on a small box. "Oh, chocolate covered cherries. I *love* chocolate covered cherries." It had been so long since she'd had any she'd actually forgotten.

"They're all yours." It was said without sacrifice.

She dug deeper. "Look, there's Brie . . . and crackers . . . and apples . . . and salads . . . and wine . . . "

"I see your appetite has returned."

"It appears it has."

"Grab your coat and let's get going."

She hadn't yet made the mental connection between having the picnic basket and actually using it. "But it's foggy outside."

"It'll burn off by the time we get where we're going." He closed the lid.

"Where's that?"

"No crowds, I promise."

It almost seemed that she'd said no so often, she didn't know how to say yes anymore. Even though the word had become automatic, something deep inside wouldn't let her say it this time. A strange peace settled over her.

She'd failed miserably at dying, she might as well try living again.

"Give me a couple of minutes," she said.

"Okay, but do me a favor and leave your hair the way it is."

"It's shaggy," she protested. He'd known her less than a week and he could read her as easily as the morning paper.

"It's still beautiful," he countered.

Beautiful wasn't a word she was accustomed to hearing, at least not in reference to herself. Aggressive, assertive, powerful, determined, those had been the words of choice, the ones that had made her feel good inside. How had she changed so much that something as simple as Adam's offhand compliment could make her flush in pleasure? Or was she so hungry for human contact that she could no longer distinguish what was important and what was not?

"Do you want to take my car?" she asked, changing the subject.

"Not where we're going."

"Sounds intriguing." It wasn't brilliant, but it was a good enough exit line. She headed for the bedroom.

Fifteen minutes later, they were on Highway 1 headed north.

Adam's special place was an isolated redwood grove. He set the picnic up on a sandbar beside a slow-moving stream. But he'd been wrong about the fog, it didn't clear. Great, dense clouds clung tenaciously to the towering trees that surrounded them. It was as if they were encompassed in a gentle, gray cocoon.

A freezing cocoon.

Adam offered Miranda the last wedge of apple. She shook her head and snuggled deeper into her jacket. "Cold?" he asked.

"Just a little."

"I'll get some more wood." He'd only brought enough for a small fire, thinking they'd be using it for the dessert he'd planned, not to keep warm. By the time he returned, Miranda had repacked the picnic basket and had pulled the blanket over her shoulders.

"We can leave if you want," he told her.

"What about this other surprise you said you had?"

"It can wait for another time." He lowered himself to his haunches but held off adding the wood he'd gathered.

"I don't want to go back yet," she finally admitted.

"Pioneer spirit, I'm impressed." He laid the branches crosswise. Considering how damp they were, they caught faster than he'd expected.

Miranda shifted out of the smoke. "Did Matt and Susan ever have their talk?"

"As of this morning they hadn't. I called Susan like I promised but she told me if I even mentioned Matt's name again she would hang up on me."

"Sounds serious."

Adam stood and shoved his hands in his jacket pockets. "It's not the first time they've split up, but they're usually back together in a day or two. I've never seen him this upset or her so angry."

Miranda took a corner of the blanket in her hand and held out her arm. "I'm willing to share," she told him. "Especially considering it's your blanket."

Adam tried not to show his surprise. Up until now she'd done everything she could to keep distance between them. He settled in beside her. The arrangement was awkward, the blanket wasn't big enough for them to sit shoulder to shoulder. He put his arm around her and tucked her into his side. Initially, she resisted, holding herself stiff. After a few minutes she relaxed.

"You smell good," he said.

"I'm not wearing anything—no perfume, I mean."

"I know." He leaned his cheek into her hair. "I like that you're not."

"Adam, I don't want you to get the wrong idea . . ."

"About what?" He let go of the blanket, put his hand under her chin and tilted her face up. Before she had a chance to react, he kissed her. Her lips were warm and supple, and for an unguarded moment, hungry. He pulled back and looked her straight in the eye. "It was time we got that behind us, don't you think?"

"Somehow I must have given you the wrong impression. Just because I agreed to come with you today didn't mean I was interested in *seeing* you. We're not—I mean, I'm not—it just wouldn't work out, Adam."

"You've got to get over this age thing, Miranda. Trust me, I'm not the kid you seem to think I am." To prove his point, he kissed her again. This time he let the kiss deepen, not forcing, but leading, opening his mouth, touching the tip of his tongue to her lips,

waiting for her to respond. And she did, not hesitantly as he had anticipated, but with a melting
need.

She abruptly changed and became the aggressor
leaning into him with a deep-throated cry of release
and desire. Her hand went to his waist and then his
thigh. Slowly she began to inch her fingers upward.

Again Adam was the one to pull away. "What's
going on here, Miranda?"

She put her hand to her mouth as if she could
wipe away what had just happened. She was angry
and embarrassed and lashed out at him. "I thought
your generation invented meaningless sex."

"That happened a good nine years before I came
along."

She looked as if he'd hit her. "I deserved that,"
she said.

"No you didn't." He put his arm around her and
brought her back into his side. "I started this thing
way too soon." He smiled. "I suppose you could
attribute it to my callow youth."

"I feel so old," she said softly.

Adam had a feeling she hadn't meant to say the
words out loud. "A couple of years ago I went to
Africa with a relief group. We were sent there to
make sure the food supplies got through to the people who needed them. I wound up working the
camps, learning how to feed children who no longer
wanted to eat because they were starving to death. I
lasted a year." He still couldn't face the memories. "I
don't know what it is to be young anymore."

"We're quite a pair."

"Two tramps on a steamer to nowhere . . ." he
said.

"With three shoes and a coat between us," she finished for him.

He laughed. "That song is ancient. How did you know it?"

"I'm ancient, too, remember?"

"That's right. I nearly forgot." He brushed an enormous red ant off the blanket then glanced back at her. "Damn, I hope I look as good as you do when I'm your age."

It was her turn to laugh.

Adam took her shoulders and held her away from him. "Was that really you?"

"What are you talking about?"

"There's been a couple of times I've almost seen you give out with a real smile, but I've never once heard you laugh."

"You're right," she said softly. "I thought I'd forgotten how."

Adam reached in his pocket, brought out a sandwich bag and held it aloft. "I have just the thing to mark the occasion."

She peered at the bag. "What is that?"

"Marshmallows. We're going to roast them."

The announcement didn't bring another laugh, but her smile was genuine. "I don't know how I ever could have doubted your maturity."

"Hand me that stick." He indicated a thin branch he'd set aside earlier. When two marshmallows were securely stuck on the end, he held them near the fire, turning them slowly, taking his time so they didn't burn. As soon as they were evenly browned, he offered the first one to Miranda.

"I like mine after it's caught fire a couple of times," she said.

Adam handed her the stick. "Have at it."

"You want to take yours off first?"

He smiled. "I like mine burned, too."

"You know what this means, don't you? We've actually found something we have in common."

He thought about the kiss they'd shared only minutes ago. "It's the second thing we've found, Miranda."

It took her an instant to pick up on his meaning. When she did she turned her face away from him, focusing her attention on the now nearly cremated marshmallows.

"I think they're done," Adam said. "As a matter of fact, I think they may be a little over done."

"No, they're perfect." She brought the sizzling mini torches out of the fire and held them aloft for his inspection. Their disagreement became a moot point when Miranda gave the stick a sharp shake meant to extinguish the flame and the marshmallows flew off the end into the fire. "Well, they *were* perfect."

"Clever way to win an argument," Adam said.

"You should see me in a—" She didn't finish.

"In a what?" Adam prompted.

"Nothing. It was a long time ago and doesn't matter anymore."

The look in her eyes told him different. "There are things I don't like to talk about either. But if you change your mind, I'm a good listener."

"I won't."

Adam turned his wrist to look at his watch. He had an appointment with a leaky toilet in Fort Bragg in another hour. He was tempted to call and cancel, but he'd already put the guy off twice.

"Time to go?" Miranda asked.

"Yeah, I'm afraid so." Reluctantly, Adam finished gathering the remnants of their picnic.

Miranda folded the blanket and poured water on the fire. When she was sure it was out, she scattered the ashes, then covered them with sand. As they left, she scanned the area. It was as if they'd never been there. Her intention had been an environmental statement—the effect struck a deeper cord. Had she left footprints in her life? Did she care whether there were any, or was she willing to leave nothing of herself behind?

On the way down the mountain Miranda noticed the CD player in the truck. "Mind if I play something?" she asked.

"I should warn you my taste in music is a little to the left, but you're welcome to look through what I've got." He reached across her and opened the glove compartment.

She pulled out several CDs and started going through them. "I've never heard of any of these people. What kind of music is this?"

"I used to play the oboe."

"Why?" It was as much an opinion as a question.

"My parents had a good friend who played oboe in the San Francisco Symphony. He came to dinner all the time and . . ." Adam shrugged. "One thing led to another."

Miranda selected one of the CDs, put it in the player and sat back to listen. After several minutes she turned to Adam. "It must take a while to grow on you."

He put his hand over hers. "You don't have to like my music, Miranda."

She turned her hand palm up and gave his fingers a gentle squeeze. After what he'd done for her that day, she would listen to his music until it became as familiar as the motivational tapes she had once listened to on her way to and from work.

"Tell me about Jason," she said.

"What do you want to know?"

"How did he come to be in Mendocino?" She hadn't stopped thinking about him since the night they'd met.

"It's pretty simple. He had a friend, more a mentor really, who was deep into the art community here. He invited Jason to visit after he got out of school. One thing led to another and he decided to stay."

"Is that where you met Jason, in school?"

"God, no. Remember, I'm a year and a half Stanford man. I have trouble snapping a straight chalk line, let alone putting something on canvas. Jason and I grew up in the same neighborhood. We've been best friends since second grade."

"Is he the reason you're here?" she asked.

"Yes."

He wasn't going to make it easy. Which was strange. Until now Adam had been open and forthcoming in all their conversations. "Would you rather not talk about him?"

"I don't mind. But you have to understand Jason is a private person. There are certain things I feel would intrude on that privacy and I won't talk about them to anyone, including you."

"Fair enough." She liked his answer. And, a little to her surprise, she was discovering she liked Adam Kirkpatric.

Adam pulled off the highway onto the road that led to Miranda's house. "Looks like the fog is starting to lift," he said.

Now that she was only seconds away from home, she realized she didn't want to be there, at least not alone. "Would you like to come in? You never did get your cup of coffee."

He pulled into the driveway, put the truck in park and turned to look at her. "I'd like to, but I can't. I've got a job this afternoon."

She reached for the door handle. Not counting their dinner, the last time she'd been on anything resembling a date had been seventeen years ago. She didn't know what to do next, how to say good-bye. "I had a nice time. Thank you for asking me."

Adam got out and came around to her side. "Does that mean you'll make it a little easier the next time I decide to come callin'?"

This was how she'd felt her sophomore year in her small-town high school when she had a crush on the senior class president. She'd hated that he had control of the situation, that she was supposed to wait to see if he would ask her out again rather than letting her make the call. When she hadn't heard from him by the end of the next week, she couldn't stand waiting any longer and took things into her own hands. She asked him to the movies. He turned her down, telling his best friend later that it was because he didn't like pushy women.

"It depends," she said, finally answering Adam's question.

"On what?"

"How soon you show up."

"That can be taken two ways. I'm going to assume you're telling me I better not keep you waiting."

"Smart man." She was amazed at how sure she seemed, how at ease with the conversation when she was falling apart inside. This business of learning to live again was harder than she would have believed possible.

"I'm going to be out of town for a couple of days."

"I didn't mean—"

"But I'll call you as soon as I get back."

She made a dismissive gesture with her hands. "Do what you want."

He pinned her with a stare. "Seeing you again, and as soon as possible, is precisely what I want, Miranda. I'd be back here tonight if I hadn't made other commitments."

What was it about him that could make her believe every word he said? She hadn't put that much trust in anyone, other than Keith, for so long it was hard to remember the last time it had happened. "I thought you said you had a job you had to get to."

"Are you going to be all right?"

Sudden, irrational anger flared. "Don't you dare treat me like that. Why wouldn't I be all right? Even if I weren't, it's my business, not yours."

"Cut the crap, Miranda," he said, unruffled by her mercurial behavior. "And while you're at it, you might as well stop pretending you're just another tourist. I don't give a damn why you came to California, only that you did." He slammed her door and went back around to his side to get in. Adam was backing out of the driveway when he stopped and leaned out the window. "The phone lines run both ways, you know. There's no reason you can't call me."

Miranda watched him leave, standing on the gravel walkway until the truck disappeared in the fog. Feeling confused and alone, she headed for the house. When she reached the back door, she realized she didn't want to go inside.

Until that morning the impersonal rental she'd never thought of as home at least had been a refuge, a place where she could keep the rest of the world at bay. Now it only seemed empty and lonely.

Five

Adam stepped out of the elevator on the thirty-fifth floor of the Chapman-Hall building and through a set of massive glass doors. "Morning Lu-Ann—is Mary in?"

The receptionist checked a board in front of her. "She's in her office."

"How's Jim?" he asked, before heading through another set of doors.

"Driving me crazy since he retired."

The news didn't surprise Adam. Jim had been his Little League coach. He wasn't the type to sit around with nothing to do. "Say hello to him for me."

"Will do," she said and reached for an incoming call.

Adam smiled and waved to several people in offices he passed, surprised both at how many he knew and how many he didn't. The hallway ended at a door marked with simple gold lettering spelling out, Mary Kirkpatric, President.

He knocked at the same time he opened the door. "Busy?" he called.

Mary swung around in her custom-built leather

chair and looked at him over her half glasses. "Never too busy for you." She tossed the papers she'd been reading on the desk. "To what do I owe the honor of your presence?"

Adam crossed the room, gave his mother a kiss and perched on the corner of the desk. "Jason has a two-day outpatient appointment at the hospital."

She took her glasses off and laid them on top of the papers. "It's been a couple of weeks since I talked to him. How's he doing?"

"He looks the same to me, but then I see him every day so it's hard to tell. He came through that spell he had with pneumonia better than Vern Lansky thought he would."

"Are you making sure he's keeping up with his exercise?"

"If it's too foggy to bicycle, we walk a couple of miles."

The intercom on Mary's desk buzzed. She hit the button. "What is it, Patty?"

"Michael Ericson is on line one."

"Would you tell him I'm with Adam and ask if there's a number where I can reach him later?"

Adam was instantly on the alert. He'd never heard his mother's voice soften that way for a mere business associate. He gave her a questioning look. "Michael Ericson . . . I don't think I know him."

Mary tried to suppress a grin, but only half succeeded. "He's a man I met at the Delponte's Christmas party."

"I thought they canceled last year when Jason threatened to show up."

"*Two* Christmases ago."

"Is he a slow starter, or were you as stubborn as

always?" The suitors had started gathering almost as soon as Adam's father was buried. In the beginning, overwhelmed with grief, Mary had been incapable of handling the attention. Later she'd immersed herself into the business and was suspicious of any man who approached her on anything but a professional level. Only lately, it seemed, had she become confident enough in what she'd accomplished to fit a personal relationship into her schedule.

"We've been seeing each other off and on for several months now."

"Off and on?" Adam was intrigued.

"Do I question you about the women you're seeing?"

Adam laughed. "All the time."

"That's different."

"Only because you keep hoping I'll pick some nice girl who'll make me want to settle down to the corporate life."

She shuddered. "You make me sound so self-serving."

"But lovingly so."

Her expression changed. She grew serious. "I don't mean to harp on this, but your birthday is only a couple of months away. You promised me you'd make a decision when you turned thirty."

Adam got up and went to the window. The sight was spectacular—the bay, the Golden Gate Bridge, the sun reflecting off a million windows in buildings planted on an undulating landscape. In all of his travels, he'd never seen a city that could supplant this one in his heart. Still, as much as he loved San Francisco, he just couldn't imagine himself looking at the same view the rest of his life.

"Three months isn't going to make any difference. I can't do it, Mom."

She moved to stand beside him. "I'm disappointed, but not surprised." She didn't say anything for a long time. And then, "I can wait. There's nothing says you have to take over when you turn thirty. Maybe by the time you're thirty-five you'll be ready."

He put his arm across her shoulders. He was always a little taken aback at how small she was. If toughness and tenacity went hand in hand with size, she'd have been a contender on the professional wrestling circuit. "You could be right. I might turn thirty-five and realize what an idiot I was for not taking over when I was thirty, but if that happens, it will be my problem, not yours. Whatever you decide has to be what you want, not what you think I might want someday."

She slipped her arm around his waist. "I love you, Adam, but you are one major pain in the ass when you talk that way."

"Thanks, Mom." He pressed a kiss to her temple. "I knew you'd understand."

"Understand hell. If I thought I could pull it off I'd have you kidnapped and reprogrammed. And don't think I couldn't find a psychiatrist to go along with me. What man in this day and age would turn his back on a thirty-two million dollar business?"

"My God, is that how much you're worth?"

"It's how much *we're* worth, Adam. Your name is right up there with mine."

"I haven't earned one dime of that money."

"Oh please don't tell me you've turned into one of those 'inherited money is dirty money' fanatics. I've gone along with most everything you've done until now, but I swear when I die I'll come back to haunt you if you give all my hard work away to some weird religious sect."

He gave her shoulders a reassuring squeeze. "Don't worry, I'll keep a *little* for myself. I'm still hedonistic enough to occasionally enjoy the finer things in life." He glanced back at the enclosed bar. "Speaking of which, do you still have a bottle of Ancestrale Cognac hanging around?"

"Special occasion?"

"Could be."

"Oh, now I am intrigued." She went to the cupboard and brought out an unopened bottle. "Maybe we can work a little trade. My Ancestrale Cognac—"

"Yes?" Adam said, dragging the word out. He leaned backward against the safety rail that circled the window.

"For information."

"What do you want to know?" His mother had the subtlety of a bulldozer when it came to even the hint of a prospective daughter-in-law.

"Who she is and when do I get to meet her?"

"Miranda Dolan."

She brought the cognac over to her desk but kept her hand tightly wrapped around the neck. "And?"

"And I don't know," he said honestly. "She's not like any other woman I've ever met. I don't have a sense yet whether it's going anywhere, or even if I want it to."

"Uh huh," she said skeptically.

Adam laughed. "Don't go getting your hopes up. Miranda's got some problems she's trying to work though. When she does, she just may see me as part of the past she wants to leave behind."

"Not if she's got the sense God gave a flea."

"Spoken like a true mother."

"So, when do I get to meet her?"

"You better give me a while."

"What does Jason think of her?" Mary pulled a canvas bag with Kirkpatric Ltd. printed on it out of the bottom cupboard and put the cognac inside.

"It was really strange. They only met once and only for about a half hour, but it was as if they'd known each other all their lives."

"Why is it that everyone can see what a wonderful young man Jason is except the two people who brought him into this world?" She set the cognac down on her desk with a heavy thud. "I get so damned impatient with those two I could just throttle them."

Adam glanced over to see if any of the four-hundred-dollar cognac was leaking out of the bottom of the bag. "I was going to ask you if you'd seen any softening in their attitude, but I think you just answered my question."

"Every time I try talking to Barbara she changes the subject. If I persist, she asks me to leave. I came close to telling her exactly how I feel about the way she and Fred are behaving, but had sense enough at the last minute to keep my mouth shut. I'm the only link they have to their son. If I shut the door where does that leave Jason?"

"He never talks about them anymore, but I know he thinks about them all the time."

I wish to hell I knew what happened to cause the break." Mary made a face. "Not that it would do any good."

"Jason has never said, but I think it has something to do with Tony."

"But Tony's been gone over a year."

"Do they know that?" Adam asked.

"I told them myself—not that it was any of my business."

"I don't know what else we can do." Adam tried not to dwell on things he had no control over. Jason and his parents fell in that category.

"Thank God you're there for him." The intercom sounded again. Mary answered, "I know, Patty. Tell them I'll be there in a couple of minutes."

"Are you free for lunch?" Adam asked.

"Can we make it dinner? I have a feeling this meeting might go on for hours and I don't want you waiting around for me."

"I'll pick up Jason and we'll meet you at the house at six. I'm going to be here until tomorrow and thought I'd stay the night with you, if that's all right."

"Of course it is. As a matter of fact, there's some mail at the house for you. It arrived yesterday. I think it's from one of those Amish people you worked with last spring."

The possibility brought a smile. The months he'd spent working with the Red Cross mopping up after the floods had brought him in contact with several Amish families. He'd become particularly close friends with one of them despite the obvious differences in their backgrounds. Because he never knew where he would settle next, he left his mother's address with the friends he made in his travels. A gratifying number followed through with their promises to keep in touch.

Adam's smile turned to concern when he realized it wasn't always good news that came in a letter. "I hope nothing's wrong," he said.

"If there is, it took a long time to tell," Mary said, picking up on his concern. "It's really a fat letter, more the newsy kind." She stopped and considered something. "You didn't say where Jason was staying."

"With a friend. I should probably try to reach him at the clinic to make sure he hasn't already made plans for dinner. Now that I think about it, if he is going to join us, it probably would be better if we met you here."

"Oh, I didn't even consider that. Of course you wouldn't want to take him by the house. But then who knows, maybe Barbara would be outside with the gardener when you passed by and you could have car trouble or something."

"It's not going to happen, Mom. If Barbara and Fred want to see Jason, they're going to have to come to him. They damn near destroyed him the last time he tried to see them. I won't do anything that could give them that opportunity again."

"You're right, of course. I just keep hoping . . . "

Adam gave her a quick kiss and started for the door. He had his hand on the knob when he remembered the cognac.

Mary met him halfway, the bag in her hand. "It's nice to see some things never change."

"Now would you really want someone like me running your company?"

"Is that an offer?" she asked.

"Will you never give up?" It was said with an indulgent sigh.

She ignored Adam's obvious attempt to put her off. "I've still got three months."

"It isn't time you need, it's a miracle."

She smiled. "So what's wrong with believing in miracles?"

The next day Jason was nodding off by the time they hit Petaluma and asleep by Santa Rosa. Adam had the rest of the way back to Mendocino to think about the gnawing sense of anticipation at seeing Miranda again that had started the minute he got out of bed that morning. Not even the long, breezy letter from Hans and the rest of his family had provided more than a brief distraction.

He rolled down the window. Dry, hot inland air filled the cab. The coastal route home was the more beautiful, the inland route far faster. It was late and he was in a hurry even though he knew there was no way he could get back in time to see her that night.

The air tugged at the brim of his baseball cap. He took it off and laid it on the seat beside him. The cap was a prized possession, a gift from his father, the last. Every year, eighteen straight, from the time Adam was a year old, they'd attended the Giants' season opener together. The streak ended when Gerald Kirkpatric died in his sleep the night before the big game. Eleven years and Adam still hadn't been back to the ballpark. He doubted he ever would.

As the miles passed in pleasant silence Adam began to realize that everything he saw, did, or heard triggered thoughts of Miranda. Their relationship was like a map without roads and he was stuck trying to find a way to get from one place to the next. Until she trusted him enough to open up a little, he had no idea how to help her. All he knew with any certainty was that he was drawn to her in a way he'd never been drawn to another woman.

It was going on ten when Adam dropped Jason off at his house, too late to show up unannounced at Miranda's. Adam took the long way home, driving past Vern Lansky's house. He saw Vern sitting on the front porch and decided to stop.

"You just getting back?" Vern asked as Adam got out of his truck.

"About ten minutes ago." Adam came up to the porch and sat in the wicker chair next to Vern's. "We've had so much fog lately I hated to go inside when we finally got a clear night."

"It always takes me a while to unwind after a long drive, too. Seems the older I get, the farther away San Francisco gets. I don't go much anymore, not if I can avoid it."

"I think the trip was hard on Jason."

"I suspect it was more the two days of being shuffled around the hospital. That in itself is more'n enough to wear down someone's who's healthy." He propped his feet on the porch railing. "How's Miranda Dolan doing?"

"What makes you think I'd know anything about Miranda Dolan?" Nothing ever happened involving any of the locals that Vern didn't know about. Adam just didn't want to make the fishing expedition too easy.

"Word is you been seeing her." It was said in a slow drawl.

Adam tilted his head back against the flowered cushion and smiled. "You might have the rest of these people fooled with that hayseed routine, but I'm not buying."

"Then stop being so goddammed tight-lipped and tell me what I want to know. Have you found out if I was right about those scars?"

"No. She doesn't trust me with the time of day. Hell, I don't think she trusts anyone."

"I've done some asking around to see if she's been out and about more'n we thought. There's no one I can find who knows the first thing about Miranda Dolan. If she's made any friends while she's been here, they aren't talkin' about it."

Even though it was said in Vern's typical laid-back style, Adam could hear concern in his voice. He was the closest thing Adam could imagine to a modern-day country doctor, intimately involved with the people in the community, as caring with the weekenders who cut themselves exploring tide pools as he was the local children who came to him for vaccinations. His interest in Miranda wasn't acquisitiveness, it was simply an extension of the man he was.

Adam felt uncomfortable talking about Miranda as if she were a specimen that needed studying. He changed the subject. "Anything happen with Susan and Matt while I was gone?"

"Matt's been by a couple of times, but Susan still won't see him. Poor guy's running around town lookin' like his world collapsed down around him."

"What's it been, a week now?"

"At least that. I figure it must be serious this time. None of their fights have ever lasted this long." Vern stretched his arms over his head and let out a low groan. "I'm getting stiff. I need to think about starting an exercise program."

"You're welcome to come bicycling with us in the morning."

He hesitated, as if giving it some thought. "I'll let you know."

Adam laughed. "I won't hold my breath."

"Say—I never did get a bill for all that work you did last week."

"It's sitting on my desk." Along with a month's worth of paperwork he kept telling himself he really ought to get to, but somehow never did.

"You're never gonna get rich that way."

"I know you're good for it."

"Well, I got another project I want you to do," Vern said. "I been thinking that house Miranda Dolan's living in could use another coat of stain before winter gets here."

"Have you been by there lately?" Adam asked. "The siding looks okay to me."

Vern set his chair rocking. "I know what I'm doing. Upkeep is everything when it comes to rentals." His speech settled into the rhythm of the chair movements. "I'm not saying there's any rush to finish. Matter of fact it might be good if you took it kind of slow and only went over there an hour or so every morning. That way you'd have the rest of the day to take care of your other business."

Adam started to protest that what Vern was saying didn't make sense and then it hit him. Vern was worried about Miranda's reclusiveness. "When do you want me to get started?" he asked, testing his theory.

"There's nothing wrong with tomorrow, unless you've got something else going, of course. Then the next day's just as good."

Adam's throat went dry. "If you've got something you think I should know, Vern, just spit it out."

"I've been putting the pieces together and something tells me the lady's been carrying a lot of baggage around with her and it's finally wore her down. I talked to the doctor who took care of her in the hospital and she agrees with me, said while she was there, Miranda never spoke a word that wasn't necessary."

Adam leaned forward, raked his hand through his hair and planted his elbows on his knees. "She's hurting, that much I've been able to see for myself."

"It's not that I think you should be taking on every stray that happens by," Vern said. "God knows you got your hands full with Jason. I just thought you being around might get her to open up a little. Besides, like I said, the house could always use another coat of stain."

"Well, if nothing else, you've given me something to think about." Adam stood. "Now that I have a job to do in the morning, I suppose I should be heading home."

"Let me know if there's any way I can help out," Vern said. He got up and walked Adam to the edge of the porch.

Adam paused before climbing in his truck. "I like her, Vern."

"I picked up on that, Adam."

When had he become so obvious? "Take it easy," he called as he backed onto the road.

Ten minutes later he pulled into Miranda's driveway.

Six

Adam saw a light in the kitchen in Miranda's house and tapped on the back door. There was no answer. He knocked again, only louder this time. Still there was no response. He tried the door, found it open, and went inside.

An eerie quiet greeted him. Not even the sound of the refrigerator motor broke the silence. He called Miranda's name, not because he expected her to answer, but bound by some screwy sense of protocol.

One by one he went through the rooms. Everything seemed in its place. The bed was made, the counter in the bathroom was clear and the magazines on the coffee table in the living room were precisely placed. Nothing personal stamped the house hers, not even a grocery-store plant, or a sprig of wildflower stuck in a drinking glass. The house had the look of a motel room waiting for the next guests. Even though her car was out front, Adam had a nagging feeling she didn't live there anymore. He went back to the bedroom and opened a dresser drawer. Inside was an assortment of silk and lace, lingerie more in keeping with the clothes she'd worn to dinner than the designer sweats that he'd come to think of as her uniform of choice.

Adam returned to the living room, looking for clues, something, anything to indicate where she might have gone. He checked the closet. Her jacket was missing, but her purse was there. Frustration gave way to fear. He glanced at his watch. It was midnight.

Where in the hell was she?

He went outside and examined her car. The engine was cold, the windows covered with mist. Because he couldn't think of anything else to do, he took a flashlight out of the truck and walked the yard. A feeling of apprehension came over him as he neared the cliff and heard the sounds of waves hitting the rocks below.

The tide was out, the water relatively calm. Adam deliberately moved the light back and forth in a sweeping motion, covering as much of the water as a three-quarter moon and four D-cell batteries would allow.

"Looking for something?" The voice was female and antagonistic.

Adam turned and saw Miranda walking toward him. His relief left him unreasonably irritated. "Not some*thing*, someone," he shot back.

"Me, by any chance." She stopped and stared at him, her hands on her hips.

She'd come from the trail that ran along side the cliffs. "Where've you been?" he demanded.

"Here and there," she said dismissively.

"Damn you." Adam's irritation exploded to anger. He wasn't some stranger who'd happened by. "I deserve better than that."

"Why?"

"Because I care. And as far as I can tell, people like me are in short supply in your life right now."

"And that's supposed to make me accountable to you?"

"Maybe not accountable, Miranda, but sure as hell civil." They were right back where they were the first day he'd come to her house. He refused to rehash an argument he'd believed settled. "I've got better things to do than stand around here and—"

"I was walking," she said when he started to leave. "It's how I put myself to sleep."

"Every night?"

She hesitated. "Sometimes all night."

"Don't you know how dangerous that is?"

She just stared at him.

"The paths get wet and slippery. You could fall . . . again."

Long, agonizing seconds passed. "I didn't fall, Adam."

She'd only told him what he'd already suspected. Still, having it confirmed was like a fist slammed into his midsection. "Why?" was all he could think to ask.

She ignored his question. "I know now why it was so hard for me to thank you for what you did. It wasn't thanks I owed you, it was an apology. You shouldn't have had to risk your life for me. If I had seen you out there in your boat, I would have waited until you were gone."

"Are you telling me you're sorry I was there?"

"No," she said softly. "At least not now. I think I'm finally on the other side of the depression that put me over the edge."

Death wasn't an alien thing to him. He'd seen it

in the cruelest terms in jungles and deserts and ghettos, and his best friend was in the process of coming to terms with it, but he'd never known anyone who purposely sought it out. "What happened? How did you wind up on that cliff?"

"I can't talk about it." Her voice grew softer. "Not yet." And softer still. "Maybe never."

He closed the distance between them and took her hand. "Let's go inside."

"It's late," she said. "I think you should go home."

"I'm not leaving you."

"Don't make me sorry I told you, Adam."

He put his hands on the sides of her face and stared deeply into her eyes. "You can't fight me on this, Miranda. There's no way in hell I'll let you win. Besides, you don't want to be alone tonight anymore than I want to leave you."

He came closer, lowering his face until he could feel the warmth of her breath against his skin. For a second she tensed and it seemed she would pull away. He waited. She didn't move again. He closed the final distance. Just before he kissed her, he brushed her lip with the tip of his tongue.

The meeting was instantly explosive, deep and filled with unchecked hunger. His tongue plunged into her mouth as his hands moved to her waist. She pressed herself closer, fitting her hips into his, moving in primal, unmistakable invitation. Adam cupped her buttocks and brought her closer still unable to get enough of the feel of her.

He had never experienced a lack of control and it left him shaken. He was near the point of not caring when a voice told him to slow down, to allow Miranda time to consider what was happening. He heard, but didn't listen. Something more basic drove him. He wanted her, more than he thought it was possible to want anyone.

Miranda wrapped her arms around his neck and stood on her toes. "We shouldn't do this," she said, her actions belying her words. "It isn't right." He reached for her legs and she eagerly wrapped them around his waist. There was a catch in her voice when she said, "I'm using you, Adam. This doesn't mean anything."

"I don't care," he said against her mouth.

"Please," she said in an agonized whisper. "Make love to me. Make me forget."

Adam didn't understand what was going on between them, but he knew she was wrong about it not meaning anything. If he didn't move, if he waited just a few minutes longer, they would make love on the grass—the hell with the cold and damp and propriety.

Instead he carried her to the house, through the kitchen and into the bedroom. He stood her on the bed, hooked his thumbs into the waistband of her sweatpants and pulled them down.

She caught her breath when he touched his tongue to her navel then slowly traced a moist, hot line downward. When she realized what he was doing, what he intended to do, she reached out to stop him. He caught her hands and held them at her sides keeping her still while he moved lower yet, exploring the apex of her thigh. His breath, hot and invasive, went beyond, to the hard, throbbing core of her sex. She ached with the need to be touched and wantonly pressed herself against him. This was not the kind of sex she knew, safe and comfortable and restrained. A part of her held back and warned of the embarrassment that would follow when the erotic flight from reality was over.

But the rest of her just didn't give a damn.

This loss of reason was her escape. She needed something this powerful and beyond her control to enable her, for a few precious moments, to forget.

Adam reached to turn on the lamp. She put her hand on his to stop him. There couldn't be light. He would see the scars and he would ask questions.

He hesitated, as if about to say something, then let it go. Effortlessly, he lowered her to the bed and finished undressing her, not hurriedly, but with slow, deliberate movements. His hands touched and explored her body in a proprietary way as if they had traveled the secret, guarded paths many times, as if he were there by right and not privilege.

He came up on his knees and removed his shirt. Moonlight illuminated him and she was struck anew at his beauty. He had the body held as the standard in advertisements for everything from cola to workout machines—the body but not the ego. He didn't pose or preen or show the least awareness that he was different in any way from the tourist walking around town in Bermuda shorts with his potbelly hanging over his belt.

The buttons on his jeans transfixed her as one by one he worked them free. When he was done he stood and finished undressing. But he didn't lay down next to her right away. Instead, as if by impulse, he touched the hollow behind her ear with the tips of his fingers. Slowly, exerting no more pressure than a drop of rain sliding down a window, he traced a path from her neck to her pelvis.

Miranda closed her eyes and bit her lower lip to keep from crying out. He hadn't touched her breasts or dipped his hand between her legs but she had never been caressed more erotically or been more aroused. Her skin felt on fire.

"You take my breath away," he said. "I've never known a woman as beautiful as you."

They were extravagant words, stored away to be brought out and spoken during moments of passion, no more true than those uttered at the sight of a brand-new baby. But she gloried in them. No one had bothered to tell her the tender lies that fed the soul in a long time.

She reached out to feel his erection but, suddenly shy, pulled back at the last minute. He caught her hand and brought it back. She liked that he wanted her to touch him and slipped her hand around the hard shaft. A low moan escaped the lips at her breast. He was as ready for her as she was him.

And then she remembered.

A hollow feeling hit her. For sixteen years she had made love to only one man. Protection for them had been her birth control pills. "Are you . . . " she stammered. "I mean do you . . . " What was wrong with her? She was a thirty-eight-year-old woman, for Christ's sake. Too old to play these kinds of games.

"I have protection if that's what you're asking."

She flinched, hating the way his answer made her feel. Did he have condoms with him because he'd come there that night with expectations? Was what she'd believed natural and spontaneous in reality a calculated encounter? Or did Adam always carry protection on the off chance he might get lucky?

"Miranda, what's wrong?"

"Nothing."

"Don't give me that. You're doing one of your disappearing acts. Tell me what happened."

"Why are you carrying rubbers?"

An inner battle reflected in his eyes, as if he were trying to decide how much to tell her. "I bought them in San Francisco yesterday."

"You were pretty sure of yourself." She moved to sit up. "Or is this something you had planned all along?"

"Yeah—right. Those were my exact thoughts when I pulled you out of the water."

She swung her legs over the side of the bed. Adam grabbed her by the waist and brought her back to him. "I've never known a woman I couldn't walk away from—until you. Now you can hold that over me or you can admit you're just as confused about what's happening between us as I am. Either way, it's not going to change one damn thing. You're still going to want me every bit as much as I want you."

"Maybe," she acknowledged. "But not tonight. I just don't feel like—"

"Bullshit." He brought her to him and covered her mouth with his own. When she began to respond he deepened the kiss, making no effort to hold back. "I can give you what you want," he murmured against her lips. He moved to her neck and then lower. "Let go, Miranda." He caressed her breast with his tongue then teased the nipple with his teeth.

Without conscious thought she swayed against him. "Yes," she said on an exhaled breath. "Do whatever you want . . . make me forget."

Adam rolled to his back. With her straddling him, he said, "Say my name."

"What? I don't understand."

"I don't give a damn who or what you forget as long as it isn't me."

"Adam . . . " She lowered her face to his. "Adam . . . " she murmured against his lips. "Ad—" The rest was lost as she plundered what he so readily offered.

A shadow moved across the ceiling, its character defined and shaped by the curtain and gradually disappearing moon. The duck had become a swan and then a flamingo. Now Adam saw a road; it had a distinct beginning, but an unformed end.

"You were right," Miranda said.

She was curled into Adam's side, her head resting on his shoulder. He pulled her closer. "I thought you were asleep."

"Maybe for a while. I don't know."

"What was I right about?"

"Me wanting you. I just didn't know how to get through the maze of confusion and insecurities."

He pressed a kiss to the top of her head. "But they're gone now?"

"They could be hiding somewhere, I suppose."

"How am I going to know if you want to do this again?"

She propped herself up on her elbow and looked at him. "Can we?"

Adam smiled. "When did you have in mind?"

"Now?"

It wasn't passion he heard but a quiet desperation. He grew serious. "Is it me you want, or is it sex, or is having sex the only way you can think to keep me from asking questions?"

"Why can't it be all three?"

"Because I can't get it out of my head that I almost didn't go fishing that morning."

"Don't do that." She sat up and wrapped her arms around her knees.

"You would have been a statistic, someone I read about in the paper or heard about in a bar. I might have wondered about you for a minute or two, but no more."

"Think how much easier that would have been."

He sat up beside her. "Maybe at one time, but not anymore."

"My grand gesture failed. Once was enough. I won't try again."

"Why should I believe you?"

"Because you don't have any choice."

"That's not good enough, Miranda. What am I supposed to do? Hell, what am I supposed to think if I show up and you're not here when you said you would be?"

"If I intended to try again, I wouldn't have told you about the first time."

What she said made sense but failed to reassure him. Needing the contact as much as wanting it, he laid his open hand against her back. "Grand gestures demand audiences. You were alone."

"Obviously not as alone as I thought."

"Are you sorry I was there?" He'd already asked and she'd already answered the question, but not to his satisfaction. There had to be more, something that would give him the reassurance he needed.

"I was furious when I woke up in the hospital and realized everything I'd gone through had been for nothing. After the nurse explained how I got there I made elaborate plans to tell you exactly what I thought of your heroics when I realized that, for the first time in months, I was actually looking forward to something. Of course it occurred to me after a while that I couldn't say anything about how I felt without admitting how I got in the water in the first place."

She brought the sheet up to cover her nakedness. "Then I got to know you and it hit me how easily you could have died doing what you did. That was when the guilt set in."

"Going after you was my idea. You have nothing to feel guilty about."

"And all's well that ends well." She'd used the brightly spoken cliche to close a door between them. "You've been wonderful, Adam. Tonight was—"

"Tonight was a beginning," he forcefully finished for her.

"That isn't what I was going to say."

"I know what you were going to say and I didn't want to hear it." He leaned forward and kissed the arch of her spine.

She jerked in surprise and moved away from him. "You should probably go. It's late and you have work in the morning."

"Understand something." He turned her to face him. "I won't be dismissed like some casual lay you picked up at a bar. If I'm good enough to fuck you, I'm good enough to sleep in your bed."

"That isn't what I meant."

"The hell it isn't."

"You're making too much out of tonight. I told you it didn't mean anything."

"That was before."

"Nothing's changed, Adam. It can't. I won't let it."

"Meaning?"

He wasn't going to let it go. "We can never do this again," she said, leaving no room for doubt.

"Because you don't want to?"

"Yes."

"You're lying."

"Is your male ego so—" She gasped as his hand slipped between her legs. "Damn you." Her words, her determination became mist, her explosive need a wind that blew them away.

Adam laid her back and moved over her. She wasn't trapped or confined, but free to get up and leave if she so chose. Instead she put her arm out and reached for the foil packets on the nightstand. When she brought her legs up and took him inside her, the cry of pleasure was a call of surrender.

At least one thing was settled between them.

Seven

After purposely staying away from Miranda for three days to give her the "space" she'd insisted she needed, Adam had finally decided the idea had about as much merit as the belief aliens were responsible for circles in wheat fields. Convenient or not, since the night they made love she'd become an increasingly important part of his life. She was going to have to find a way to deal with it.

That morning he'd scheduled his day to be through work by early afternoon planning to surprise Miranda with a trip down the coast to Gualala for dinner. But then he hadn't counted on running into Faith Spencer when he'd gone to the deli to pick up a sandwich for lunch. She'd cornered him, asking if he would fix the flashing on her fireplace and replace some shingles that had blown off during the last storm.

Actually *pleaded* with him was more the way it had gone. She'd told him she'd heard a storm was on its way and was terrified a leak would ruin the new drywall in her family room.

An absolute sucker for a hard luck story, Adam agreed to do what he could. He figured the job wouldn't take more than a couple of hours and he and Miranda could still make dinner, if not in Gualala, at one of the local inns.

Adam strapped on his tool belt, pulled the ladder out of the back of his truck, and headed for the side of the house. His optimism about finishing the job early lasted to the top of the ladder. With the shape the roof was in it was amazing there weren't leaks all over the house. God, he hated jobs like this. When he did something, he wanted to do it right. Faith needed her roof replaced, not repaired.

But Faith was a single mother and barely making it month to month on what she earned in the gallery. There was no way she could afford a new roof, even if Adam didn't charge for the labor.

Three hours later he was still working when he heard someone calling to him from the backyard. He walked over to the edge of the roof and looked down.

"Hey, Susan. What are you doing here?"

She stood with her hands on her hips and glared up at him. "When are you going to join the modern world and get a pager? I've looked all over town for you."

"Why? What happened?" Two weeks ago the natural end to the sentence would have been "to Jason." Since then he realized he'd subconsciously added Miranda.

"Nothing," she said quickly. "Jason's fine. I just needed to talk to someone and you're elected."

"Could it wait a couple of hours—at least until I finish up here?"

"I'll go crazy if I have to wait that long."

Susan lived at one extreme or the other, there was no middle ground. Her life was either in crisis or ecstasy and it didn't take much to set the swing in motion. Since the breakup with Matt, she'd been even worse than usual.

"I'll be right down." Adam worked his way back across the roof to the ladder, careful not to cause more damage then was already there. He climbed down, removed his tool belt, put his arm across Susan's shoulders and led her to a set of patio chairs. When they were seated, he said, "I'm all yours."

Her chin-up attitude disappeared, leaving someone who only looked lost. "I don't know where to start."

"Just jump in. If I get lost, I'll ask questions." He leaned back in the chair and stuck his legs out in front of him. After crouching on the roof all afternoon it felt good to stretch.

"You know Matt and I broke up."

It didn't require an answer but he nodded anyway.

"But you don't know why."

"I figured if you wanted me to know you would have told me."

She shifted position, leaning forward and then back again. "We started sleeping together last winter. It was the first time for both of us but he knew how I felt about Jason so we agreed nothing would ever happen unless Matt was wearing something." She stopped to take a breath and let it out again as a sigh. "After a couple of months he said I should go on the pill, just to be sure. I did because I know rubbers break sometimes and the last thing we needed was for me to get pregnant."

"I don't know about you being on the pill," Adam said. "But you were smart to protect yourself."

"Yeah—I even told Matt he was great for thinking of it. Of course that was back when I thought he was looking out for me."

Even taking into consideration Susan's tendency to over-dramatize, Adam had decided the length of her and Matt's separation had to involve a breach of trust. He hadn't been able to piece the clues together.

Her hands knotted in her lap. She looked down at them when she said, "Turns out he wasn't thinking about me at all. He wanted to see what it was like to make love without wearing anything. He didn't even ask, just pretended to put the rubber on and then fucked away."

She blinked several times. Her bottom lip trembled when she said, "God, I'm so dumb I didn't even know he'd done it until afterward. You'd think I would've been able to tell."

"You were probably too caught up in what was happening." Adam wasn't so far from Matt's age that he couldn't understand the stupidity that came with a surge of testosterone. Still, he was furious with Matt for treating Susan and her feelings the way he had.

When she looked up her eyes were filled with unshed tears. "I don't know what to do. I miss him so much. But I can never trust him again, and I won't be with anyone I can't trust." She covered her face with her hands. "How could he do that to me? Damn it he *knows* how I feel about Jason. We talk about it all the time."

"What did he say when you confronted him?"

"That he thought I was making a big deal out of

nothing. He said it shouldn't matter since neither of us had ever slept with anyone else, that it was no different than people who were married."

"And you said?"

"That I knew about the stripper his friends hired for his birthday."

Adam let out a low whistle. This was the first he'd heard about a stripper.

"Of course he swore nothing happened," Susan went on.

"You don't believe him?"

"I want to. But if he lied to me about putting on a rubber, how do I know he isn't lying about that, too? Jason trusted that guy Tony and look what happened to him."

"Have you told your dad?"

"No."

"But you're going to," Adam insisted.

"He would kill Matt."

"You have to be tested, Susan. And so does Matt. And not just once."

"I know," she said softly. "That's one of the reasons I've been looking for you. I was hoping you would take me with you the next time you and Jason went to San Francisco. I could get tested at the clinic and no one would ever have to find out. You know if I went anywhere around here, it would get back to Dad before I walked out the door."

"What about Matt?"

"That's his problem."

Feeling a sudden, overwhelming weariness, Adam sat up and ran his hands across his face while he tried to decide what to do. "I know you're mad at him," he finally said. "And you've got every right, but it's more important to find out whether or not he's positive than to prove a point."

"What do you mean?"

"I think we should take him with us."

"No way. I'm not sitting in the same car with him all the way to San Francisco."

"You don't honestly think he can go for testing around here without someone figuring out what's going on and saying something to your dad, do you?"

"He can go over to Ukiah. Nobody there would make the connection between him and me."

"What if he decides he doesn't give a damn who knows? I understand why you want to keep this a secret, but why should he?"

"Because he loves me." There was a catch in her voice.

He took her hand. "Maybe you should try to find a way to get past what happened, Susan."

She glared at him. "I might miss Matt, but I wouldn't forgive him if he crawled all the way to San Francisco and back on his hands and knees."

"That's not what I'm saying. You and Matt live in the same town. You have the same friends." Unbidden, Adam saw a mental picture of how devastated Matt had been at the restaurant and when he came over with the picnic basket. Now he knew why. "Christ, you're even going to the same college in another month. What are you going to do, head the opposite way every time you see him coming? Do you really want him to have that much control over you?"

"I'm afraid if I'm around him I'll . . ." She made a small, helpless gesture with her hands. "How can you love someone and hate them, too?"

She'd come to him for answers and all he had
were more questions.

It was the third time Miranda had driven by Adam's
house and he still wasn't there. She'd passed time visiting the shops in Mendocino, even bought a new
outfit that was so unlike anything she'd ever owned
she had doubts she'd ever wear it.

She wasn't the "peasant look" type. Muslin skirts
and off-the-shoulder blouses belonged on women
with free spirits and fewer years. Still, she had to
admit she'd liked the person who'd stared back at her
in the dressing room mirror. There'd been a glow
Miranda hadn't seen for longer than she wanted to
remember. But then she had a feeling the glow had a
lot more to do with Adam than the clothing.

She made one more swing by Adam's still-desert-
ed house and was headed back to the highway when,
on impulse, she decided to visit Jason. Normally she
would never drop in on someone uninvited; it just
wasn't the kind of thing you did in her circle of
friends—at least not in her old circle of friends. But
these people were different. She hadn't quite
believed Jason about liking drop-in guests, but
instinctively felt he wouldn't be displeased to see her.

Having second thoughts by the time she arrived,
she sat inside her car trying to decide what to do.
Simply driving away wasn't an easy option. What if
he'd seen her? How would she explain her peculiar
behavior?

Finally it was something the old Miranda
wouldn't have noticed or taken the time to appreciate
that enticed her to move. The myriad flowers

between her and the front door were a reflection of the man inside. He would be as welcoming.

The common—petunias and daisies and marigolds—were casually mixed with the exotic— plants Miranda couldn't identify. She stopped to admire and smell and touch them all the way up the steps.

The door opened before she had a chance to knock. "I'm sorry it took so long to get here," Jason said. "I saw you coming but I was in my studio and it's over the garage."

"I've interrupted you." She felt like an idiot. Of course he would be working. "I should have known you'd be busy this time of day. Why don't I come back later?"

"You'll do no such thing." He took her arm and guided her inside. "I was just about to fix tea. Would you like some, too? Or, I have coffee if you prefer."

She smiled. "Tea is fine."

"Come in the kitchen with me while I fix it. The sun is wonderful there in the afternoon."

She followed him down a hallway and into a large room with a Spanish tile floor and washed oak cupboards. A large bay window looked out over another garden, this one filled with vegetables. There was a free-form flagstone patio with a knee-high brick wall running along one side that separated it from the garden. Beyond was the forest.

"Have a seat," Jason said.

Miranda pulled a chair out and sat at the table, positioning herself so she could see Jason and the view from the window at the same time. "What is that smell?" she asked, taking an appreciative breath.

"Banana nut bread," Jason told her. "Laced with

oat bran and wheat germ and all kinds of good stuff."

She shuddered. "Why would you do that to something as wonderful as banana nut bread?"

"Ahhhh, a cynic. Just wait another" —he bent to check the timer— "fifteen minutes. I promise you'll change your mind."

"I don't know . . . " She'd purposely used her most skeptical voice knowing he would not take offense at the teasing. What was it about him that made her feel so at ease?

"A year ago you wouldn't have wanted to eat anything that came out of this kitchen, but since then I've become a hell of a cook. Even Adam thinks so, and he was always the first to complain."

"I've never been much of a cook. Maybe there's hope for me."

"You have to have a reason." He took an ornate metal box out of the cupboard over the stove. "At least I did. Without something to goad me I'd probably still be eating candy bars for breakfast and popcorn for dinner."

"Sounds like me."

He eyed her. "I'd believe the popcorn, but not the candy bars."

"I've lost a little weight this past year," she admitted.

"There's nothing wrong with being on the thin side if that's your genetic programming, but—"

"Can we talk about something else?" Why was it conversations in a kitchen and at a restaurant always led to discussions about weight? She hated it just as much now as she had when she was fighting going up a size.

"Sure. You name it."

"I went to the Sea Change Gallery this morning," she said.

"Find anything interesting?" He filled a kettle with water and put it on the stove.

"There were a couple of paintings I liked." She smiled. "Actually, I thought they were wonderful."

Jason smiled. "You're really good at this."

It was only then that she realized how coy she must sound to him. "They were yours, of course. I like everything I've seen so far."

"Thank you. I'm not where I want to be, but at least I'm finally moving in the right direction."

"Are there any other galleries around here that handle your work?"

"Not anywhere close. There's one in Carmel and one up in Portland. I keep the best pieces, at least the ones I consider the best, here with me in my studio. They're like old friends I can't bear to lose."

She wasn't surprised. It was something she would have done, too. "I would love to see them. That is if you ever allow—"

"Usually I don't. But for you, I'll make an exception."

"I'm honored."

"And well you should be." He hunched over and rubbed his hands together, the epitome of the mad scientist. "You alone will know my secret formula for making gray skies come alive."

Responding to his playfulness, she laid her hand over her heart. "I shall carry the secret to my grave." The words were no sooner spoken than it hit her how close she'd come to that grave—to never saying them or anything else. She would have missed spending the afternoon in Jason's kitchen if Adam hadn't pulled her out of the water. Not that there was anything monumental about her being there—world peace would not come out of their conversation—but with a new-found certainty, she believed her tomorrow would be brighter and fuller.

The kettle began to whistle. "First we'll have our tea." He opened the tin and scooped several spoonfuls of loose leaves into a ceramic pot. "It's a special blend," he told her, "created exclusively for me by a Chinese herb doctor I met at a conference on holistic medicine. His shop is in the center of Chinatown but impossible to find without a map."

"One of those 'knock three times' places?" Miranda asked and grinned.

"Four," Jason said. "Hajin said three was cliched and if he's nothing else, he's an original."

The smell was less than wonderful. She considered asking for coffee instead, but before she had a chance, the mug was sitting in front of her and Jason was waiting for her reaction. She had to at least try it. If it tasted as bad as it smelled, there was always milk and lemon and sugar to disguise the flavor.

She took a sip. Her taste buds recoiled. She swallowed—fast. "Specially blended for you, huh?"

"You don't like it?"

Words failed her. "It's different."

"I don't understand," he said. "I keep trying, but so far I'm the only one I know who can stomach the stuff."

"Thank God." She set the cup on the far edge of the place mat. "I thought I was going to have to drink the whole thing."

"Just to be polite?" Jason asked, incredulous.

"Something like that."

"Life's too short, Miranda. You have to say what you think."

"The tea is terrible, Jason."

He smiled. "Good for you."

"Can I have something else?"

"Coffee?"

"Strong and black." Maybe it would get rid of the taste the tea had left behind.

Two hours later they were still at the table talking. The bread had been every bit as good as Jason promised—they'd eaten half a loaf between them, Miranda, uncharacteristically, consuming more than her share.

The telephone rang and Jason got up to answer. He was back before Miranda had a chance to finish clearing the table. "That was Adam," he said.

A disquieting warmth spread through her at the mention of his name. "Is he coming over?"

"Actually, he drove by but said he was too dirty to stop in. He saw your car and wanted you to know dinner was on him and he'd be by your place at six-thirty to pick you up. If that isn't okay, you're to call him." Jason put the tin of tea back in the cupboard. "I had no idea it was this late. Would you rather I showed you the studio another time?"

She glanced at the clock on the far wall. "I've taken up half your day, Jason. Why didn't you say something?"

"I didn't notice the time either." He leaned his back against the counter, bracing his hands on the tile. "What is it about us, Miranda?"

The question caught her off guard. She took a minute to answer. "You mean because it seems as if we've known each other forever?"

"You feel it, too, then?"

She nodded. "Almost from the moment we met."

"Maybe we shouldn't try to figure it out. Sometimes when something special is examined too closely in the process it becomes ordinary."

Miranda wasn't used to talking about intimate thoughts and feelings. To do so was considered a sign of weakness in the world she'd inhabited. "Would it be all right if I came back on Friday?"

"Friday's fine. Make it about eight-thirty, I'll be back from my bike ride by then. Don't eat—I'll fix us breakfast."

"I'll be here." She was making plans. And actually looking forward to something. How strange, how good, it felt.

He walked her to her car, lingering in the driveway until she turned at the corner. She'd never had a friend like Jason Delponte. But then it had been a long time since she'd allowed herself the time to put into making new friends—partners, business associates, acquaintances, but not friends. Adam didn't even qualify. He was her lover. Keith wouldn't have fit securely on either list. How could she have done that to herself? How could she have done that to him?

She pulled up to the stop sign. Her hands clamped the steering wheel and she blinked several times to clear her vision. She didn't understand what was happening. Why tears? And why now, after all this time? Where was her famous iron will and emotionless demeanor?

This sadness that had stolen over her when she'd believed the day so good, would it always be there lying in wait?

Would the day ever come when she could think about Keith without suffocating with guilt?

And Jenny . . . how could she not have realized how very special her daughter was until she was gone? How had she taken something so invaluable for granted?

Adam checked the messages on his answering machine before he headed for the shower. There were the usual assortment of weekenders wanting phone estimates for "minor" repairs to their cabins, but there was also a strangely cryptic call from his mother.

He considered calling her back right away but opted for the shower first, hoping a little scalding spray would work the tightness out of the muscles in the back of his neck and ease the headache that had started with Susan's visit, and grown to a pounding beast as he drove home.

As much as he was looking forward to seeing Miranda, he couldn't get Susan and Matt off his mind. Susan was hurt and disappointed, but more than anything she was scared shitless. And he didn't blame her. Jason was a daily reminder to all of them of love gone wrong.

And then there was Matt.

Plainly the "it always happens to the other guy" attitude was as pervasive among Matt and his friends when it came to AIDS as it had been about drinking and driving when Adam was his age. The feeling, if not the subject, was worn like a protective mantle and passed from generation to generation.

Maybe it was the only way to stay sane in an insane age.

Whatever the reason, Matt would bear the consequence. If he was lucky and the birthday present from his buddies turned out to be clean, at least he'd learned a lesson, one that might save his life down the line. But without a miracle, there was no way he would ever set things right with Susan.

Adam stepped into the shower, leaned forward against the tile, and let the spray hit the back of his neck. God, he felt old. It was as if a generation separated him and Susan and Matt, not a decade.

A half hour later he was dressed and on his way out when he remembered the message his mother had left on the answering machine. He'd call her in the morning. She was a patient woman, she had to be with him for a son. Besides, if it had been an emergency, she would have said so.

He had his hand on the doorknob when the phone rang. As he headed back to the living room, he flung his jacket over his shoulder, determined whoever it was wouldn't keep him long.

"Hello." It wasn't his most pleasant greeting.

"Oh, Adam. I thought for sure I would get your machine again."

"As always, your timing is amazing, Mom."

"You were on your way out, weren't you?" she asked. Not waiting for an answer, she went on, "I had a feeling you might put me off until tomorrow."

"What's up?"

"I was wondering when you were coming to the city again."

It was more a lead into something than a question, but he answered anyway. "I don't know. Why?"

"I need to talk to you."

This was not going to be quick and she was not

going to be put off. Adam sat on the arm of the sofa. "Isn't that what we're doing now?"

"I'm serious, Adam."

"Sorry." He had promised Susan he'd take her to the clinic, but not for another week or two. It would mean rearranging both their schedules, but would put an unpleasant task behind her a little sooner. "How about Friday?"

"That would be wonderful. Can you stay the weekend?"

"Not this time. I'll have someone with me."

"They can stay, too."

His mother loved company, the more the better. It was the bane of her life to have her only progeny a wandering son. "That wouldn't work out," he said. "It's someone I'm taking to the clinic who doesn't want anyone to know."

"Oh, dear. Not another friend."

"She just wants to be tested," Adam said.

"She?" Her concern was instant and palpable.

"It's complicated, but nothing you need to worry about. And no, it isn't Miranda. Now, what time Friday?"

"Can you be here for lunch?"

He should take the opportunity to stop by Sea Ranch. Several homeowners there had gotten together and wanted to hire him. Normally the travel time would be too great for him to even consider the job, but they were willing to put him up at one of the condos and make sure he had eight hours of work a day. He'd have to arrange to meet them another day. "I could probably get there by then."

"Great. I'll make reservations at some place special. Dress up."

"Wait a minute," Adam protested. "You're not even going to give me a hint?"

"It's too complicated to go into over the phone. But there is something I want you to do for me. Be thinking about the possibility you might change your mind some day and want to take over the business."

"Mom, I told you—"

"I know. But it's important that you're absolutely sure this time."

He'd heard the same thought in various forms for the past ten years, but somehow this time was different. "I'll think about it," he promised. A strange feeling came over him. He'd made up his mind about entering the business world a long time ago.

Or had he?

Could it be he'd made his decision knowing the door would always be open should he change his mind? Was what he'd heard in his mother's voice the sound of that door closing?

Eight

Miranda was on the back deck waiting for Adam when he arrived. He didn't say anything when he saw her. Instead he stood with one foot propped on the step and stared appreciatively. The early evening sun reflected off her hair and made it look more golden than brown. She had on a long gauzy skirt made nearly transparent by the backlight. The matching blouse hung low on one shoulder, not in a calculated way, more as if it had slipped there unnoticed.

Nothing was revealed that he hadn't already seen, that he hadn't caressed or kissed or come to know by the touch of his tongue. Still her shadowed legs and bared skin were incredibly, almost unbearably, erotic. Beyond that was the deep pleasure of finding her waiting, knowing she had put on the dress for him and that he was the reason her eyes shone with anticipation.

"I see you bought more fuchsias," he said. There were five of them sitting on the railing.

"Hooks, too," she said. "But I couldn't get them to stay up when I hung the plants."

"Sounds like you need someone who's done that kind of thing before."

A smile tugged at one corner of her mouth. "I'm pretty new around here and don't know a lot of people. Is there someone you could recommend?"

"I'm not sure. Was hanging a couple of hooks all you had in mind?"

"Oh, no," she said innocently.

"Maybe you better tell me what—"

"There's this other problem I'm having . . . I planted several packs of petunias around the trees yesterday, but when I got up this morning they were gone."

"Deer," Adam said.

"Yes?"

"D-E-E-R."

"Oh . . . " She grinned and moved to pull her blouse back over her shoulder.

"Don't. I like it that way."

Her fingers touched her bared skin. "I bought the size I've always worn." Now she nervously fingered the material. "But the top is too big. I don't know what came over me at the store. I've never worn anything like this."

He came over and gently pulled on the opposite sleeve until both shoulders were exposed. "This is the way it's supposed to look."

It wasn't until her hand flew up to cover the newly exposed skin that he realized what he'd done—revealed one of her scars. He covered her hand with his own and looked deeply into her eyes. "I know what's there. You don't have to hide it from me anymore."

"How could you?" She tried to pull away.

"Vern."

Her eyes opened wide in anger. "He had no right. I'll sue him. He'll never be able to get insurance—" The words died in her throat. "My God," she whispered. "What's wrong with me?"

"What happened to you, Miranda?"

"I won't tell you." There was no equivocation in the statement. The scars she carried inside and out would stay hidden.

If he pushed, he was afraid he'd lose her, and wouldn't take that chance. "Then I won't ask again. But I won't pretend they aren't a part of you."

To prove his point, he moved her hand and touched his lips to the scar on her shoulder.

She held herself rigid as if enduring his touch rather than needing or wanting it. With slow deliberate movements, he lowered her blouse farther, exposing the gentle mound where her breast began. He made a thin moist trail with the tip of his tongue as he moved across her chest. When he moved lower still, he realized she wasn't wearing anything underneath the gauzy material. The knowledge was intoxicating, its message unmistakable. She'd made her own plans for the evening.

"God, I've missed you." He brought her arms up and put them around his neck.

"Why did you stay away?" It was more accusation than question.

"Because I thought it was what you wanted." He bent, placed his arm behind her knees and lifted her into the air. "Because I'm an idiot." He captured her mouth in a deep, plundering kiss.

An hour later, the storm that had been lingering offshore finally moved inland, lashing the bedroom windows with dime-size pellets of rain. "I love the sound of rain," Adam said.

Miranda came up on her elbow and looked at him. She ran her hand across his chest in a hesitantly possessive gesture. "With me, it's snow."

"But you can't hear snow."

"I can."

He smiled, caught her hand and pressed a kiss to the palm. "Come winter I'll take you to the mountains. You can listen to it snow there."

"Winter's months away. I may not be here then."

She was warning him, telling him not to get too involved.

"It's not going to work, Miranda. I don't scare easily."

"I only thought it fair to warn you."

The next morning Miranda was still in bed when Adam brought her a cup of coffee. "What are your plans for today?" he asked, sitting down beside her, his back propped against the headboard.

"I don't know. I'll probably go for a walk if it isn't too wet."

He blew gently on his coffee. "And?"

"And nothing. Why are you asking?"

"There's a bike shop in Fort Bragg. I saw in yesterday's paper they were having a sale."

She eyed him. "So?"

"Don't be obtuse. If you had a bike you could go riding with us."

"Gee, thanks. But I think I'm going to have to pass on that offer." She had him hold her coffee while she readjusted her pillow to sit up beside him. "I could just see me on one of those mountain bikes you guys ride. The whole town would be laughing."

"What are you talking about?"

"Come on, Adam. I'm thirty-eight years old. Those things are for kids."

Adam let out a groan. "There are times you drive me crazy. When are you going to get it through your head I don't give a damn how old you are and neither does anyone else?"

"All this because I don't want to go biking with you?" she snapped.

"It isn't that you don't want to go, it's the reason."

"Pretending we don't have an age difference won't make it go away. I'm *thirty-eight* years old, Adam. You're twenty-nine."

He tried to ease the tension. "Would it make you feel better if I told you I'm going to be thirty in a couple of months?"

"It's more then the years, Adam. It's how we think. If you live to be a hundred, you won't be as old as I was at twenty. I'm not saying there's anything wrong with that, although I might have a while ago," she admitted. "Now, I wish I could be more like you. I've finally begun to understand how much I missed." Her voice faded to a whisper. "But it's past and there's nothing I can do to change it."

He could feel her mentally leaving him. "I'll let the bike thing go for now, but I reserve the right to try again later."

"So, now that we've settled what I'm not going to do today," she said too brightly, "what about you?"

"I've got a meeting with a group of homeowners in Sea Ranch." When he'd called to postpone their meeting, they'd arranged to have it sooner instead.

"Why a group?"

The conversation had turned meaningless, but it was what they needed to save the morning. "I told the man who wanted to hire me that the job wasn't worth the three hours it takes in travel time. He got several people together who had work they wanted done and he even arranged a house for me to stay in while I'm there. Supposedly there's enough work lined up to last a week. That's what I'm going down there to check out."

"When would you go?" she asked carefully.

"I'm not sure, the end of the month maybe, depending on how things look around here." He wanted her to ask to go with him, or at least say she would miss him when he was gone.

"I guess you have to take whatever work you can during the summer. I wouldn't imagine there was much to do around here after Labor Day."

He hated polite conversation. It was as artificial and demeaning as phony compliments. "Are we only going to be good in bed, Miranda?"

She got up, grabbed her sweater off the chair and jammed her arms in the sleeves. "What do you want from me?"

"Honesty would be good for starters."

"I haven't lied to you."

"Then tell me how you feel about my being gone for all that time."

"It's your life. What possible difference—" She stood with her back to him. With jerky, impatient movements she tied the belt tightly around her waist. "I'll miss you."

Adam got up and came around the bed. "You could come with me."

She shook her head. "I'm not ready for anything like that. Not yet."

It wasn't what he'd wanted to hear, but it could have been worse. "If I hadn't promised, I wouldn't go."

"Don't worry about me, Adam. I know how to be alone."

"I have to go into the city Friday. Want to come along?" He would work out the arrangements with Susan. If she felt awkward having Miranda along, he could take her to the clinic the following week.

Miranda laid her hands against his chest and forced a surprisingly successful smile. "Believe it or not, I'm busy Friday."

Adam cocked an eyebrow at her. "Anyone I know?"

"Jason. He's going to show me his studio. I thought I'd take him to lunch afterward."

The news brought a swell of pleasure. Jason and Miranda would be good for each other. "If I'm back by eight or so, would you happen to be free for dinner?"

She stood on tiptoe and gave his earlobe a playful nip. "Why don't we eat in."

"Put a candle in the window." His hands slipped over the wool material coming to rest on her buttocks. He brought her closer. "Come hell or high water, I'll be here."

Friday morning Miranda got up early in anticipation of her meeting with Jason. It was one of those crisp, clear days where everything, even thoughts, seemed in sharper focus. Off shore there was the usual fog bank, but inland the sky was a robin's egg blue, not a cloud in sight.

Miranda started for her car, but as she opened the door it struck her that it was simply too beautiful a morning to drive. She went back in the house and called Jason, leaving a message on his answering machine that she'd decided to walk over and would be a little late arriving.

She was only a mile from town when she glanced at the road and saw Adam's truck coming. Her heart quickened and she smiled at the automatic reaction. Could it be her body knew something her mind refused to acknowledge?

She glanced at her watch. He'd obviously waited until after the bicycle ride to head for San Francisco. But why was he coming from behind her? Unless . . . Of course, he'd stopped by her place to tell her good-bye.

A twinge of guilt hit at the thought of the long lonely ride ahead of him. Surely Jason wouldn't have minded if she'd put off the tour of his studio a few days more. The temptation to take Adam off guard when he'd asked her if she had plans had been too great to resist.

If nothing else, she could have him drop her off at Jason's and then send him on his way with a promissory kiss for that evening. She quickened her pace and cut across the grassy slope that separated the path she was on from the highway. As she neared the road she brought her hand up to wave but checked the motion at the last minute. Adam wasn't alone.

He drove by without noticing her, but not so fast she wasn't able to see who was sitting beside him. Susan Lansky must not have had a prior commitment, or if she had, it was one she was willing to cancel.

An unreasonable surge of jealousy swept through

Miranda. What she was feeling was stupid and groundless but there was nothing she could do to rein it in.

Adam and Susan were friends. They'd known each other long before Miranda was in the picture. Besides, Susan was only eighteen years old and had a boyfriend who worshiped her. What could she and Adam possibly have in common?

But were the eleven years that separated them so different from the nine that separated herself and Adam? Damn it, she didn't want to feel this way. Adam had given her no reason to doubt him. It was her that he made love to and it was her he was coming back to that night. Where was her self confidence, the ego that had put her on top in a male-dominated world?

How could a morning that had started out so beautiful turn so tarnished?

It was a foolish question, especially coming from her. She more than anyone else knew how easily the best of worlds could be irrevocably shattered.

Nine

"Mary, I honestly think it would be easier on all of us if I wasn't here when Adam arrives." Michael Ericson came up to Mary where she stood looking out the window and put his arm around her. "I don't want you worrying about me if Adam says something negative. He's bound to be upset at first. I know I would be if I were in his place."

She looked up at him and smiled. "I keep telling you Adam isn't like anyone you've ever known. He never reacts the way you think he will, or even should."

"Then why are you so nervous?"

She considered his question. "I'm not sure," she admitted. "Maybe it's because I don't just want his approval, I want him to see you the way I do."

He gave her a suggestive grin. "Within reason, I hope."

"He's going to know I would never become involved with a man who wasn't as stimulating at home as he was in the office." She lifted her chin to receive his kiss.

"I wasn't aware I'd been put through such extensive testing."

Mary laughed. "Oh, yes you were."

Michael took her hand and led her back to the burgundy and green plaid sofa. He sat down and pulled her into his lap. "Would you rather put off telling him?"

"So he can read about us in the paper?"

"Am I supposed to believe Adam reads the society page?"

"No, but he does read the business section."

"Why would a man who has absolutely no interest in—"

"He thinks he's looking out for me." Michael started to say something, but she held her hand up to stop him. "I know, it seems impossibly naive, but he has this sixth sense about things. He doesn't call unless he has specific questions or thinks I should be aware of something that's happening in a foreign market."

"And is he right?"

"Every damn time. That's the frustrating part. He has all the instinct and talent and wants nothing to do with the business."

"I think you're as confused about where he belongs as he is. You probably don't hear it yourself, but there's a distinct note of pride in your voice when you talk about Adam and his projects."

"I know he likes to think of himself as a citizen of the world, whatever the hell that means, but he's bound to want to settle down some day. He was born and raised in this country. If he wants to do good deeds, there are plenty of them that need doing right here."

"Spoken like a true mother." He shifted position to give her more room. "Is it the places he goes or the work he does that bothers you?"

"Both. I know the world needs people like Adam—"

"You just don't want it to be him."

"Can you blame me? He's my only child. And don't tell me he could get run over by a bus right here at home. I'll play those odds over the odds of getting shot while feeding refugees or ending up in a shallow grave for mouthing off about some political injustice."

"He's a grown man, Mary. And from everything you've told me, capable of taking care of himself."

"Most of the time. I hate to think what losing Jason is going to do to him." They'd been best friends since they were old enough to walk. Jason told Adam he was gay long before he broke the news at home. And he was the first person Jason had turned to when the HIV became a case of full-blown AIDS.

"There are some people who are capable of being around suffering without taking it into themselves. And there are others who die a little every time someone else does. Adam couldn't do what he does if he wasn't more the first than the second. He'll come through this thing with Jason all right."

She put her elbow on his shoulder and leaned her head against her hand. "I know you're right, but I can't get past the idea that Adam will change his mind some day and want what he can't have. Once the business is sold, even if he could buy it back, it wouldn't be the same. Ever since Gerald died Adam has been looking for something. I don't think he knows what it is, only that he can't stop until he figures it out. How is he going to feel if it turns out to be his father's business and some corporate conglomerate has taken it over by then? Or if, God forbid, it's gone bankrupt through poor management?"

"Hold on just a minute," Michael said. "This company stopped being Gerald's a long time ago. You're the one who successfully expanded and you're the one who tripled the revenues. If Adam is as savvy about business as you think he is, he's well aware that this is your company and not his father's." He pressed a quick kiss to the tip of her nose. "Or is that what's really bothering you?"

"I don't know what you mean."

"Never mind. I'm probably way off base on this."

"Don't do that, Michael. If you have something to say, say it."

"You did something no one believed you could do and made more than a few bankers eat their words."

"Get to the point." She gave his tie a none too gentle tug.

"It would only be natural for you to want to pass your own accomplishments on to your son."

The thought stopped her cold. For eleven years she'd mentally put herself into the roll of executor of Gerald's estate, maintaining the fortune until it was time to pass the business on to its rightful heir. But Michael was right. Through time and effort and pure determination, she'd made the business hers. She wanted Adam to know what she'd achieved and the only way that would ever happen was if he took over from her. How could she have been so blind to the obvious?

"Assuming you're right," she began, disconcerted at the revelation, "what do I do now?"

"That's up to you, sweetheart. I'm staying clear of this. As far as I'm concerned, this is between you and Adam."

A buzzer sounded on her desk. "He's here," she said.

"There's still time for me to slip out the back."

She stood and held out her hand. "Don't tempt me."

Despite Patty's assurances his mother was waiting for him, Adam tapped lightly on her office door before going in. "Now what's this big surprise you—" The words caught in his throat when he saw his mother was with someone. "I'm sorry," he said, "I thought you were alone."

Mary smiled nervously. "Adam, I'd like you to meet Michael Ericson." She turned to Michael. "Michael, this is my son, Adam."

So this was the mysterious man in his mother's life. He extended his hand. Adam had always believed you could tell a lot about someone by the way they shook your hand. Michael passed. Easily. "It's nice to meet you," he told the older man. "Mom's been decidedly circumspect where you're concerned, which can only mean there's something serious going on between you two."

"*Adam*," Mary said sharply.

Michael smiled. "I'm as serious as can be where she's concerned."

"So much for taking time to get acquainted," Mary said. "I should have known better."

Adam gave his mother a hug. "Congratulations."

"Just like that?" she asked, hugging him back. "You aren't going to question Michael or ask if his intentions are honorable?"

"You're the smartest woman I know. You'd never get involved with a man you didn't investigate first."

She laid her forehead against Adam's shoulder and let out a groan.

"Is that true?" Michael asked her. "Did you have me investigated?"

"Just a little," she admitted without looking up.

Adam liked the amused look in Michael's eyes. He guessed him to be around his mother's age and with a bank account at least the equal of hers. He was tall, and had an athletic build. His black hair was well on its way to gray and there were strong laugh lines around his mouth and eyes. They would make a good pair.

"So have you set a date?" Adam asked.

"Not yet," Mary answered.

But at the same time Michael said, "The second of November."

Adam looked into his mother's eyes. "Well, which is it?"

"I was going to talk to you about it first . . . before we made an official announcement."

"November sounds great to me," Adam said. "You won't have to worry about fighting the crowds on your honeymoon."

"You don't have to sound so eager," Mary told him.

"Having doubts, Mom?"

Michael interrupted the byplay. "I think I'll leave you two alone now." He directed the next to Adam. "If you have the time, I'd like you to come over to my offices later so I can show you around."

"I'll make the time," Adam said. He extended his hand again. "Welcome to the family."

Michael's face lit up with a warm smile. "Thank you, Adam. You're everything I was led to expect."

Adam made a face at his mother. "You've been at it again, haven't you?"

"Shut up," she said with mock sternness. "And sit down. I'll be right back." She left with Michael.

Adam wandered over to the window. He was more surprised and thrown off balance by his mother's news than he'd let on.

She'd been the one constant in his life—all of his life, as much a friend as a parent. He was happy for her but he was confused, too. Why had she waited until now to tell him something this important?

Mary returned in less than a minute. She closed the door and stood with her back pressed against it. "Well?"

"I like him," Adam said. "At least what I've seen so far. But then I'm not the one who counts. Why don't you tell me why you like him?"

"We met at the Delpontes' Christmas party two years ago, but then I already told you that. He was as bored as I was and we found each other in the library. We started talking about books, he's a reader, too. Which is surprising considering how busy his business keeps him."

"What kind of business?"

"Computer software. He owns Jelcon."

Adam let out a soft whistle. "*That* Michael Ericson. I'm impressed." Which took care of any concern Adam had been subconsciously harboring that Ericson might be after the Kirkpatric fortune.

"He's a simple man, Adam. You'd never know he owned something like Jelcon." She went to her desk and took out a folder. "I had Felix draw up a prenuptial agreement for me saying our companies were not and never would be community property. Michael refused to sign."

Adam took the papers she extended and saw that it contained his mother's signature but that the space left for Michael's was blank. "I'm not following you. Why did you do this?"

"I thought it only fair. I had nothing to do with building his company, why should I get half just because I married him?"

There were a lot of people who would think his mother a few cents short of a dime for her beliefs. Adam would have been surprised had she behaved any other way. "What did Michael say when you told him how you felt?"

Her face became flushed and she smiled shyly. "He said everything he had was nothing without me."

"But what about your company?"

"He knows that I consider Kirkpatric Ltd. yours, not mine, and insists everything be worked out between you and me before the wedding. He doesn't want your assets caught up in some legal entanglements with his."

"Sounds like you've got a winner, Mom. Someone who really understands what you're all about," Adam said. "I'm happy for you. You've been alone too long."

She sat back in her chair, her hands grasping the arms. "Since we're on the subject, aren't you going to ask me what I intend to do with our company?"

Adam shrugged. "I assumed you were going to keep it."

"I don't need my work to fill up my life anymore, Adam. Michael conducts business all over the world and I want to travel with him."

"I see," Adam said softly. The moment they'd been talking about for years was finally here. There would be no more reprieves, no more postponements.

"I don't know the first thing about running this company," he said.

"I would stay until you felt you were ready to take over."

Again, as he had only weeks ago, he tried to picture himself the one behind the desk day after day, held there by obligation to an idea and commitment to a memory. The mere thought made the room grow smaller as if the walls were closing in on him.

"This is not who I am," he said at last. "I wish it were, at least for you and Dad, but I'd go crazy knowing my life was planned out for me." How strange it had been to discover there was a value, namely the thirty-two million dollars listed in the accountant's last report his mother had given him, that could be put on something as ethereal as his mental freedom. He wished there were a way he could communicate his feelings, a way to lessen the blow that came with the destruction of his mother's own dream, but there were no words. "I'm sorry."

"I won't lie and tell you I didn't harbor a secret hope you would change you mind when it actually came down to the wire, but I think now that I'm going to be starting a new life of my own, I have a better understanding of how you feel."

Adam sat on the edge of the desk and took his mother's hand. "How did I get so lucky?"

"Damned if I know."

He smiled. "I hope your Michael Ericson appreciates you."

Another flush accompanied her return smile. "Trust me, he does."

"So, what will you do with the company?"

"Look for a buyer who won't come in and dismantle everything. It could take quite a while, but I feel we owe that to our employees. After the sale the money will be yours, of course."

He recoiled at the idea. "What in the hell would I do with it? I don't want it. I've done nothing to earn it."

"One doesn't earn one's inheritance, Adam. It just is."

"You aren't dead," he shot back. "I hardly ever use the money in the trust fund Dad set up. I haven't made a major draw on the account in years."

"I'm not saying you have to spend it."

"So what am I supposed to do, let all those millions make more millions for some bank?"

"It's your money." Her voice remained reasonable and calm in direct contrast to Adam's excitement. "You can do whatever you want with it."

He took a deep breath and let it out slowly. There was time yet. The sale would take months. One way or another he would convince her.

"Why does the idea of having money scare you?" she asked.

"It's not who I am."

"Are you afraid it might change you?" Her expression was thoughtful. She was trying hard to understand.

"It could," he admitted.

"Not if you don't let it."

"Tell that to all the lottery winners."

"Now you're being ridiculous. You were born

with money. It's been a part of who you are all your life. I can't see where it's done you any harm."

She was right, of course. Adam was having trouble understanding the strength of his reaction himself. "I need some time to think this through."

"Just don't put it off the same way you have in the past, Adam. This time the deadline is real."

The phone rang. Because his mother usually had her calls held when he was there, he said, "That's probably Susan. I told her to let me know when she was through shopping."

Mary picked up the receiver. "Yes," she said. "He's right here."

Adam took the phone. "That was fast."

There was a long pause before Susan said, "Actually I was wondering if it was all right if I stayed a little longer."

His promise to Miranda to be back early enough for dinner made him hesitate. "How long did you have in mind?"

"The rest of the afternoon?"

"The shopping isn't going well, I take it?"

"Wrong—you wouldn't believe what I've found." Her voice was animated with excitement, a nice change from their recent conversation. "They have the coolest clothes in Nordstrom—not what I expected at all. And there's this really great lady, Julie, who's going all over the store with me helping me pick out stuff. If I just had a little more time I could get everything I need for school today."

"How about if I pick you up out front at 4:30. Is that enough time?"

"You're the best, Adam." She started to hang up and then added, "By the way, the people at the clinic were great. I told them to send the results of the test to your house. I hope that's all right."

"No problem. Now get shopping. I don't want you calling me at 4:00 telling me you need more time."

She hung up without saying good-bye.

"If you start for home at 4:30," Mary said, "you'll be sitting on the bridge for an hour."

"Damn it," Adam groaned. He'd only considered the travel time, not the traffic. There was no way he'd get back early enough to take Miranda out for a decent dinner that night.

"Is this the same Susan I met last Christmas?" Mary asked. "Dr. Lansky's daughter?"

"Uh huh," Adam said.

"You had to bring her all the way down here to be tested?" And then, "Oh . . . she doesn't want her father to know."

"She doesn't want anyone to know," Adam said.

"Don't worry, I won't say anything." She gathered the papers she'd shown Adam earlier and put them back in her desk. "It's just so sad. How many more young people can we afford to lose? When will they get it in their heads that—"

"Not now, Mom," Adam said. "I live with it every day. I come here to get away from it for a while."

"By bringing Susan to the clinic?"

"It's a one time thing." At least he hoped to hell it was, but they wouldn't know that for another six months when she had her second test at the school clinic.

"Let's see, you don't want to talk about Jason or Susan or selling the business . . . " She smiled brightly. "So, how was the cognac?"

"I haven't opened it yet."

"I thought—" She looked up and saw the expression on his face. "Never mind."

The door opened and Michael Ericson came in.

"Just in time," Mary murmured.

"Ready for lunch?" Michael asked.

Mary turned to Adam. "I am. How about you?"

"I have a phone call I'd like to make first." With any luck he could still catch Miranda at Jason's.

"While you're doing that," Mary said, "I'll check my schedule with Patty. Maybe we could get in to see Felix this afternoon and start things rolling."

A strange heaviness settled in Adam's chest. Felix Hansen had been the family attorney as long as Adam could remember. He would be the natural person to help with the sale.

"Sounds good to me." Adam could see by his mother's reaction that his attempt at enthusiasm had been only marginally successful.

"We'll meet you by the elevators," Michael said.

"I won't be long."

Michael waited for Mary to get her purse out of her desk and then opened the door for her. He guided her through with his hand at the back of her waist. They stopped by Patty's desk and then went into the conference room where Mary had left her raincoat. When they were alone, Michael asked, "How did it go?"

"He refuses to have anything to do with the money."

"But isn't that what you expected?"

"What's the old saying? Hope springs eternal?" She put her arms around Michael's waist and her head against his chest.

"I've been giving this some thought," Michael said. "And I believe I may have come up with a solution."

"Please—let me hear it."

"Let me do some checking first," he said. "I want to find out if what I have in mind is even possible."

She didn't wait easily but wouldn't push him. "You're good for me," she said and gave him a kiss. "I forgot how special it is to have someone to share my problems with."

He deepened their kiss. "I aim to please."

"Oh, you do that, Mr. Ericson. Yes indeed."

Ten

Adam didn't reach Miranda before lunch and decided against leaving a message on Jason's machine. He tried again at 1:30 from Michael's office and then at 3:00, after the meeting with Felix. Finally, just before he was to leave to pick up Susan, Jason answered.

"I've been trying to get you all afternoon," Adam said.

"We went shopping," Jason told him with an air of mystery.

"God—you and Susan."

"Hmmmm, you sound a little out of sorts. Susan get lost in Macy's?"

"Nordstrom. Or at least that's where she was when she called me four hours ago."

"The girl has good taste. You have to give her that."

The mood Adam was in, he wasn't ready to yield anything. "Is Miranda there by any chance?"

"You just caught her. She was about to walk out the door."

Seconds later, Miranda's voice greeted him. "Where are you?" she asked. "On the road, I hope."

The anticipation in her voice was an undisguised invitation. Adam wondered if Jason had picked up on it. "I'm still in San Francisco. And probably will be for another couple of hours."

"Oh," she said softly.

"I'll explain when I see you."

"Would you like me to call Vern and tell him you're going to be late?"

Jason must have told her that Susan had gone with him. "I don't think it's necessary, he's the one who loaded her down with the credit cards she's been using all afternoon. But then it might keep him from waiting up for us."

"Susan went with you to go shopping?"

The question confused Adam. What other reason could Miranda think she'd gone with him? Jason wouldn't have told her about the testing without checking with Susan first. "She wanted to get some things for school."

"And Fort Bragg isn't exactly a fashion mecca," she said as if it were some kind of revelation.

"Are you all right?" Adam asked.

"I'm fine, just a little disappointed you're getting such a late start coming home."

"I'll make it up to you." He wasn't convinced his not being there was the only thing bothering her. "Maybe we can do something tomorrow. I'll call the people with the wiring job and—"

"You don't have to do that, Adam," she said. "Thanks to Jason, I'm going to have plenty to keep me busy from now on."

"What's going on with you two?"

"What do you mean?"

"First you're gone all afternoon on some mysterious shopping trip . . ." Their relationship had had so few moments of lightheartedness, it felt good to be able to tease her about something. "And now you're telling me you don't care whether you see me tomorrow or not."

"I'm sorry, Adam, but that's the way it is with us artist types. We need uninterrupted time in order to create."

"So, Jason signed you up for lessons."

"He said he's never seen anyone with such natural, raw talent."

"You've already painted something? I'm impressed."

"Well, not painted exactly," she equivocated. "More like appreciated. Jason showed me his portfolio."

Adam laughed out loud. "What am I going to do with two of you spouting that artist stuff?"

Her voice lowered to a whisper. "I know what you can do with one of us."

The muscles in his groin tightened. "Hold that thought."

"Until when?"

"Somewhere around ten, maybe eleven."

"Are you sure you want to do this? Don't forget you have that wiring job tomorrow."

"I can handle it."

"I'll be waiting."

An hour later Adam was on the Golden Gate Bridge headed home. It was Friday and the traffic was even worse than usual. After stopping in Santa Rosa for something to eat, it was almost eleven when he dropped Susan off at her house.

Feeling hot and sweaty, he decided to stop by his house for a quick shower and change of clothes before going to Miranda's. The instant he pulled into the driveway he saw that he'd made a mistake.

Matt was there waiting for him, sitting on the trunk of his Mustang, his back propped against the window.

There was no way he could tell Matt that Miranda was waiting for him without their late-night meeting becoming a subject of gossip. It wasn't that Matt couldn't be trusted with a secret, it was more that Adam didn't want to tell him. He was reluctant to give his and Miranda's meetings a clandestine tag.

Adam got out of the truck and walked over to Matt's car, determined whatever had brought him there that night wasn't going to take long to settle. "How long've you been waiting?"

"A couple of hours," Matt said. "I thought you'd be back sooner."

"Me, too." Adam shoved his hands in his back pockets. "What can I do for you, Matt?" Even in the dim light of the filtered moon he could see how distressed Matt looked.

"How'd it go at the clinic?"

Adam let out a deep sigh. "I don't think that's something you should be asking me."

"You're the only one I can ask. Susan still won't talk to me except to nag me about being tested."

"She's going to be a long time getting past this, Matt."

"Did you talk to her?"

Adam knew what Matt was asking and it made him want to deck him. But on the slim chance he might be wrong, Adam asked, "About what?"

"You know, about how she's making too big a deal out of this." Adam pulled himself to the edge of the trunk and propped his feet on the bumper. "What's so wrong with wanting to know what it feels like to have sex the way God intended? She's got to know I wouldn't have done it if I'd have thought there was any chance I had something. I love her too much to do something like that to her."

To keep his hands still Adam folded his arms tightly across his chest. "If you were so sure what you were doing was okay, why didn't you talk to her about it first?"

Matt didn't answer.

"Well?" Adam insisted.

"You know as well as I do she would've said no," Matt said almost angrily.

"What you're saying is that you getting your rocks off was more important than her consent."

"It wasn't like I planned it."

"Oh?"

"Well, not a long time. And I told her I was sorry." He slammed the side of his fist against the trunk. "Why can't she just let it go?"

"About the stripper, Matt . . . "

He looked up. "Yeah?"

"How far did it go?"

"I was drunk."

"And?"

"There was a lot going on that night." He shrugged. "I don't know for sure."

"The hell you don't."

"God damn it, what do you want from me?"

"The truth." Adam needed to know how hard to push Matt about the testing, and for his own peace of mind, how concerned he should be about Susan.

"She was doing it with all the guys."

Adam's peace of mind took a nosedive.

"What was I supposed to do?" Matt sent Adam a pleading look, begging him to understand.

The tragedy was in the understanding. Matt and his friends were only upholding a long tradition of stupidity. Trouble was, the consequences had outpaced the behavior. "You've got a lot of the same thing ahead of you in the next few years, Matt. I'd suggest you work it out before it happens again."

"But what am I going to do right now about Susan?"

"I don't know that there is anything you can do. Someday you're going to figure out what this trust thing she keeps throwing at you is all about. Until then I'd say you're out of luck where she's concerned."

"Did she tell you that?"

Nothing he could say was going to get through to Matt. His world was too small, his experiences too limited. In his eighteen years this was the first time he'd come up against something he couldn't change or make go away just because he wanted it to.

"It's late," Adam said. "And I'm tired."

"Will you talk to her again for me?"

"There isn't anything more I can say."

"Yes there is. Just keep telling her that I'm sorry and that I love her. Maybe if she hears it enough it'll wear her down."

"I'm not the one you want pleading your case, Matt."

He reacted as if Adam had hit him. "Why not?"

"Because I agree with Susan. If you don't have trust in a relationship, you don't have anything."

"Jesus, I didn't do anything any other guy

wouldn't have done in my place. I don't know what—" He couldn't go on. For long seconds he sat perfectly still, his face contorted in pain. Tears spilled from his eyes and landed on his blue NIKE T-shirt, the one with the logo, JUST DO IT.

"You've learned a hard lesson," Adam told him. "Don't waste it."

"I ain't giving up." He swiped at his cheeks with the back of his hand and slid the rest of the way off the car. After several seconds he went around to the driver's side and got in. Without saying anything more, he backed out and drove away.

Adam stared up at the night sky. The Milky Way was like a creamy blanket on a field of black. He found a star, one so small it blinked, and made a wish. He didn't believe in such things anymore than he believed in horoscopes, but what the hell? Who was he to say there wasn't anyone up there listening?

By the time Adam got to Miranda's house it was after midnight. She'd left a light on and the door unlocked but there were no sounds coming from inside.

He found her on the sofa, curled up with an open magazine on her lap, her head tilted to the side, resting on the wing of the high back. She was wearing something peach colored and satiny. Lace covered her breasts, held in place with thin straps loosely draped over her shoulders. The gown left the scars on her shoulder and arm visible and Adam was oddly pleased that she'd done nothing to try to hide them from him.

She'd put on weight in the past few weeks, but not so much he couldn't still see the outline of bone under too-thin flesh.

Fragile and vulnerable weren't words he would have ordinarily used to describe Miranda, yet they were the ones that came to mind.

He went to the sofa and took the magazine off her lap, glancing at the cover as he did so. It was something called ART WORLD; Jason's name and address were on a sticker at the bottom.

Adam touched her arm. "Miranda . . ." he said softly.

She stirred but didn't wake.

"Come on, sweetheart," he went on. "Let's get you to bed."

Her eyes blinked open. "Adam?" She sat up and swept her hair from her face. "What time is it?"

"Late."

She touched the side of his face, her hand lethargic from sleep. "I missed you."

"I missed you, too." The half-closed lids and slow speech told him she was only half awake. He reached past her to turn off the lamp then picked her up in his arms.

She snuggled against him, nestling her head on his shoulder. "Hmmm, you smell good."

"I stopped by the house to take a shower."

"For me?"

He smiled. "For you."

She yawned. "What a nice thing to do."

"What can I say, I'm a nice guy." The bedroom was dark and he had to feel his way. After several slow, hesitant steps, his shin came in contact with the mattress. She'd already folded the bedding down. "I'm not going to find a chocolate stuck in my hair in the morning, am I?"

She didn't answer.

He listened to the steady rhythm of her breathing. She was asleep again. He put her on the bed, stripped off his clothes and carefully got in beside her. Within seconds she had curled into his side, her arm possessively flung across his waist.

When Adam woke in the morning Miranda was still next to him, curled up to his back, spoon fashion. He turned to face her. She made a soft groan at the loss of position and rolled to her other side.

Adam glanced at the clock. He had ten minutes before he was due to meet Jason. Reluctantly, he got out of bed, picked his clothes up off the floor and went in the living room to get dressed. He was tying his shoes when he heard a noise behind him.

"Would you like me to make you some coffee?" Miranda asked from the doorway.

He turned to look at her and his reply caught in his throat. Her hair was disheveled from sleep, the strap to her gown had slipped off her shoulder, leaving one breast exposed to the top of the nipple. Peach satin clung to the curve of her hip. The slit from the hem showed a sliver of thigh.

He wanted her—not slowly or gently or with subtle seduction. In his mind he'd crossed the few feet that separated them, stripped the gown from her body and wrapped her legs around his waist. Her breast was in his mouth and he felt the hard peak of her nipple pressed against his tongue. She called his name as she rode him; he moved deeper and harder into her until she exploded with the sweet pain of climax.

But it wasn't enough. With Miranda it was never enough. Awake he was thinking about her; asleep she was a resident in every dream. When they were apart, he was filled with a keen anticipation of being with her again. When they were together, they inhabited a wondrous cocoon, special in its isolation.

"Adam?"

"Jason's waiting for me."

"He wouldn't mind if you were a few minutes late. Call him and—"

"He's meeting me at my house." His need to be with her was becoming a physical ache. "Afterward I have that job in Fort Bragg."

She smiled. "And I have my first lesson with Jason this morning."

"Is this artistic bent something new or are you one of those closet painters who always wanted to run away to a South Sea island?"

"It's new, but Jason insists the inclination has always been there." She put her arms behind her back and leaned into the wall. "Speaking of closet, why didn't you tell me Jason was gay?"

He was dumbfounded at the question. "I guess I just assumed you knew. It isn't something he's ever tried to hide. Hell, he came out when he was sixteen." Another thought struck. "Does it matter?"

"Of course not. I was surprised, that's all. He isn't . . . he doesn't act . . . " She frowned. "You know what I mean."

Obviously she hadn't been around many gay men if she still believed there was a type. "How did you find out? Did he say something?"

"He showed me the paintings in his studio. There were several of the same man and they were painted with an unmistakable intimacy. Just looking at them had an effect on Jason. I could tell the man was someone he'd loved a great deal. I would have had to be pretty thick not to have figured it out."

The rest wasn't his to tell. He went to her, put out his finger and hooked the strap lying on her arm. With great reluctance, he brought it back up to her shoulder. "This is nice. Is it new?"

She shook her head. "Lingerie used to be an indulgence of mine."

"You mean you have more of these?"

"Dozens—but not with me," she quickly corrected. "I only grabbed what was on top when I packed to leave."

Someday he would ask why she'd run away, but it was still too soon. "How long is your lesson?" he asked.

"Jason didn't say. Why?"

"I thought I'd come by this afternoon."

"Tell me what time and I'll be here."

"I'm not sure how long the job will take." He didn't want to leave. "I'll call as soon as I get some idea."

"You better go now," she said. "Jason and Susan will be worried about you." The thought brought a flicker of a smile. "By the way, how do you intend to explain not being there when they arrive?"

"I'll come up with something."

"Maybe they won't ask."

He smiled. "And Madonna will join a nunnery."

She walked him to the door. "Thank you for last night."

At first he thought she was being sarcastic, then he looked in her eyes and saw she meant every word. "In what way?"

"For holding me—and staying."

"You're welcome." He didn't understand why she was grateful for something so inconsequential, but knew better than to question her. He was learning, slowly to be sure, but at least he'd passed the point where he felt every step forward only added more distance to the end.

When Adam was gone, Miranda went into the kitchen and made coffee. She lingered at the sink to watch a deer eyeing her fuchsias. After several minutes the doe reared up on her hind legs, balanced herself with her front feet on the railing and stretched her neck. Her mouth nibbled air as a brilliant red and white blossom swayed gently in the breeze less than an inch from her outstretched tongue.

Miranda could feel the doe's frustration when it dropped to the ground and stared at what should have been its breakfast. Convinced the show was over, Miranda left the window to get a cup out of the cupboard. While her back was turned, she heard a soft thud on the deck.

She looked outside again. The doe had both front feet on the middle step, poised to move toward the fuchsias. Miranda drew in a breath of surprise. She'd never been so close to anything wild. It was tempting to let the scene unfold even knowing the hummingbirds would have to forego their morning meal.

The plants were replaceable, the moment was not.

But was the pleasure she would receive from witnessing the scene worth the potential consequence to the doe? Deer didn't belong on decks.

Reluctantly, Miranda opened the window, moving slowly to warn rather than frighten the doe. For long seconds they stared at each other, the deer's eyes huge and questioning.

"You don't belong here," Miranda said softly. As if it understood, the deer backed away. Still, Miranda and the deer looked at each other. Finally, unhurried, it turned and disappeared into the cypress. As she watched it leave, Miranda's own words echoed in her mind. She left the window and let her gaze sweep the kitchen, settling on appliances and dishes and utensils that weren't her own. "Anymore than I do . . . " she added in a whisper.

Eleven

Two weeks later Adam left for his job in Sea Ranch. It took forty-eight hours before Miranda's need to see him seeped into her every waking moment. Uncharacteristically, she refused to question that need, accepting it as a natural progression of their friendship. She even tried to convince herself that she could handle his absence by marking the days on the calendar until he returned.

And then early one afternoon, as she returned home from a lesson with Jason, she acknowledged she felt Adam's absence to the core of her being and nothing short of seeing him was going to make it any better. She went into the bedroom, packed a bag, and drove south. Her reluctance to travel beyond the small world she'd come to know had been overpowered by something deeper and more basic.

The surprise on Adam's face made the anxiousness she'd suffered on the way fade into a dull memory; the night they spent making love erased all doubt about her welcome. The next night she did something she never imagined possible—after he'd finished work for the day, she met him at the door wearing nothing but a nasturtium in her hair.

Sex with Adam was uninhibited and spontaneous. It wasn't that she hadn't enjoyed making love with Keith or had gone to sleep dissatisfied, it was more that she'd never felt the loss of control that she did with Adam. There was something almost primitive in the way they came together. Nothing was held back. Adam made love to her in ways she had refused Keith. With him she became an eager participant, even, at times, the aggressor. She didn't want to consider what about her had changed. There were questions she didn't want answered. Not now. At least not yet.

After she returned to Mendocino, she called Adam every night, updating him on her progress with her lessons—or more often, lack of it. Jason insisted her natural talent was in sore need of patience. Remembering their lovemaking, Adam told her he refused to consider her lack of patience a negative.

With Labor Day the last major holiday of the tourist season, Jason told Miranda it was time to have a party to celebrate the return of Mendocino to the natives. Miranda liked that she was considered a "native" even if only by Jason.

She helped with the planning, taking quiet plea-sure in Jason's oft-repeated comments about her organizational skills. It felt good to be doing some-thing constructive again, if only putting together a party.

Adam came home the afternoon of the big cele-bration, two days later than he'd planned, but with several hundred dollars more in his bank account.

"I could have stayed another month," he told Miranda as he helped her load her car with the cookies and brownies she'd picked up at the bakery for the party. "Once word got around that I was there, it seemed everyone had something that needed fixing."

"You don't realize how hard it is to find someone to repair the small things that go wrong around a house. Washer and dryer and air-conditioner repairmen are all over the place but who do you call when the light switch in the bathroom doesn't work or there's a loose board in your hardwood floor?"

"Sounds like I'm listening to the voice of experience."

She braced a towel around the tray of cookies to keep it from sliding around in the trunk. "Oh, the tales I could tell. I remember one time we . . . " The memory had arrived unbidden and far too easily.

"I'm listening," Adam said.

"It's not important." She lowered the trunk lid.

"You're closing me out again, Miranda."

"No I'm not," she said too brightly. "I could just feel myself getting upset all over again thinking about what happened. I don't want your homecoming ruined because I'm grumpy over some long-ago incompetent repairman." Not exactly the truth, but close enough that she could forgive herself the small lie. She gave him a quick kiss before going around to the driver's side.

"Time's a wastin', Mr. Kirkpatric," she said when he was slow to move.

Adam got in beside her. "I can think of a dozen things I'd rather be doing tonight than going to this party."

She grinned. "Name one."

"How about if I show you instead?" He slipped his hand under her skirt.

Instant heat shot up her thigh. "Stop that," she said and clamped her hand over his.

"Okay, so you didn't like that one. I still have eleven others I can show you."

"Later." The waiting would be hell. What had possessed her to promise Jason she would stay and help clean up after the party?

Adam snapped his seat belt in place. "I like your hair."

"Thanks. I do, too." Her hand automatically went to the shorn locks. She'd had it styled a week ago at a shop in Fort Bragg—shoulder length, parted at the side and turned under at the ends. Her bangs were feathered across her forehead. It was the kind of style that looked simple but in reality took a highly skilled cutter. Not expecting much, she'd been delighted at the result, and the cost. Eighteen dollars for something she would have paid eighty for at her old salon.

"Any more surprises you'd like to tell me about?" he asked.

She put the car in gear and backed out of the driveway. "Let's see, did I happen to mention I'm having my first showing at the Henderson Gallery in Carmel in a couple of weeks?" She looked at him out of the corner of her eye. "Laugh and it will be your last."

"Hey, I believe in miracles." He leaned over and nuzzled her neck. "How could I not when you came into my life?"

"Corny, but effective." She came to a stop sign, put the car in park and gave him a kiss, opening her mouth in invitation.

"Don't do that again if you really want to make

the party," Adam warned. "Or if you feel shy about asking Jason to borrow his bedroom."

His hand cupped her breast and caressed it. She was filled with a sweet yearning. "*Uncle*," she murmured against his lips.

"How late is this thing supposed to last?"

"The invitation was open ended."

Adam groaned. "What say we slip out for an hour or two somewhere in the middle?"

"Wouldn't you be surprised if I took you up on that offer?"

"Not so surprised I wouldn't have you out the door before you could change your mind."

She liked being desired. It made her feel young again, and a little bit wild. God, had she ever really been young or wild? She couldn't remember either.

By the time they arrived at the party several guests were already there. Jason met them at the front door.

"What kept you?" he asked and then grinned. "Never mind. It was a dumb question."

Miranda felt her face grow warm. The time when she'd believed her and Adam's relationship could be kept quiet had long passed. It was disconcerting to think everyone knew what they were doing.

"I was late getting to Miranda's," Adam said. "I think half of San Francisco decided to take the scenic route north this morning."

Jason leaned over and gave her a kiss on her cheek. "Early or late, I'm glad you're here."

She smiled. "Me, too."

A new wave of guests came up the walkway. "Where do you want the cookies?" Adam asked.

"In the kitchen," Jason told him.

"Adam," came a squeal from across the room. "You're home. *Finally*."

Adam turned to see Susan headed toward him.

Miranda laughed and took the tray. "You say hi to Susan. I'll take care of the cookies."

"I'll be there in a minute," he told her.

"Take your time."

Of all the changes Adam had seen in Miranda the past few weeks, the growing independence pleased him the most. She was like a newly-sided house ready to face the elements.

Susan flew into his arms. "I was afraid you wouldn't get back before I left."

"I had another week," he said.

She put her arm through his and led him out of the traffic flow. "Debbie and I decided to leave early."

"For any particular reason?" He hadn't heard from her or Matt the entire time he'd been gone.

"It's not what you think. We just decided to get a head start fixing up our dorm room."

"Did your results come in?" He'd had her pick up his mail while he was away so she could intercept her letter.

"It was negative." She plucked a piece of lint from his sleeve. "Five and a half more months to go."

"Have you heard whether Matt went in?"

Her smile faded and she looked away. "He brought the paper over to the house a couple of days ago. I guess he thought if I saw he was okay it would make a difference."

Adam had to strain to hear her. "Did you get anything settled?"

"I told him for the umpteenth time there was no way we were getting back together but he won't listen.

He just keeps saying everyone is entitled to one mistake." She moved away from Adam and sat on the arm of the camelback sofa.

Adam had a feeling her early departure for school had more to do with escaping Matt than fixing up a room. He sat on the cushion next to her. "So now what?"

"I wait five and a half more months then get on with my life." She brought her foot up and laid it across her knee. "I don't know about Matt. He was crying when he left last time. I've never seen him cry before."

"It was a tough lesson." Adam didn't know what else to say.

"Did I do the right thing?"

It was the first time he'd heard her express doubt. "All you can do is go with how you feel. And for both of your sakes, don't try to second guess yourself five years from now."

"I never asked you this"—she hesitated—"but could you, *would* you, ever have done what Matt did?"

"No," he answered truthfully. "But then I'm not eighteen."

"Being eighteen makes it all right?"

"That's not what I'm saying. It's more that you look at things differently when you're nearing thirty than you do when you're in your teens."

"You mean getting old changes you?"

Susan could only stay serious for so long. It was one of the things Adam liked about her. "I'll tell you about it someday. But I gotta warn you, it isn't pretty."

"I'm going to miss you and Jason and our bike rides."

"That's nice to hear, but I bet it doesn't last for long."

She slipped off the arm of the chair and onto the cushion beside him, laying her head on his arm. "You better write to me."

"I'll tell you what, I'll answer every one of your letters." They would stop coming after a while and that was all right with Adam. He wanted her to be too busy with her new life to write home. Her father, she would call.

"And you'll tell me what's happening with you and Miranda?" she said innocently.

"What is it you think you want to know?"

"Oh, stuff like when you move in together." Before he could say anything, she cut him off. "And I want you to let me know how Jason's doing—really doing. Whenever I ask him he always says he's feeling fantastic. You've got to promise you'll tell me the truth."

Being the daughter of a doctor, and losing her mother when she was only eight, had exposed Susan to sickness and death, but Adam doubted she was prepared for what lay ahead for Jason. AIDS could be a slow, gruesome killer. "I won't have to tell you, you'll be seeing him yourself when you come home for holidays."

"But if something happens when I'm not here you'll let me know?"

"Yes." It wasn't something he wanted to do, Susan deserved to hang onto what little naiveté she had left. But how could he not?

Across the room Miranda stood in the doorway and watched the exchange between Susan and Adam. The affection they had for each other was evident in the animated way they talked and how comfortable they were being close. Adam seemed to have no boundaries where his friends were concerned. He was as at ease with Susan as he was with her father, with women as men, with gay as straight. He moved as easily in the social climate of a place like Heritage House as he did the Fish and Chowder restaurant in Fort Bragg. His taste in music ran to the weird side of classical but he listened to country or rock on the radio. He had a limited education but had more knowledge on more subjects than anyone she'd ever known.

Jason waved to her from across the kitchen. "Miranda, come here, there's someone you haven't met."

He was clearly determined to introduce her to everyone at the party. Over lunch one day he'd told her he had no interest in the "why" of her reclusiveness, only in helping her get over it. Friends were as important to him as his painting.

She snaked her way through the crowd. "Do you really know all these people?" she asked.

"By next year you will, too," he said.

The statement gave her pause. She couldn't imagine herself still in Mendocino a whole year from then. But if not there, where?

Jason put his arm around her in an affectionate gesture. "Miranda, this is Sharon and Colin Baker. She's a writer and he's in the leasing business."

There was too much noise for any but the most rudimentary conversation, still Miranda immediately took to the Bakers. But then she liked all of Jason's friends, even the woman who had cornered her earlier with a speech about eradicating non-native plant life and establishing fines for anyone caught bringing them into the area.

The noise level grew in direct proportion to the drop in temperature as the less hardy souls who'd started on the patio began drifting inside. Miranda watched to see if the crowding encouraged anyone to leave, but claustrophobia didn't seem to be a problem with this group.

Several times during the evening Adam had signaled her and headed her way only to be cornered by someone who insisted they'd been looking for him all night.

The louder and more crowded the house became, the more Miranda wondered about the wisdom of her staying. She wasn't ready to be around so many people.

A dull pain started in her neck and progressed up the back of her head. Experience told her if she didn't take something soon for the oncoming headache, nothing would work. She'd just have to wait it out in a dark room with a bag of ice on her forehead.

She went looking for Jason to ask him for some aspirin and found him talking to Susan. As she came closer, she saw there were tears in Susan's eyes. Miranda hesitated intruding. She waited to see if he would notice her, but his focus was locked on Susan. After several minutes, he took Susan's hand and led her outside.

"*At last.*" Adam slipped his arm around her waist. "Having a good time?"

It was on the tip of her tongue to tell him she'd had enough fun and wanted to go home, but there was such enthusiasm in the look he gave her she didn't have the heart. "Do you know where Jason keeps his aspirin?"

"Is something wrong?"

"Not yet, but I can feel a headache coming on."

"Do you want to leave?"

A stunningly beautiful young woman with long curly hair, dressed in a full skirt, knit halter top, and open cotton blouse came up to them, clasped Adam's free hand and gave him a kiss on his cheek. "Where in the hell have you been keeping yourself?" She pointedly looked at Miranda. "And why haven't you introduced me to your friend?"

"Cindy Harper—Miranda Dolan," Adam said.

Cindy smiled expansively. "Adam's one of my all-time favorite people. I hope you're taking good care of him."

"We're just friends," Miranda protested. She cringed at the lie and how quickly it had come to her.

Cindy's smile stayed in place for an artificially long time as she glanced from Miranda to Adam and back again. "I didn't mean to imply anything else."

Miranda prayed for a hole to open up and swallow her. But her prayer went unanswered. She was still there and still needed to extricate herself. "How do you and Adam know each other?"

"We're about the only two Trekkies north of San Francisco, or at least the only two I've been able to find," Cindy said. "I'd go crazy if I didn't have Adam to talk to."

Before Miranda could ask, Adam supplied, "Star Trek fans."

"Oh, you mean the television show," Miranda said. "I didn't know it was still on."

Cindy laughed. "I can see you're not one of us either."

"I'm sorry, but I don't watch much television."

Miranda pressed her fingers against her temple. "I have this headache coming on. Adam was about to tell me where Jason keeps his aspirin."

"I'll check the bathroom," Adam said.

"I can do it," she told him. "You stay with Cindy."

Cindy moved to let Miranda pass. "It was nice meeting you."

"Thank you," Miranda said. "It was nice meeting you, too." Another lie. She'd give the pink slip on her BMW to buy back the last five minutes. How would she ever explain to Adam why she'd been so quick to deny their relationship? How could she when she didn't understand herself?

The bathroom door was closed and there were two people waiting. The man smiled, said he was sure they hadn't met, and introduced himself. Miranda waited long enough not to offend him and then excused herself. She'd remembered the bathroom off Jason's studio and headed upstairs. As she'd hoped, no one was around.

Finally alone, she sat on the edge of the bathtub and tried to figure out how an evening that had started out so well could have turned into such a disaster. It hadn't been necessary to look at Adam to know she'd hurt him when she'd denied their relationship. Could it have been she didn't want to face the questioning look from Cindy, a woman who looked as if she was the one who belonged with Adam, who looked and acted as if she might have something in common with him other than great sex?

There were a dozen or more people at the party Miranda's age, some even older. She knew them not by how they looked, but by their tendency to cluster into groups, their conversations centered around health care, taxes and politics. They ate carrots and celery and sipped glasses of wine.

The people Adam's age, however, seemed to reject anything serious. They were there to party. They laughed and joked and teased each other, and ate cookies that they washed down with cans of beer.

Her headache was getting worse.

Bracing her hands on the cool porcelain, she pushed herself up and opened the cabinet over the sink. What she found was so far from what she'd expected, she frowned in confusion and struggled to make sense out of it. There was none of the normal paraphernalia—the toothbrush, razor, aftershave, or Band-Aids. Instead the bottom two shelves were filled with dark orange plastic bottles, fat and skinny, tall and short, their labels neatly lined up and facing out. The top shelf contained a variety of square and round white bottles; these, too, held labels. Outside a pharmacy, she'd never seen as much prescription medicine.

There was no way they could all belong to Jason. He was the picture of health, athletic and energetic. What in the hell was going on here?

She knew about the underground market for legal drugs. One of her first cases after being hired by Coker/Standish had been defending the son of one of the firm's long-time clients. But that didn't make sense. Jason exhibited none of the signs of a drug user.

The smart thing to do was close the door and forget what she'd seen. How and why the drugs had come to be in Jason's bathroom had nothing to do with her.

The argument was reasonable, even compelling,

but she wasn't buying it. She picked up one of the bottles and read the label. The only thing she recognized was Jason's name. Moving closer, she saw his name on all of the bottles. The dates ranged from two years ago to just the day before. There were capsules and tablets, some so big they looked impossible to swallow.

She recognized an antibiotic and an antacid; others seemed familiar, but she couldn't . . . oh, dear God. She backed away from the sink, her hand clasped over her mouth.

It wasn't possible. She had to be wrong. Not Jason.

But why not Jason?

Because he was handsome and young and full of life.

Because he was her friend.

She tried to look away from the silent accusers, to make the evidence go away, to deny what she'd seen, but she couldn't stop staring. Her mind denied her shelter, demanding she see it all, that she imprint the image of the row upon row of medicine, to be called up again and again—just the way it had the afternoon her world was taken apart piece by piece.

She couldn't watch someone die. Not again. Not ever again.

The carefully constructed barriers she'd built to protect herself began to crumble. A familiar knife-edged pain hovered, ready to settle into its old home around her heart. She battled the pull but it was like trying to fight the sucking winds of a tornado.

No, she begged whatever malevolent force it was that reached for her, *please, no*. But it was useless. She was back in the conference room. More easily than she could summon a mental image of her daughter's first smile or word or step, she saw the blood dripping from the side of Jenny's mouth . . . Keith trying to hold Jenny upright to keep her from choking . . . Jenny mouthing the words, I love you, to her father . . . Jenny dying . . . Keith dying.

The white bathroom walls turned crimson, the sounds from the party below became screams of terror and pain.

An inner voice demanded she escape.

Run . . . fast and far and don't look back.

But where to go? She'd already stepped off the edge of the earth. It hadn't worked. Adam had been there to pull her back.

Damn him.

Twelve

Adam smiled automatically at Cindy's description of one of the "crazies" she'd run into at the last Star Trek convention she'd attended in Sacramento. He was only half listening, his thoughts on Miranda and how long she'd been gone.

"Well?" Cindy prompted a short time later. "What do you think?"

Adam blinked in surprise. There was no way to fake an answer; he didn't have a clue what she was talking about. "I'm sorry," he said. "My mind was on something else."

"That's okay. It wasn't important."

"Why don't you drop by the house sometime this weekend and I'll give you that article we were talking—" He broke off when he glanced up and saw Miranda at the top of the stairs. Her gaze was fixed on him, but it wasn't recognition in her eyes, it was desperation—or was it panic? She looked away, first at the people below and then, longingly, at the front door. She hesitated for a heartbeat before lunging headlong down the stairway.

"Excuse me," Adam said to Cindy. He shouldered past her to intercept Miranda. But Miranda was faster and reached the door before he'd made it half way across the living room. He called to her, not loud enough to draw attention, but too loud for her not to have heard. She bolted outside without a backward glance.

She hadn't been away from him more than ten minutes. What could have happened in so short a time?

A fear he'd managed to keep under control until then abruptly leaped its boundaries. He was momentarily paralyzed by its force. The feeling wasn't new or unfamiliar, but the result of a seed that had been planted the day Vern told him about Miranda's scars. It had sprouted when she told him her fall from the cliff hadn't been an accident. Now, within seconds, it burst into full bloom.

With sheer force of will he made his legs obey the command to move. He heard someone call to him as he moved through the doorway, but paid the person no more heed than Miranda had paid him.

He expected to see her once he was outside, instead it was as if the utterly black night that hovered beyond the festively-lit house had opened and absorbed her.

He couldn't just stand there. Without action his fear would become all-consuming. He was halfway down the flagstone steps when he heard a sound at the side of the house. She was headed for the forest, an area of towering trees and dense foliage without landmarks or clearings. If she made it a hundred yards, she would be lost to him.

Adam cut across the flower bed and hurdled the

boxwood hedge that marked the yard's side bound-
ary. The peripheral light from the party rapidly faded,
a few more feet and he would have only his hearing
to guide him.

He had to find her—soon.

A canopy of layered branches closed over him
when he entered the forest, leaving only an occasional glimpse of the night sky lit by a quarter moon. He
went on until all traces of the party were gone.
Silence surrounded him. He stopped to listen and
heard only the sound of his own breathing.

She had stopped, too.

But he could feel her.

If he believed people had auras, he would have
said he'd stumbled into hers. He held his breath to listen harder. Somewhere a pinecone fell; a startled bird
took flight. A breeze whispered through the tops of
the trees. The sound of his heartbeat echoed in his
ears.

And then he heard what he'd been waiting for—
a smothered, almost imperceptible crying. He closed
his eyes and concentrated. The sound came from his
left.

"Miranda?" he called.

Silence.

"I know you're there." Were there words she
needed to hear? Ones that would drive her farther
away? How could he distinguish? "Please, talk to
me."

Again, he waited.

Finally, her voice came to him. *"You should have
told me."*

It was an accusation said with a pain he couldn't
conceive. He turned toward the sound of her voice.

Slowly, an image took shape. She was almost beside him, sitting at the base of a tree, her legs drawn up to her chest, her back pressed against the trunk.

"Go away," she said when he moved toward her. "I don't want you here."

"I don't understand. What should I have told you?" He lowered himself to his haunches and reached for her arm.

She jerked away when she felt his touch. "You knew. All along you knew and you never said anything. You had no—" The words were cut off as a low keening cry rose from her throat.

Adam had never heard a more desolate or heartbreaking sound. It scared the hell out of him. "I don't know what you're talking about. What is this thing you think I knew?"

"*Jason.*" She pulled her legs closer, folding into herself. "He's dying. You didn't tell me . . . you let me care about him." Her head came up. "Damn you for that, Adam Kirkpatric. Damn you to hell."

His eyes had adjusted to the dark and he could see her clearly now; but it was more curse than blessing. The sight of her pain laid him bare. "How did you find out?"

"What difference does it make?"

"None."

"Why didn't you tell me?" It had become a mantra.

He didn't have an answer, at least not one that would satisfy her. Still, he tried. "I didn't know you would care this much." Could she possibly be afraid Jason would somehow infect her? "And I didn't think I should be the one to tell you." Whom to tell and when to tell them was Jason's right. "Are you afraid of him? If you are—"

"I'm terrified," she flung back, "but not for the reason you think." She put her head down. "Go away, Adam."

He'd never felt such helplessness. "You're not going to get me to leave, so you might as well stop trying."

"Then stay." She got to her feet and started toward the distant glow of light coming from Jason's house.

She hadn't gone ten feet before he caught her. She was trembling, violently. In his surprise, he almost let her go.

She put her hands against his chest and pushed, hard. A desperate look radiated from her eyes. "Don't touch me," she told him. "Don't ever touch me again."

He was beyond listening or responding to such words. A deeper need drove him. He pulled her into his arms. "For me touching you is like breathing," he whispered into her hair. "I can no more stop one than I can the other."

She held herself stiffly at first, but at least she didn't continue to fight him. Then, slowly, her own need broke through her defenses and she laid her head against his shoulder. "How long does he have?"

"I don't know," Adam answered truthfully. "I don't want to see him in those terms, so I've never asked."

"Does that make it easier for you to pretend he isn't dying?"

She was asking him to give words to what until then had only been nebulous thoughts and feelings. "Somewhere inside my mind I know that one day Jason's life is going to end, it's inevitable and I've accepted it. What I won't accept is wasting what time he's got left, worrying about him dying. Even if he only has another year, that's three hundred sixty-five days he has to live." He hesitated. "I'm not explaining this very well."

"And I suppose you think this mind set of yours will let you walk away from his death unscathed?"

"I've known all along I'll be a different person when this is over." Losing his father had changed his life in ways no one could have predicted. There was no reason to think losing his best friend would have any less effect.

"You sound like a kid playing a grown-up's game. Your theory is laudable, Adam, even touching, but it doesn't have a thing to do with real life. You can't compartmentalize tragedy and you sure as hell can't control grief. It's visceral, not cerebral." She moved away from him. "I want to go home."

"If we try to get to the car now, we're going to run into someone at the party. They're bound to ask questions."

"You can pick me up down the road."

"Get it through your head, Miranda, I'm not leaving you alone."

"You're being stupid. What could possibly happen to me—" She caught herself as if just then realizing what he was thinking. "I should never have told you about that."

"But you did."

"And now I'm suffering the consequences." Her anger was swift and complete. "God damn it, Adam, what do I have to do to convince you that you're not responsible for me? And you can't control me. If I ever decide to jump off another cliff, there isn't a thing you can do to stop me."

"Is that really what you want? Is your life so terrible you can't find one reason to stick around?" Just thinking about her answer made him sick to his stomach. "Talk to Jason. I'm sure he'd be glad to change places with you."

"You have no idea what my life is or isn't."

"Then tell me."

Her voice faded to a choked whisper. "I can't."

"Yes you can." He put his hands on the sides of her face and made her look at him. "It's time to let go of whatever it is you've got locked inside."

She closed her eyes. "I can't."

"Why would you want to hold onto something that hurts you this badly?"

Long, agonizing seconds passed. Finally, so softly he had to strain to hear, she said, "It's my punishment."

Adam had prepared himself for anything, at least he thought he had. "What crime could you possibly have committed to deserve what you're doing to yourself?"

"I killed my daughter . . . and my husband." She twisted away from him and leaned her shoulder into the rough bark of a pine tree. "And Dan, and Harold, and Delores." Slowly she collapsed to the ground. "Margaret didn't die, but she'll never walk again. Robert moved away. No one knows where. And Phillip . . . I don't know what happened to Phillip. He just stopped coming to the hospital one day. I never saw him again." Her voice was monotone now, and strangely distant, as if she were speaking from some far away place where her mind had taken her.

For over a year Miranda had fought the memory of that day, closing her eyes and mind to images that swirled through every conscious and unconscious thought like a pervasive, encompassing mist. She couldn't let herself remember. To do so would be to witness the horror and feel the loss all over again. She'd barely survived the first time.

But her defenses weren't strong enough to protect her from Jason and her memories. Her barriers had been breached. The limb she'd been clinging to snapped and she was swept into a dark, swirling current that took her to another time, another place.

It was the Friday before a three-day holiday. In an uncharacteristically generous gesture, the senior partners had decided to close the offices early. While most of the attorneys and their staffs had taken off at noon, a few stayed behind to catch up on work. Miranda was there because she'd dropped her car off for an oil change that morning and was waiting for Keith and Jennifer to pick her up.

She was on her way back to her office from the copy room when she heard her secretary's raised voice followed by a loud thump and then another. Seconds later a man stepped into the hallway in front of her. He had on a long overcoat, which seemed strange because it had been an unseasonably warm day. Her gaze shifted to the man's face. It was Tobias Trout. Had his eyes been weapons, she would have been bleeding.

"Did we have an appointment?" she asked, knowing full well they hadn't. When he didn't answer, she added, "I'm sorry, Tobias, but I wasn't expecting you. If you could tell me what—"

He raised his arm. His hand held a large black gun, automatic and menacing. Taking careful aim, he pointed it at her head.

Miranda went cold. "You don't want to do this,

Tobias." Her mind frantically worked to bring reason to the scene. Tobias was a long-standing client, the firm's most lucrative and litigious, as crazy as he was rich. She'd been given the job of handling his never-ending lawsuits two years ago. "Is it the apology Dawson's demanding? If you just give me a little more time, I'm sure I can work something out."

"You should have thought of that before. It's too late now."

"It's never too late."

"Shut up. I don't want to hear it." He motioned her forward with the gun.

"Why don't we go into my office?" She came toward him. "Just you and me. I'll tell Joni not to let anyone disturb us. No one has to know this ever happened."

His lips turned back in a malevolent smile. "Joni isn't going to tell anyone anything."

Miranda's fear for herself shifted to her secretary. "What do you mean?"

A man's voice came from the hallway to his left. Tobias pressed himself against the wall and slowly inched forward until he could see around the corner.

A wild hope soared in her that somehow, some-one had seen the gun and had called for help. And then she heard Keith's voice and was catapulted deeper into the nightmare.

"Excuse me," Keith called out. "Do you know if Miranda Dolan is in her office?"

She couldn't just stand there. She had to do something. Reacting to her intense panic, she lunged at Tobias while she shouted to Keith, "Get out of here—*run*."

With a violent backward motion Tobias shook

Miranda free, grabbed her as she began to fall, and swung her in front of him.

He jammed the gun against her head. "I wouldn't go anywhere if I were you," he told Keith. "Not if you care what happens to her."

"Miranda, what in the hell is going on here? Are you all right?" Keith asked.

It was then she saw Jennifer come up behind Keith. "Let her go," she begged Tobias. "She's just a little girl. She'll only get in the way."

"Mommy?" Jennifer said, sounding more confused than frightened.

"Wait for us outside, Jennifer."

"If she tries to leave, I'll shoot her," Tobias said coolly. "It's your call."

Miranda was struck with the sure, sickening knowledge Tobias meant what he said. "We'd better do what he wants," she told Keith.

Keith nodded, never taking his eyes from Miranda's. Keeping Jennifer close to his side, he followed Tobias's direction and gathered everyone left on the floor into the conference room.

For the next hour, Tobias paced the long room, clutching the large black gun with one hand, the front of his coat with the other. In a continuous monologue he recited the injustices he believed he'd suffered at Miranda's hands, detailing her inept handling of his lawsuits. His hatred for her built on itself until it became a living, palpable thing. She was terrified and utterly helpless to do anything to appease him.

Jennifer cried quietly. Miranda couldn't tell whether it was from fear or embarrassment at the venom directed at her mother. Keith attempted to comfort her but there were no words.

For a long time it seemed the phones in the offices rung continuously, and then they just stopped.

Miranda tried to figure out if anyone had escaped, but it was impossible to know who had still been in the office. Periodically she imagined she heard sounds. She gave them elaborate meanings, convincing herself rescue was imminent. For a while she even allowed herself to believe Tobias would simply talk himself out and let them go.

That hope died when he stopped pacing, took off his coat and emptied the pockets of their guns and ammunition, laying them in what seemed a predetermined order. Someone moaned in fear. She turned at the sound, and out of the corner of her eye, saw Margaret Kinnion reach for the phone on the side table. Without warning an explosion erupted. Margaret jerked backward and fell. The cream colored curtain swayed, as if to rid itself of the splattered crimson.

Miranda turned to look at Tobias. She saw him mouth the word, "Bitch," and then felt something strike her shoulder and force her backwards. Shouts and screams mixed with rapid, rhythmic explosions as Tobias ran from one side of the room to the other, the gun rocking in his hand. The air rained fragments of wood. It seemed an eternity as the scene played itself out one frame at a time. And then, abruptly, it was over.

Across from her Keith sat with Jennifer cradled in his arms. Blood stained their clothes and pooled on the polished oak floor beneath them. He looked up at Miranda, his eyes filled with a pain that went beyond tears. "I tried to shove her under the table . . . she wouldn't go . . . she was so scared." Keith awkwardly brushed the hair from Jennifer's face. "It's all right, sweetheart," he said softly. "Daddy's here. I promise I'll take care of you. Everything will be all right."

Jennifer opened her eyes then, and for an instant, Miranda's hopes soared. Then she saw a trickle of blood stream from the corner of her daughter's mouth and heard her say, "I can't breathe, Daddy. I'm trying, but . . . "

Keith moved to give her more room. "Is that better?"

She looked at him for a long time before she said, "I love you, Daddy."

"I love you, too, Jenny," he whispered. Seconds later she closed her eyes. Keith leaned forward to kiss her.

His lips touched Jennifer's forehead with such infinite tenderness it stole Miranda's heart. And then she realized he was saying good-bye and she cried out, "No—don't let her go. Damn it, Keith. *Make her fight.*"

He leaned his head against the table leg and closed his eyes. For a long time after that Miranda watched his chest move but it was automatic. He died when Jennifer did. She was his world. He simply could not go on without her.

In the black, cold of the Mendocino night, Adam knelt beside Miranda, his mind struggling to understand something that was incomprehensible. "I don't understand how you can blame yourself when you were shot, too."

His words brought her back to the present. It took her a second to recognize she'd traveled her journey alone, that Adam had seen the scars, but there was no way he could understand what had happened unless she took him back with her. "He was my client. He came there because of me. I should have known." A sob caught in her throat. She covered her face with her hands. "It was my fault, every bit of it. I should have known."

Adam sat down next to Miranda and took her in his arms. She didn't move to make it easier for him, but she didn't fight him either. As he held her and felt her heart beat against his own chest, a hundred questions dogged him. But they would have to wait. Now wasn't the time or place for asking.

It was a good excuse, a seeming kindness. Never mind the voice that insisted he wasn't asking the questions because he didn't want to hear the answers.

Thirteen

As an afterthought, Adam went back into his kitchen and shoved a couple of the cinnamon sticks Jason had left behind after a party into cups of cider he'd heated in the microwave. He was out of tea, and didn't need or want the edge coffee brought, either for himself or Miranda, especially not at 2:30 in the morning. Carrying the mugs into the living room, he found Miranda burrowed in the corner of the sofa, incommunicative but no longer aggressively hostile at his refusal to drop her off at her own house.

He didn't try to give her the cup but put it down on the end table beside her and went to the stove to add a fresh piece of oak to the fire. He left the doors open and propped the screen in place.

When he turned around again he caught Miranda looking at him. She immediately shifted her gaze to the untouched cup. "You have a domestic side," she said with unmistakable sarcasm. "I'm impressed."

She was striking out to protect herself. He'd seen her do it before; now he understood why. He went to the sofa and sat on the center cushion, close, but not touching her. "And you have a bitchy side. I'm not impressed."

"You don't like being called domestic?"

"Save your breath, Miranda. I'm not going to let you bait me into a fight." He took a drink of cider. It burned his mouth. "Damn it." He put the cup back on the table.

"Are you okay?" she asked.

The concern seemed genuine. They were making progress. He decided to push a little harder. "Tell me about your daughter. What was her name?" He almost stumbled on the "was." It seemed so wrong.

"Jennifer."

He waited.

"She was eight years old . . . she had blue eyes and blond hair,"—Miranda took a deep, shuddering breath— "like her father's."

"She was in third grade?"

"Fourth. I had her put up a year. Keith didn't want her to leave her friends, but she was so far ahead of the rest of the class that I—" She didn't finish. She reached for the cider. The regret was like a weight, making her movements slow and clumsy.

"How long were you and Keith married?" It was a guess, but who else would this Keith be?

"Sixteen years. It would have been seventeen last May."

"You must have been in school when you got married."

"Keith had graduated, but I still had a year to go—four actually. Law school took three."

"So, you're a lawyer. It fits now that I think about it."

"What's that supposed to mean?" she asked defensively.

"There's just something about lawyers. The way they—"

"What? Manipulate? Lie? Cheat?"

"Analyze and question everything," Adam finished evenly.

She was quiet for a long time. "The other people who died were lawyers, too."

He waited for her to go on.

"They all had families." She stared into the steaming liquid as if it were a screen filled with images of this other time and place. "I saw the funerals on the news. The processions went on for miles." Her hand started to shake. The cinnamon stick slid from one side of the cup to the other. "The kids in Jennifer's class made a wreath out of paper flowers. All of the flowers had notes written to her on them. Clifford brought it to me in the hospital." Her eyes closed against the memory. "He thought it would make me feel better to know how much everyone had loved my daughter."

Adam took Miranda's cider and put it back on the table.

"Who is Clifford?"

"One of the senior partners."

"The one who took you under his wing when you first joined the firm."

She looked up at him. "How did you know that?"

Several of Adam's friends at Stanford had gone on to law school. They were still new enough to the profession that it was all they could talk about whenever Adam visited. "You don't move up in a large firm without a mentor. It's obvious from what you've said that you were on the fast track at your firm so I assume this Clifford was an important partner and that he attached himself to you. My guess is that he spotted you at the interview."

"Not that soon," she admitted, "but not long after. Clifford liked to tell people he knew I was a winner when I'd been there less than a week and he heard me chewing out a law clerk that I'd overheard giving a secretary legal advice."

The questionable compliment was repeated in a self deprecating way. "I've never thought ambition was a dirty word, Miranda."

"Not even when it's to the exclusion of every-thing, and everyone, else? I was a success junkie. I couldn't wait to get to the office every morning for my daily fix. Keith and Jenny became secondary. I knew what I was doing, but I thought I could make it up to them once I was on top and could spare the time."

"So how does the guy,"—he assumed it was a man—"with the gun fit in?"

"Tobias Trout . . . " Miranda ran her hand through her hair in a nervous gesture. "He was a client who liked to sue. I thought he was crazy, the senior partners insisted he was a harmless eccentric."

"How were you chosen to handle his lawsuits? Luck of the draw?" He didn't believe it for a minute but was interested in her answer.

"It was Clifford's idea. He considered me the best 'people handler' the firm had. Of course I was thrilled when he told me how he felt. I was embarrassingly easy to control back then, like some god damned donkey chasing a carrot on a stick."

"Ambition can make you blind to a lot of things."

The statement made her angry. "How in the hell would you know what ambition is or isn't?"

"Because I'm only a handyman?"

"Like it or not, Adam, it's a long way from repairing leaky roofs to arguing a case worth millions to a client."

"Why does it always come down to money?"

She got up and moved to the fire, holding her hands out to the flame. "Your age is showing, and your naiveté. Money is power and—"

"Power is everything," he finished for her. The small part of him that had been vacillating over whether or not to hold off selling the family business, died a quick, painless death. He was more sure now than ever that he wanted nothing to do with that life or that world.

With her gaze fixed on the fire, she said, "I got sloppy, busy actually, and didn't give Tobias the attention he expected. At times it seemed as though my entire career centered around him. I was constantly filing these idiot lawsuits for him and negotiating settlements on his behalf. Then one day we lost one he thought we should have won." She slipped her hands into her skirt pockets. "He didn't give a damn about the money, it was the apology the judge insisted be published in the *Post* that infuriated him."

"And he went berserk."

It was time, she couldn't put him off any longer. He had bits and pieces and had put them together in a logical order, but he needed to be told the whole story. "He arrived at the office late Friday afternoon . . . " she began. Her voice became remote, as if she were reciting something she hadn't lived, but had read in the paper.

"When did the police get there?" he asked after the telling, prompting her to finish when she became lost in remembering how Keith and Jennifer had died.

"Not until after it was over." She frowned in concentration. "Did you mean when did they get to the building or to us?"

"To you."

"When it was over," she repeated, "but I found out later that they'd been there almost from the beginning. One of the secretaries escaped and called them. They had a SWAT team set up for an assault when they heard gunfire. No one knew whether Tobias was firing wildly to scare us or had actually started shooting at us, so they didn't break in right away. When they finally made their move, Tobias was sitting in the middle of the conference table holding a machine gun.

"I'll never forget the look on his face," she went on, "his eyes were bright and he had this excited smile on his lips. He acted as if he were in the middle of one of those games where people chase each other through the woods with guns that fire paint balls. He shot himself before the police could reach him."

She'd said enough. Or he'd heard enough. He needed time to work through what she'd told him and to deal with her reflected pain. "No more tonight, Miranda."

She nodded.

He stood and held out his hand. "We'll finish this in the morning."

She put her hand in his and slowly came up beside him. "Call me before you come over."

"That won't be necessary."

"It's late, Adam. I want to sleep in tomorrow—if I can."

He brought her arm up and placed it around his neck. "You can sleep as long as you want right here."

She started to protest, but the words caught in her throat. Desperately needing the comfort he so willingly offered, she put her other arm around him and leaned her head against his chest. In a whispered voice she told him, "I hate it when you do that. I should tell you to go to hell . . . and I would, but I'm afraid you might listen to me, and I don't want to be alone tonight."

With a fluid, effortless motion he picked her up. "You can tell me in the morning. I promise I'll act properly chastised."

"You could at least pretend to care how I feel."

He stayed where he was for a long time, holding her in his arms, his chin pressed against the softness of her hair, his lungs filled with her essence. Finally, he said, "I do care, Miranda."

The words were from his soul and heart as much as his mind. Instead of their power frightening him, Adam felt a sense of discovery, a new understanding of his years of searching. A wondrous peace came to him.

Fourteen

Somewhere in the distance Adam heard a dog bark. He glanced at the clock on the nightstand. It was barely five, it would be another hour before the sky began to lighten with false dawn.

He'd slept fitfully, conscious of Miranda's every movement, his mind filled with bloody, violent images as he tried to picture what it must have been like for her to witness the deaths of her husband and daughter and friends. He understood now that her grief was a wound that would not heal until she found a way to deal with the guilt. Adam didn't know how to help.

It was no wonder discovering Jason's illness had terrified her. Every day had become a personal battle of survival for Miranda as she sought reasons to believe the next would be better. How could she believe that while watching a friend slowly dying? It wasn't remarkable that she had ended up on the edge of a cliff, the wonder came that she'd struggled as long as she had before giving up the fight.

She began to move beside him, rolling from side

to side. His T-shirt twisted and rode high on her waist from the constant movement. Seconds later, a low moan escaped as she brought her legs up and curled her body into a fetal position. With a start she came fully awake. Even with her face turned to the wall, she was aware that he had been staring at her.

"Adam?"

"I'm here." He brought her into the curve of his shoulder.

She came eagerly, pressing herself into his side. "I couldn't remember where I was."

She was still trying to hide her thoughts from him. "Bad dream?"

She hesitated. "Yes."

"Does it come often?"

"Every night." She pressed the flat of her hand to his chest. "Make love to me, Adam."

The request was more desperate than seductive. He had become her drug, her escape, someone to chase the nightmares away. But there was too much at stake to let things go on as they had.

"Tell me about Keith," he said.

Her body grew rigid. "Why do you want to know about him?"

"Because he's a part of you."

"There are things about me that are none of your business, Adam. Last night was—"

"A beginning, Miranda. I won't go back."

"You want too much."

"Tell me about Keith," he insisted. The rigidness left her. Her shoulders sagged, in defeat or weariness over fighting him.

"He was patient and unassuming and a wonderful father." She spoke the words by rote. In her day to day life, she did everything possible to keep from thinking of Keith. If she allowed real memories, the guilt almost paralyzed her.

"Not your type at all," Adam said. "Why did you stay married to him?"

She tried to see into his eyes, but the window was to his back and the room too dark. Was he guessing? He had to be. There was no way Adam could know how it had been between her and Keith. "I loved him."

"Really—a man you describe as unassuming?"

She rolled away, not stopping until she was at the other side of the bed. "What do you want from me?"

"I want you to let me in, Miranda."

She was afraid, more afraid than she'd been since the shooting. Adam wasn't like anyone she'd ever known. His moral code and caring were throwbacks to another time. How could she expect him to understand the compulsive, work-driven woman she'd been before he met her? "I did love him," she said defensively. "I just didn't know that I did until after he was gone. When it was too late."

She pulled the blanket up to her chin. She was cold, but it was the kind that came from inside. A down comforter would do her no good. Adam reached over to cover her shoulders, but otherwise didn't touch her.

"I was a terrible wife," she said. "Is that what you wanted to hear?"

"By whose standards?"

Already he was offering her a defense. She could quit now and his image of her would be intact. But it wouldn't be honest and would always be between them. "Don't try to protect me, Adam. If I'm going to do this, it has to be my way."

"All right—but not from over there." He moved to the middle of the bed and put his hand on her arm.

Miranda knew he believed he was making the telling easier by removing her from the purgatory of isolation, but it was a familiar place and she gave it up reluctantly. Finally, she yielded and leaned her back into his chest. "We were happy in the beginning, but everyone is when they're first starting out. I suppose it helped that we never saw each other. I was either in school, with my study group, or at the library. And then I was on law review and working my summer law job. It seemed my time off never coincided with his, especially with the two jobs Keith took on to pay the bills and get me through school."

"What kind of work did he do?"

"By day he was an architect, at night he waited tables." Needing something to hold on to, she caught the edge of the pillow. It wasn't enough. She took his hand from her waist, knitted her fingers with his and held on tightly.

"Keith had a blind spot where I was concerned." A lump formed at the base of her throat. "He never stopped telling everyone how proud he was of me . . . not even when I would say terrible things to him . . . "

There were mornings since Keith's death that she would wake up hearing the words she'd used to humiliate him. She'd desperately try to convince herself her memory had corroded the incidents, made them worse, made her part crueler. It never worked. In her mind she would tell Keith how sorry she was, over and over again. And she would ask his forgiveness. It never came.

"Were you purposely trying to hurt him or just make him mad?"

Adam's uncanny insights into her past didn't startle her as much as they had when she'd first known him. She'd come to realize that for all his participation in life, at heart, Adam was an observer. "I didn't realize what was happening at the time, but later, when I looked back, I could see that I was embarrassed to be with him. I guess I thought if I made him mad enough, he would change." She brought Adam's hand close, holding it tight against her chest. When she realized she could feel her own heartbeat through him, she loosened her grip. "Outside of the movies or comic strips, how many fathers do you know who gave up their careers to stay home and take care of their child?"

Adam gave it some thought. "None."

"Neither did I. Keith was one-of-a-kind. He became a standing joke at the office. Not to my face, of course, but the subtle, and sometimes not so subtle questions and comments clued me in to what was happening behind my back. I didn't know how to explain him, and didn't have the strength of character to defend something I didn't understand." Her father hadn't been as circumspect as her coworkers. He had no qualms telling her exactly what kind of man he thought she'd married and what a burden Keith was to her. She still struggled to understand the man she'd married and come to love more after his death than before.

"Why *does* a man give up everything that society says should be important to him in order to become something no one respects?" She didn't expect an answer.

"No one?" Adam asked.

"Not anyone I knew."

"And I assume these people felt the same way about women who stayed home to take care of their children?" He paused even though he already knew the answer. "Kind of sexist for supposedly educated people, wouldn't you say?"

Adam's words could have come from Keith's mouth. How had she missed something so obvious? There was a lot of Keith in Adam, a disconcerting amount. Was that the basis for her attraction? Was she using him as a substitute for Keith, hoping he would give her the absolution Keith couldn't?

"What is it, Miranda? What are you thinking?"

She was too stunned at the revelation to keep from blurting out the truth. "How much you're like him."

"Something tells me that wasn't meant as praise."

She felt like a skydiver whose parachute had just failed. With abrupt, panicked movements, she swung her legs over the side of the bed and sat up. "I can't talk about this anymore."

He sat up and reached past her to turn on the light. "Yes you can, and you will. I'll be damned if I'm going to let you run away again."

"You have no claim on me, Adam. I owe you nothing."

When she started to get up, he grabbed her shoulders and turned her to face him. She tried to twist free. "Look at me," he insisted.

Her eyes narrowed in fury. "Let go of me."

In response, his grip tightened, not enough to hurt, only to get his message across. "Not until you promise to finish this."

"I'm not promising you anything. You're nothing but a God damned bully."

"And you're nothing but a God damned coward."
He was taking a terrible chance. No matter how the
confrontation ended, she would never forget how
he'd treated her. "What are you afraid of, Miranda?
What demons are you nurturing in the hope they'll
grow strong enough to force you back to the edge of
that cliff?"

"Don't play psychiatrist with me, Adam. You
don't have the education."

A slow smile was his only answer to the cutting
remark. He released her and waited.

"I fight when I'm threatened," she said.

Still, he didn't say anything.

After a long, tense minute, she said softly, "Now
do you understand?"

"No," he answered.

"I hurt the people I care about. It's second nature
with me."

"Why?"

"It's just the way I am."

"There has to be a reason. What drives you to be
the way you are?"

She'd never ascribed motives to something she'd
fought admitting. The conclusion was as startling as it
was obvious. "I guess it's some kind of warped sense
of self defense."

"You're going to have to do better than that."

"If I let people in . . . I give them power."

"Power to do what?"

He wasn't going to let it go. "To hurt me."

Adam touched the side of her face. "How could
you possibly be hurt any more than you are now?"

She looked down at her hands knotted together
in her lap.

"I don't know any other way to be."

His resolve to make her talk about her past was in sudden battle with his need to comfort her. He slid his hand down her arm, felt a rash of goose bumps and brought her back down on the bed and into his arms.

Later, Miranda broke the silence by asking, "How long does he have?"

"I don't know," Adam said.

"Is Jason the reason you're here?"

"Yes."

"You came to watch him die?"

"No, Miranda," he said gently. "I came to be with him while he was alive."

"He will take a part of you when he goes." She had to warn him.

"I know."

"I don't have anything left to give, Adam."

He pressed his lips to her forehead and then her temple. "It's all right. Jason will understand."

"You'll tell him for me?"

"If that's what you want."

It was exactly what she wanted. Adam was right. She had become a coward. "Give me a couple of days."

"What about your lessons?"

"I'll think of something."

"Don't let it go too long," Adam said. "Jason's had too many friends just stop calling. He deserves an explanation from one of us."

"He never mentions his family." She didn't want to talk about Jason, didn't want to think about what was ahead for him, but she was tired of running away.

"They cut him out of their lives a couple of years ago."

"Maybe someone should tell them he's sick. It might make a difference." She was thinking like a mother and what she would give to have just one more day with Jennifer.

"They know."

"Are you sure?" It was inconceivable to her that a parent could stay away from a dying child.

"I'm positive."

"I don't see how—" But she did. Her own father could hold a grudge with more passion than he could love. He hadn't attended Keith's and Jenny's funeral and never once came to the hospital to see her. Her brothers and sister came, which, sadly, surprised her. But their visits were awkward. After a lifetime of the wedge driven between them growing larger by the year, they discovered they had nothing to offer but sympathy to a stranger.

Her mother had phoned several times, finally, accidentally revealing the reason her father had stayed away. He had read in the paper that Tobias Trout was her client and could not get over the fact that the shooting, that the loss of all those lives, had been her fault.

She hadn't spoken to her father since and doubted she ever would again.

Adam rolled to his back and tucked his arm under his head. "I've known for a long time now that my being here isn't enough to get Jason through this with any real peace of mind. He needs something I can't give him, mainly a real understanding for what he's going through. He'd never say anything, but—"

"Am I hearing you right? Are you beating yourself up because you're not gay or that you don't have AIDS?"

"It's more than that."

"I'm sorry to be the one to tell you this, Adam, but you can't be all things to all people. It just isn't possible."

"Is this the voice of experience talking?"

She moved to her side, bringing her leg over his, her arm across his chest. Sometime during the night they'd become more than lovers. Now they were friends, too. "You try, I never did. Whenever I came to the place on one of those forms you fill out in doctors' offices where they ask your occupation, I never thought beyond attorney. I was only incidentally a wife and mother."

"I don't believe you. There may have been problems between you and Keith, but I saw how you looked when you were talking about Jennifer."

Just hearing her name spoken aloud was enough to send a sharp pain through Miranda's chest. "She used to make these funny little drawings for me to put up in my office. I was afraid they would look unprofessional in open view so I hung them on the inside of the cupboard door where no one would see them but me."

"Sounds like the perfect solution," Adam said.

"I cared more about what other people thought than I cared about pleasing my own daughter."

"I had a grandmother who I thought was the queen of guilt, but I think you just topped her, Miranda."

She came up to a sitting position. "You bastard. How could you say something like that when I'm trying to open up to you?"

"Here we go again." He sat up, grabbed the pillow and propped it against the headboard. "Another lesson in the care and feeding of Miranda Dolan's guilt." He leaned back and crossed his arms. "Go ahead, lay the rest of your ugly little secrets on me. Who knows, you might even convince me you're the reprehensible person you think you are. That is what you want, isn't it? But none of this hidden picture stuff. Tell me how you screwed around on Keith or how you refused to take Jennifer to the doctor to have her broken leg set because it would make you late for work. And while you're at it, I'd like to hear how you personally derailed that commuter train last week."

"I've never hated anyone more than I hate you right now."

He stared at her long and hard. "Not even Tobias Trout?"

She sucked in her breath. "Tobias was crazy."

"Bingo," he said softly. "And nothing you could do or say, now or then, will ever change that simple fact. *What happened wasn't your fault, Miranda.*"

The pain of remembering was almost more than she could bear. "Tell me again."

"Tobias Trout needed someone to blame for whatever was wrong with his life. You were a logical target, a suicide note guaranteed to get him the attention he craved. Think about it, Miranda. What other means did he have to gain national network coverage?"

"Are you saying he killed all those people just to get on the evening news?" There had to be something else. People didn't die for such capricious reasons. But she knew they did. All the time. Drunk drivers ran stop signs, drive-by shooters hit the wrong houses . . . cars needed their oil changed.

"You would have seen it yourself if you hadn't been so involved."

She held her hands out in a helpless gesture. "Without blame there's no reason. Their deaths are meaningless."

"Then blame Tobias, or the media that damn near guaranteed his fifteen minutes of fame if he made his leave-taking spectacular enough, or all the gun fanatics who can't seem to get it through their heads that the Bill of Rights wasn't referring to semi-automatic weapons. Just stop blaming yourself. If beating yourself up won't bring them back, what good does it do?"

Her eyes burned with unshed tears. "I can understand what you're telling me here," —she touched her head— "but not here." Her hand covered her heart.

He put his hand over hers. "In time," he promised.

He'd given her a wondrous gift. There was a deep need to give something in return. "Jennifer loved to ski," Miranda said with great difficulty. Why was it the good memories hurt even more than the bad? "But Keith ruptured a disc shoveling snow when she was five and the doctor ordered him off the slopes. I took over his job of teacher."

Images flooded her mind like fast moving pages in a photograph album. Little things she'd forgotten, like the time Jennifer broke her binding at the top of the hill and they skied all the way to the bottom in tandem, and the afternoon they'd simultaneously discovered a sweater in one of the shops in Aspen and agreed it was the perfect birthday present for Keith.

"She was amazing, Adam," Miranda said, a catch in her voice. "I would show her how to do something once in the morning and she'd have it mastered by the end of the day."

"You never cry," Adam said.

Her lip trembled when she gave him a sad, self-deprecating smile in response. "I'm afraid if I start, I'll never stop."

"I think we should go skiing this winter. We're not that far from—"

"I couldn't, Adam." The mere thought terrified her. "It's too soon."

"You have to create new memories. It's the only way to make peace with the old." He brushed the hair from her forehead and cupped his hand at her chin.

"I'm not ready." She turned her face into his chest, burrowing against his warmth.

He didn't say anything for several seconds. And then, "I'll make a deal with you. Go skiing with me and I'll take you to a Giants baseball game."

This time she brought her head up to look at him. "Am I missing something here?"

"The entire time I was growing up every game I attended was with my father. I haven't been back since he died—eleven years ago." He bent and softly kissed her lips. "There isn't anyone I would rather make new memories with than you."

Her heart swelled as she returned his kiss, her lips parted in invitation. "Now, will you make love to me?" she murmured. His reply was lost in the deepening of their kiss. It didn't matter. The heat of his hand on her inner thigh was all the answer she needed.

Fifteen

At the sound of a car pulling into the driveway, Jason scooted his chair across the wooden studio floor to the dormer window and looked outside. It was Susan's Celica. She'd filled the backseat to overflowing. Suitcases were strapped on top and the trunk was held closed with nylon rope. He waited for her to get out before he opened the window and shouted, "I'll be right down."

She met him at the door, her arms flung wide. "It's time," she announced.

Jason hugged her. "God, I'm going to miss you."

"I won't give you the chance. I'll call every week and send so many letters, you'll get tired of answering them. And I'll be home for Thanksgiving and Christmas—don't you dare put up the tree without me."

Another car pulled into the driveway, parking behind Susan's Celica. It, too, was loaded. "Who's this?"

"Karol Black. She lives in Wesport. We're on our way to pick up Debbie and then we're all driving together. You know, safety in numbers, that kind of thing. My dad's even making me take his cell phone."

The trip was something she and Matt had planned and talked about for months. He'd run into Matt the previous week, and after several awkward attempts at conversation, Matt mentioned he still hadn't decided when he would leave for school. Jason had wished him well and asked him to keep in touch, but didn't hold out much hope they would ever see each other again.

"Adam must have forgotten today was the big day," Jason said. "He's going to be disappointed he missed you."

"I went by his house. His truck was there, but the house and shop were locked up tight."

"He and Miranda took off for a couple of days."

Susan reared back and gave Jason a look of disbelief. "I knew they were friends, but I had no idea they were actually gettin' it on."

Jason laughed. Susan prided herself on being on the cutting edge of town gossip. It wasn't like to her to let something this big slip by unnoticed. "They've been pretty discreet. I didn't know what was going on between them until Miranda started coming here for lessons."

"I don't know about this, Jason."

He could see she was genuinely worried. "I'm a little uneasy about it myself, but then it really isn't our business. Adam's got to know what he's doing."

"Adam's the human version of the SPCA. It's his nature to take in strays."

Jason worked to keep a neutral look on his face. He didn't want her to know how close she'd hit to home. "He's been that way all his life, Susan. We're not going to change him."

"He's going to need someone around to pick up the pieces when she dumps him." She glanced back at Karol, held up her hand with the fingers stretched out and mouthed, "Five more minutes."

"What makes you think she's going to dump him?" Jason hadn't been aware his mind had been traveling the same road until Susan said the words out loud.

"They're the match from hell. She's way older than him and not nearly as good looking. And you can tell she's uncomfortable with him being a handyman—she owns a BMW for Christ's sake."

"What've you got against BMWs?"

"The people who drive them. They come up here a couple of days a year and act like they own the place." She shuddered. "It got so I could tell what kind of cars people drove by the way they acted when they came into Dad's office. People who own regular cars don't throw their weight around. I'd bet Dad on it, and I was always right."

"I know what you mean, but Miranda's not like that," Jason said. "And Adam can handle himself around money. It's the age thing that's got me worried."

"Damn, I leave town and everything falls apart."

"We're making too much out of this. It's not as if they were sending out invitations to the wedding." He put his arm around Susan and guided her back down the walkway to her car. "If and when that happens we'll put our heads together and see what needs to be done."

She seemed placated, at least for the moment. "Adam would have a fit if he knew how we were talking about him."

"Which is as good a reason as any to stop."

"Tell him good-bye for me."

"Good-bye?"

"You know what I mean. And tell him he better be here when I come home for Thanksgiving."

"I'll even do it in just that tone of voice." He opened Susan's door and gave a quick wave to her friend.

Before she got in, she gave him another hug. "Behave yourself."

Jason smiled. "I think that's my line."

"Call me if you need me."

"My line, too."

She got in, started the car, and rolled down the window as she waited for Karol to back out. "I love you."

Jason blew her a kiss. "*Still* my line."

He waited until she rounded the corner before heading back inside. When he reached the porch, the phone started ringing. It was Mary Kirkpatric.

"Jason, dear, I hope I haven't caught you at a bad time."

"There's no such thing where you're concerned." He carried the phone into the kitchen to make himself a cup of tea while they talked. "I would put the President himself on hold to talk to you."

"Do you rehearse things like that or do they just come naturally?"

"I work on them for hours, waiting for you to call." He liked that she still teased him. For most people his illness had changed the way they dealt with him, sometimes subtly, sometimes not so subtly. Mary was a refreshing constant. "What's up?"

"There's a couple of things I've been meaning to talk to you about, but first, I've been trying to reach

Adam for two days now. Do you happen to know where he is?"

Jason had no idea whether Adam had told her about Miranda, or if he had, how much. "He decided he needed a break and took off for a couple of days. You want me to try to find him for you?"

"Goodness no, it's not an emergency. I have some papers that need his signature and was wondering if he planned a trip to the city any time soon. I could stick them in the mail, but I'd rather not."

"I know he has a job in Albion the day after tomorrow, so he's sure to be back by then. As far as heading your way, I don't have another appointment for . . . " He tried to remember when he was due at the clinic again. "I think it's at least another four weeks. Of course I'm not the only reason he goes into the city, so I really don't know what to tell you."

"I just hate the thought of him being alone when he sees the end in black and white." Her tone was conversational; the words were explosive.

"I'm sorry, Mary, but you seem to think I know more than I do about what's going on between you and Adam."

"He didn't tell you we're selling the business?"

Jason sat forward in the chair. This was not some small thing Adam would forget to mention. "He didn't even tell me you were considering it."

"Then he probably didn't tell you I'm getting married two months from now either."

She could have told him she was planning a run through Golden Gate Park in the buff and he would have been less surprised. "Congratulations. I can't believe there's a man out there good enough for you, but I guess I'll have to accept your word on that."

"I love you, too, Jason. You're such a dear."

"Two months from now, huh?"

"We've decided on a small wedding, just family and a few friends. I'd like to invite your mother and father. After all, Michael and I did meet at their house, but if it would make you uncomfortable to have them there, I certainly understand. You're part of the family, Jason, they're just friends. You come first."

It would be difficult for her to exclude his parents; they had known each other since before he was born. And it would take some of the shine off the day if he were to stay home because of them. "Would you mind if I took a couple of days to think about it?"

"Of course not. I'll call you sometime next week."

The doorbell rang. "Hold on a second," he told Mary. "I'll be right back." He set the phone on the counter and made a dash for the front door.

What he found sent him reeling. "Tony—" A dozen emotions battled for supremacy. Anger won. "Out slumming and thought you'd drop by to see if I was still among the living?"

There was no immediate response to the attack. It was as if Tony had anticipated Jason's reaction and prepared himself. "I need to talk to you."

"Sorry, you're two years too late. You probably didn't notice, but my car isn't parked outside anymore." The garage had been Tony's studio where he'd sculpted high dollar pieces featured in trendy galleries on both coasts.

"I noticed," Tony said.

Jason purposely looked down at Tony's hands. They were soft, the nails healed and trimmed. He hated that it gave him satisfaction. "Not working I see."

"Please, Jason. It's important that we talk, not just for me, for you, too."

Jason had thought when he was able to go an hour and then two and finally a whole day without thinking about Tony, he'd gotten over the loss. And now, in the time it took to open a door, he was right back to where he'd been the night Tony walked out. If he had the sense God gave an amoeba he would go back to the kitchen and find a way to convince himself he'd imagined the whole thing. "I'm on the phone."

"I'll wait." Tony glanced around and spotted the wicker rocker on the far end of the porch. "Over there," he said, pointing to the rocker.

"You might as well come in the house. I don't want someone to see you hanging around outside."

Jason stepped out of the doorway to let Tony pass, then indicated he should wait in the living room. His hands were trembling when he picked up the phone again. "I'm sorry, Mary, something's come up. Would it be all right if I called you back later?"

"Certainly." There was concern in her voice but she was too well-mannered to ask Jason what had happened.

"If I see Adam before he picks up his messages I'll tell him you were looking for him."

"I'm sure he'll get back to me as soon as he can." She stared to hang up and then added, "Take care of yourself, Jason."

"Thanks—I intend to do just that."

Mary sat with her hand on the receiver for a long time after she hung up. Worrying about Jason had become as second nature as keeping him from hearing the worry in her voice. He'd never been someone who liked being fussed over, and had made it obvious from the onset of his illness that he wouldn't take kindly to questions about his day-to-day health. She'd consulted with experts in the field, both physical and mental, and their advice had been to follow his lead. They'd all said the day would come when he would reach out to those closest to him. Until then the kindest thing she could do was treat him as normal as possible.

Of course Adam had taken the completely opposite course and in his own indomitable way had proved to be precisely the friend Jason needed.

There was a soft tap on her office door before it opened and Michael came in. "Did you find Adam?"

"Not exactly." She got up to meet him and accept his kiss. "But I did find out where he is and that he's due back in a couple of days."

Michael went to the closet, took out her coat and held it for her to put on.

Mary gave him a questioning look. "Did I forget something?"

"There's a house I want you to see."

The now familiar flutter started in her midsection. "Does it have to be today? I have a hundred things on my schedule for this morning. I had no idea how much work was involved in selling a business, let alone setting up a—"

"Is there anything that won't keep until this afternoon?"

She went through all the motions of giving it thought. "I have a meeting with Edgar at 11:30."

"Edgar Rosenthal?"

She nodded.

"He's right down the hall, Mary. You can meet with him anytime."

Why was she holding back? Could it be that she was having second thoughts about their relationship? The instant the question formed, she discarded the possibility. Other than her love for Adam, the one sure thing in her life was her love for Michael Ericson.

She slipped her arms into her coat and got her purse out of her desk. "Two hours, Michael." She tried to sound stern. "That's absolutely all I can spare today."

He caught her as she headed for the door and turned her to look him in the eye. "You want to tell me what's going on here?"

"I would if I could," she said, "but it's as much a mystery to me as it is to you."

"Then your dragging your feet about finding a house isn't my imagination?"

"No," she admitted reluctantly.

"Is it just the house or is there something else happening I should know about?"

"If you mean am I having doubts about marrying you, I'm not. I love you, Michael." She hadn't realized how tense he was until he let out a heavy sigh of relief.

He pulled her into his arms and held her as if he would never let her go. "Do you suppose it's the idea of living in the city that's upsetting you? I only suggested it to cut commute time. I hate to think of being stuck in traffic every day when I could be spending those hours with you." When she didn't answer right away, he went on. "We could always look at something farther out . . . Marin . . . the Napa Valley . . ." When she still didn't say anything, he added, "Lake Tahoe?"

That brought a smile. "You better be careful. I

could get used to being spoiled. Then what would you do?"

"Exactly what I intend to do anyway."

She touched the side of his face. "Maybe it's all the details of selling the business that has me on edge."

He caught her hand and pressed a kiss to the palm. "Perhaps, but I have a feeling the real problem stems from our setting up the foundation without saying anything to Adam about it first."

She considered the possibility. In the abstract Adam would applaud the solution Michael had come up with on what to do with the money from the sale of the company, but when faced with a fait accompli she wasn't sure his reaction would be positive. He was the only true free spirit she'd ever known. No matter how noble the opportunity she and Michael planned to present Adam, it was still the road map of his future and he'd been left out of the creation. "You could be right," she said.

"Well, you'll know soon enough. I assume you're going to tell him when he signs the papers Felix prepared."

She dropped her gaze to the blue stripe on his silk tie. "I'm not sure now is the right time."

"Oh?"

Michael could convey more meaning in one word than anyone she'd ever known. "There's so much else going on."

"Worried about the wedding?"

She shot him a frustrated look. "Will I never be able to keep secrets from you?"

He grinned and kissed the tip of her nose. "Never. It's a waste of energy to try."

"Then what am I giving you for a wedding present?" she challenged.

"An amazing night of sex."

She laughed. "If we don't get out of here, we'll never get back in time for my meetings."

He lifted the strap of her purse over her shoulder. "Was I right?"

"You'll just have to wait and see." It was said with a throaty promise.

Later, when Michael parked his Porsche Speedster in the driveway of the federal style house on Nob Hill, Mary again felt the peculiar heaviness in her chest. The house was one of the gems of the old neighborhood, featured in historical guidebooks and on tours, which explained the high brick fence and wrought iron gates.

Michael came around to her side of the car and opened her door. "Well, what do you think so far?"

"It's beautiful."

"And even in the worst traffic, less than twenty minutes from the office."

It was hard to resist his enthusiasm. "Why don't we look around outside while we wait for the agent?"

"She isn't coming. I told her I wanted to show it to you alone the first time."

Mary shook her head. "I'll bet you could talk your way into Fort Knox."

"Time's a wastin'." He took her hand.

When they reached the front door, Mary stood back while Michael put the key in the lock. The closer they'd come to the house, the stronger the feeling of unease had become, until it seemed it would take all her determination to get inside.

The right side of the massive walnut doors swung

open. Michael turned and smiled encouragingly. She took a deep breath and crossed the threshold. The foyer was massive, filled with natural light and rising three stories, topped by a crystal chandelier that looked as if it belonged in the opera house. A suspended stairway circled gracefully to a second floor landing. The walls echoed their footsteps on the marble floor.

"Impressive . . . " Mary said, at a loss of words for any other way to describe the luxury that surrounded her.

"But a little cold, don't you think? It needs some warming up. I thought that table you have in the living room would look good in the middle here. Maybe with a bouquet of flowers."

Her gaze lifted to the ceiling. "A *great big* bouquet."

"Come with me," —he reached for her hand— "we've got a lot of rooms to look at yet."

The rest of the house was more in keeping with Mary's idea of what a home should be. Several rooms were still partially furnished, making them seem even more inviting. The den and office were actually on the cozy side, with fireplaces and windows facing the garden. She didn't care for most of the wallpaper and thought a couple of the bathrooms were on the ostentatious side, but these were problems with easy remedies.

In the middle of exploring the second floor, she stopped on the landing and stared down at the marble medallion on the foyer floor.

"What is it you see?" Michael asked, coming up behind her.

Slowly, room by room, she'd begun to understand the emotional battle going on inside her. If she moved into this house, or any other house, with Michael she would necessarily have to leave the house that had been her home for over thirty years behind—and with it her memories.

Adam had grown up in the house in Burlingame. The pantry door still held the pencil marks they'd made each birthday to show how much he'd grown since the last. There were a few in between, too, made at Easter and Fourth of July and any other date Adam was hit with the need to grow up faster. Even though he hadn't stayed with her for over two weeks at a time in ten years, there was a bedroom she still thought of as his. And in her mind's eye she saw Gerald everywhere, building a fire in the fireplace on Christmas morning, sending her a tender gaze over the breakfast table, making love to her in their bedroom.

It was as if she were being asked to abandon her past in order to build a future. Adam would have no history in the home she made with Michael. When he came to stay it would be in an alien room. She was selling his father's company to get on with her own life. How could she also sell his history?

"Mary?" Michael's curiosity had turned to concern.

She looked up at him. The love she saw in his eyes told her he would understand, that he would commute any distance to give her peace of mind. Adam was her child and Michael would never ask her to do anything that could change their relationship.

But Adam had a life of his own, completely separate from hers—as it should be. And Michael was her love, her companion for the rest of her life.

It was time for her to let go of her past.

"Which room would be ours?" she asked.

He smiled. "Any one you want."

"Pick one," she insisted.

"The one with the window seat. I like morning sun. And the view is—"

She put her arm through his. "Come with me, Mr. Ericson," she said mysteriously.

They climbed the stairs to the third floor. Mary opened the door and was delighted to find it was one of the guest rooms that still contained furniture, most importantly, a large, Victorian bed. What she was about to do was at war with everything she'd been taught a lady should do and be. She reached up to loosen Michael's tie. "I think our new home should have a proper christening."

He blinked in surprise before his mouth turned up in a rakish smile. "I promise this will be a day you remember."

A shiver of anticipation raced down her spine. She shrugged out of her coat and let it drop to the floor. "Enough talk . . . "

Sixteen

Miranda was on the back porch plucking dried blossoms from the fuchsias when she heard a car door slam. Deciding it was someone visiting one of the neighbors, she ignored the sound and went around the opposite side of the house to get the hose to water the plants. Seconds later the sound of the doorbell chime drifted through the open window.

Her first thought was that Jason had come to check on her. While she wasn't as afraid of him as she'd been when she first found out that he was dying, she wasn't emotionally prepared to see him again either. Her hesitation was as much for him as for herself. The last thing he needed was to have someone around him who couldn't accept his dying.

In his singular way, Adam had convinced her she was stronger than she thought. Instead of encouraging her to open up and pour out her soul to him, he'd taken her hiking in the redwoods north of Eureka. For two days they'd wandered the cathedral-like setting, both of them as reluctant to break the silence as if they'd been in a real church.

At first she hadn't understood why he'd brought her there. And then slowly she began to see past the obvious of the beauty and serenity of the ancient setting to the horrific scars from fires borne by still-living redwoods. Even in nature there was tragedy. And life went on.

She was at the deck and heard the doorbell ring again. "I'm coming," she shouted. He must have heard her because before she had completed another stride, Clifford Chambers came around the corner.

Miranda stopped and then took a half step backward. It was as if she'd run into a solid, invisible wall and it had knocked the wind out of her.

"I'm sorry," Clifford said, noticing her reaction. "I guess I should have called first."

"No—it's all right. I'm just surprised to see you." She automatically checked her wind-swept hair, straightening tangled strands with her fingers. "It's been so long."

"You look wonderful."

"Thank you." She flushed at the compliment. He looked wonderful, too, tanned and narrow-waisted—more athletic than she remembered. The gray at his temples was more pronounced, as were the lines around his eyes. But instead of aging him, the changes gave him a heightened air of importance.

It was almost a year since they'd seen each other last. Joan had sent him to ask her to Thanksgiving dinner. By then she'd been holed up in her house for weeks and had all but given up trying to return to work. The memory of that day was like looking through a partially-opened blind, the scene was familiar, but large pieces were hidden from view. Clifford had been concerned at her appearance that day . . . or had he been repulsed? He hadn't stayed long. And he'd never returned.

He took a step closer. "To be honest, I was a little afraid of what I might find today. The last time we saw each other—"

She didn't want to hear it. "What are you doing here? And why now?" What was this inexplicable pride that made her glad he hadn't come a month ago?

"I haven't been able to get you out of my mind, Miranda." It was obvious the admission didn't come easy. "I thought I would get over you in time, that eventually I would forget, but I was wrong."

She frowned, confused. For several long seconds she didn't say anything while she struggled to understand what he was telling her. And then pieces started coming back in a staggering rush, a memory so shameful it had lain buried in the recesses of her mind all these long months. She and Clifford had been more than colleagues, more than friends. Had the shooting not happened on Friday, they would have been lovers by the next Monday morning.

Clifford became concerned. "God, I don't know what came over me. I never should have just blurted it out like that." He came closer. "Forgive me?"

Whether by design or accident, with a few short sentences he had focused attention on himself again. She didn't know whether to feel grateful or suspicious. "There's nothing to forgive. You only said what was on your mind."

He gently laid his hands on her shoulders. "But I should have eased into it. I had no right to hope your feelings hadn't changed, either."

There was a haunting familiarity in his touch. An

explosion of emotions followed. She must have loved him; she couldn't let herself believe she would have agreed to an affair for any other reason. How could she have forgotten something as important as loving someone?

"Getting to where I am now hasn't been easy," she said. It was the most she would ever tell him about what she'd gone through since leaving Denver. She might not remember everything about him and their relationship, but she instinctively knew he wasn't the kind of man who suffered guilt or understood self recrimination.

He moved his hands to her back and started to pull her into his arms. She resisted. He immediately let her go. "Forgive my impulsive behavior. It's just that it's been so long. Ever since I made the decision to come here, I haven't been able to think of anything or anyone else."

"You haven't mentioned Joan." Miranda was suddenly fiercely angry at his assumption he could ignore her for a year and still find her waiting for him. "How is she?"

Clifford let her know he understood what she was doing by the look he gave her. "I hate to admit it, but I think she's happier now than when we were married."

"*Were* married?"

"As soon as I realized my feelings for you weren't going to go away, I asked Joan for a divorce. That process was the main reason I didn't come to you before now. I wanted you to know what I was willing to give up in order to get you back."

Now was the time to tell him about Adam, before he committed himself deeper, but something wouldn't let her. Clifford might accept that there was someone new in her life, he'd never accept that it was someone like Adam. She had to do whatever it took to make sure they never met.

Thank God Adam had a job out of town and wouldn't be back until that night.

Adam's stomach rumbled in noisy protest over a coffee and stale-doughnut breakfast and a skipped lunch. He'd left home before the sun was up that morning determined to squeeze an eight-hour job into five and surprise Miranda by returning early. The effort had paid off; he'd finished and had been back on the road again before noon.

As he neared the cut off to Miranda's house, he glanced down at jeans and T-shirt crusted with dirt he'd picked up crawling under a house. He tried to convince himself he should go home and clean up before he went to see her. Of course going home meant facing four days of unanswered calls on his machine. The thought was immediately followed by one he liked better. He'd stop by, pick her up and take her to his house with him. She could either wait while he returned any urgent calls and then showered—he smiled—or better yet, join him. Afterwards he'd tell her about the tickets he'd picked up the week before for the outdoor music festival in Gualala. They could make a night of it and stay at the Whale Watch Inn, eat breakfast in bed and take their time coming home.

Without conscious effort, the evening began to unfold in his mind. After the festival they'd have a late dinner then relax for an hour or so in the spa.

They'd open the cognac he'd been saving . . . and make love in front of the fireplace . . . and fall asleep in each other's arms with the sound of waves hitting the shore.

Life was good.

Damn near perfect.

Adam spotted the road to Miranda's house, flipped the turn signal and left the highway.

"How did you come to pick this place?" Clifford asked, his gaze sweeping the living room.

She wasn't fooled by the question. Vern's house fell short of Clifford's exacting standards; in his mind she was living beneath herself and he wanted to know why. "I liked the location."

"Kind of Spartan, but then I don't imagine if I had rental property I would put anything worthwhile in it either." Finally, he looked at her. "With your sensibilities, I'm surprised you've lasted as long as you have in this place."

"You get used to it after a while." Her answer was automatic and had nothing to do with how she really felt. While the decor was pedestrian at best, she'd come to like the house. It was small, but not confining.

"Don't you miss your house . . . your paintings?"

"Sometimes."

"And what about me?" he said in a passionate outburst. "Do you only miss me sometimes, too?"

She waited too long before she answered to fool him. "I try not to think about you," she admitted. "It hurts too much."

"God, I'm so sorry, Miranda." He raked his hand through his hair. "I don't know what I was doing making you wait all this time to hear from me. I was an idiot to think you'd be impressed if I came after you like some fucking knight on a white horse and announced I was a free man. It never crossed my mind that you might not be here waiting for me."

When she didn't say anything in reply, he went on. "To be honest, I thought you'd be back on board at the firm long before now. Who could have known it would take you this long to get over what that asshole Trout did?"

"Yeah . . . who could have known?" Had anyone else said something as insensitive, Miranda would have told them to go to hell. With Clifford his casual reference to her grief wasn't an insult, it was simply an expression of his own philosophy. Loss was a part of living. You dealt with it and moved on. There had been a time when she would have given anything to be more like him.

"I can see that you're doing all right now, though."

She couldn't hold back the ironic smile. "You should have seen me last week."

"No matter. Today is what counts." He put his arm around her and gave her shoulders an attaboy squeeze. "We've missed you at the office. Allen's brought in a couple of women to kind of balance things out, but they'll never make partner." In a quick, fluid motion, he tucked his hand under her chin, tilted her head back and kissed her.

It was at that very moment the back door opened and Adam came inside.

Miranda turned at the sound and saw that she and Clifford were standing in a direct line from the door. She closed her eyes against the confusion she saw in Adam's.

"It appears you have company," Clifford said. His

arm stayed locked around her waist.

Berating herself for her cowardice, Miranda looked at Adam. His hair was disheveled, his T-shirt and jeans filthy. Obviously he'd come straight from the job. He shoved his hands in his pockets and stared at her, saying nothing. Her heart went out to him. He looked hurt and vulnerable and so very, very young.

She moved away from Clifford, the lingering moisture from his kiss a brand it took every bit of her self control not to wipe from her lips. "I thought you were going to be gone the rest of the day," she said to Adam. Not until the words were spoken did she realize how scheming they made her sound.

"I finished early," Adam said.

Beside her, Clifford cleared his throat, not loud enough to be obvious, but she recognized the signal all the same. "Adam, this is Clifford Chambers, one of the partners at Coker/Standish." She motioned in Clifford's direction. "Clifford . . . " How did she introduce Adam? What title did she give him? She took the coward's way out and prayed he would understand. " . . . this is my friend, Adam Kirkpatric."

Clifford didn't move to meet Adam to shake his hand. Instead he waited, as if it were the younger man's duty to come to him.

The tension between the two men charged the air. Miranda could almost feel the static. "Clifford surprised me this morning," she said to Adam. "I had no idea he was coming."

Adam nodded. He answered Miranda, but looked at Clifford. "After all this time it's no wonder you were surprised."

"I've explained all that," Clifford snapped, instantly angry.

His reaction startled Miranda. She'd been around Clifford when he was under enormous pressure and had never seen him lose his composure. "It's been a difficult year for all of us."

"More difficult for some than for others, no doubt," Adam countered, still looking at Clifford.

Now it was Adam's turn to surprise her. She would have sworn he wasn't capable of such open and aggressive hostility. She sent him a pleading look. "Don't do this."

They were the magic words. "I guess I should have called."

"You're damn right you should have," Clifford shot back.

Miranda whirled in his direction. "*Shut up.*"

He recoiled from the attack. "I was only—"

"You're the one who should have called. You had no right just to show up and expect to find me waiting for you." When he started to say something she warned him off with a scathing look. "Don't you dare give me that shit again about waiting for your divorce to be final. You waited because you didn't want to have to deal with what I was going through."

Instead of unnerving Clifford, Miranda's attack restored his composure. "We need to talk," he said to her. "Alone."

Before she could answer, Adam said, "I have some things I have to get done this afternoon. You can reach me at home tonight."

He was trying to help, but she couldn't let him just walk out. "Have you seen Jason?"

"No. But he's on my list."

"Tell him I'm sorry about missing my lessons."

"Meaning?"

He was asking if she'd changed her mind about seeing Jason again. She desperately wished she could tell him what he wanted to hear, but she wasn't ready. After this morning, she didn't know if she ever would be. "Nothing."

"I think I'll wait a while before I say anything. He doesn't need anymore roller coaster rides." Adam opened the door and left.

Miranda willed her legs to stop shaking and went after him. As soon as she was outside, she called out, "Adam, please wait."

He stood with his back to her. "Do what you have to do, Miranda."

She put her hand on his arm. "I'm sorry. What you saw wasn't—"

"Don't explain. It isn't necessary. Either you trust someone, or you don't." He turned to her. "I trust you."

His words were a gift, one she wished she deserved. "I didn't know he was coming."

"So you said."

"Do you want me to tell him to leave?"

He touched the side of her face and looked deeply into her eyes. "I won't make that decision for you."

"I don't want to hurt you. I'm afraid I will if I let him stay."

"*Do what you have to do,*" he repeated. "I can take care of myself."

"I'll call you."

He pressed a quick kiss to her forehead and left without saying anything more.

Miranda watched him leave, wanting to bring him back, glad when he was gone. She heard the kitchen door open. It was followed by the sound of footsteps on the walkway behind her.

"I thought it had to be something more than the scenery that's kept you here," Clifford said easily. "Adam's quite a kid. I'm surprised he's up here instead of in LA."

"He isn't a kid." She hated the defensiveness in her voice.

"Oh? You could have fooled me. I would have pegged him at twenty-four, maybe twenty-five."

"He's in his thirties." It was only a small lie.

"Must be the climate out here."

She turned and confronted Clifford. "Adam saved my life."

"I'm sure he's a good listener, too." The line was good enough. Clifford only had to add a touch of snideness to his voice.

"Adam's a lot of things," she agreed, "but when he pulled me out of the surf it wasn't for a cozy chat by his fireplace." She waited until she was sure he understood what she'd said and looked properly contrite. "The fireplace came later."

Instead of rising to her bait, Clifford became thoughtful. "I can see how something like this could happen. You were cut off from the life you loved, from all your friends, you had nothing, no one. I'm sure this Adam is a nice young man, certainly uncomplicated. He was undoubtedly just what you needed at the time."

That she listened to him, that what he said sounded reasonable, made Miranda sick to her stomach.

When Adam left Miranda's he'd intended to go straight home, stand under the shower in the hottest water he could tolerate and stay there until it was cold. But the closer he came to his house, the more he realized he didn't want to be alone.

He was distracted when he arrived at Jason's, but not so much that he failed to notice the change that had occurred in the four days since they'd seen each other. Jason looked happier than he'd seen him in a long time.

"Adam—welcome home. How was the trip?"

"Great." He came inside.

"I take it you haven't been home?"

"Not yet. Why?"

"Your mom got tired of leaving messages on your machine and called here to see if I knew where you were."

"What did you tell her?" He wasn't ready to explain his relationship with Miranda yet. Hell, after today, he wasn't sure there would be anything left to explain.

"Only that you'd decided to take off for a couple of days."

"Thanks."

"She told me about selling the business—and that she's getting married again."

Adam felt as if time had become a physical force, walls of a room that were slowly, inexorably closing in on him. "I meant to say something but—"

"Hey, it's all right. I understand. You'll talk about it when you feel like it."

Every once in a while Adam received a jolting reminder why Jason was such a good friend. "Got any beer left from the party?"

"In the fridge."

Adam headed for the kitchen. "What time did

everyone finally clear out?"

Jason laughed. "Not until noon. For some reason, everyone really let loose that night. I wound up with a drawer full of keys and a house full of people. Next time I think I'll hire a bus to pick everyone up and take them home." He leaned against the counter while Adam dug through the refrigerator. "Susan came by on her way out of town. She said to tell you that you were a first class shit for not being here to see her off."

Adam groaned. "I forgot. Was she really mad?"

"More disappointed, I think. You can make it up to her when she comes home for Thanksgiving."

"She say anything about Matt?"

"Not a word." Jason crossed his arms and stared at Adam. "So . . . how's Miranda?"

Adam took a long swig of his Heineken before he answered. "It'll keep."

"Jesus, you're not fighting already?"

If he didn't want to talk, why had he come? "Fighting I could deal with."

"I can see this isn't going to be a simple fix. Sit down." Jason filled the kettle with water and put it on the stove before he joined Adam at the table. "Now tell me why you're here and not at her place."

"She has company—someone from her past."

"Male, I take it."

Adam nodded. "Someone she used to work with, but from what I walked in on, I'd say it went beyond that."

"It makes sense. She's a beautiful woman."

"Yeah, that she is."

"Let me guess. He's older, distinguished looking, and gives off big money vibes."

Adam finished his beer and got up to get another one. While he was up he fixed Jason's tea and brought it to him. "He rented a Cadillac Seville to drive up from San Francisco."

Jason shuddered. "Enough said."

"He's my worst nightmare, Jason. I left school because I was scared to death if I took over the business I'd wind up just like him."

"Not a chance. You don't have it in you."

Adam didn't argue. He preferred to let Jason keep his illusions. "So, how's it going with you?" It was a throwaway question, but Jason hesitated so long with the answer, Adam grew concerned. "Something happened. What is it?"

"It's not what you think," Jason said quickly.

Adam waited. "Then what is it?"

"Tony came to see me the other day."

They didn't talk about him often. Jason had rejected the abandoned lover role. "He's got guts, I'll give him that."

"He wants to come back."

Something in Jason's voice told Adam to tread lightly. "And you said?"

"I had to think about it."

"Is he sick?"

Jason slowly traced the design on his mug with the tip of his finger. "That's what I thought, too. It's been two years since he left. Why would he just show up again unless he wanted something."

"And?"

"He still isn't showing any symptoms."

"The bastard." Not until that moment did Adam realize how deeply he hated Tony. Jason had believed himself in a monogamous relationship and therefore safe. It turned out Tony liked an occasional walk on the wild side. He'd become infected on one of his walks and passed the virus on to Jason. Then he'd panicked when faced with what he'd done and took off.

"You don't mean that," Jason said.

"I'm afraid I'm not as forgiving as you are."

"Then we may have a problem."

Adam had a feeling he didn't want to hear what would come next, but he asked anyway. "Why's that?"

"I'm considering letting him move back in with me."

Seventeen

Adam lost himself in thought as he left Jason's and headed home. He was only peripherally aware of a horn honking when he looked in his rearview mirror and saw Matt's Mustang closing in behind him. With an abrupt turn of the wheel and a frustrated curse, Adam pulled his truck to the side of the road and got out.

"You wanted something?" he said as Matt came up.

Matt stopped midstride. "Hey, if this is a bad time, I can catch you later."

Adam leaned heavily against the side of his truck. "It's been a hell of a day, Matt. I'm afraid I'm not in a very good mood."

"I'll be damned. I didn't think things like that ever happened to you."

"Why are you still here? Shouldn't you be on your way south?"

"I'm leaving first thing tomorrow morning. Which is why I've been tryin' to chase you down. I wanted to thank you for all you tried to do for me and Susan." He shoved his hands in the back pockets of his jeans and dropped his gaze. "I know you were pretty pissed off at me through it all, but you still treated me fair," —he looked up, a sheepish smile on his face— "better'n my mom anyway. I think she would've thrown me out on my ass if my dad hadn't stopped her."

It was now that Adam should say something wise, something Matt would carry with him through life. But he'd decided to throw his pundit cap away. It didn't fit and he was tired of having it constantly falling over his eyes.

"You're welcome," Adam said. "I hope everything works out and you have a great time this year." He sounded like a frigging greeting card.

Matt tried, but couldn't hide a look of disappointment. "Yeah, everyone's been tellin' me the college years are the best ones."

"So I've heard." Now he sounded as if he were shining Matt off. "Listen—" Adam was interrupted by the sound of an approaching car. He looked up and saw that it was a forest green Mercedes 500SL, the driver hidden by the sun glaring off the windshield. Undoubtedly there had been a couple hundred identical cars imported into the States, he was even willing to bet the majority of them had been sold in California, how then did he know with dead certainty that this particular one belonged to his mother?

Matt's head swiveled as the car passed. "How much do you suppose someone has to make to afford one of those?"

"It isn't just the car, Matt," Adam said. "It's the crap that goes with it."

"What do you mean?"

"The worry about someone stealing it, the insurance, the garage to put it in, the—"

"Hey, it comes with the territory." He looked longingly at the disappearing car. "You gotta give to get."

Focused properly, it wasn't a bad philosophy. "I have to go," Adam said. "Someone's waiting for me up at the house."

Matt pulled his hands from his pockets. "You should've said something sooner. This wasn't important. I just wanted to say thanks and tell you I was headin' out."

"Come and see me over Thanksgiving."

"I'll do that." Matt grinned in pleasure and held out his hand. "No hard feelings?"

"No hard feelings." Before Adam let go of Matt's hand he said, "Just make sure you get in for that second test."

Matt nodded, went to his car and got in. "I'll do that." He waved as he drove away. "See ya in a couple of months."

Adam returned the wave, then glanced up the hill toward his house. On a normal day, under normal circumstances, he would be pleased by his mother's surprise visit. Today it was everything he could do not to get in his truck and head off in the opposite direction.

Mary was sitting on the deck in the redwood swing when Adam arrived. She got up to greet him. "What perfect timing. I haven't been here two minutes."

"Why didn't you go inside? The door's unlocked."

"I'm a city girl, Adam. It wouldn't even occur to me to try the door."

He enfolded her in a bear hug, confident she wouldn't be put off by his grimy appearance or the possibility of something rubbing off on her silk blouse. His mother was a tactile person. Growing up he'd been hugged and kissed more than any ten kids he knew. "Have you had lunch?"

"As a matter of fact, I stopped by Steve's Deli before I left this morning. I had him put together all your favorites—including cheesecake with fresh strawberries."

"Uh oh." Adam opened the door and held it for her to enter first.

Once inside, she dropped her purse on the nearest chair. "Now just what did you mean by that?"

"Steve's Deli? Cheesecake? Sounds like a bribe or bad news."

"You really should do something about that ugly suspicious streak of yours."

"I promise I'll work on it, right after you tell me why you're here."

"Oh, all right. I have some papers for you to sign."

He went to the window to open the blinds and let the sun in. "And?"

"I wanted to talk to you about something."

"You didn't happen to pick up some of Steve's special blend coffee, did you?"

"It's in the car." When Adam started for the door, she put her hand on his arm to stop him. "Can we talk first? I've been rehearsing what I would say all the way up here and I'm afraid if I wait any longer, I might chicken out."

He put his hand over hers. "Go for it."

"I think we should sit down."

"That bad, huh?" He sat in the green and blue

striped chair and propped his feet on the coffee table.

"Not *bad*, Adam." She took the chair opposite him. "Just different. More for me than you, but I wouldn't be concerned if my decision didn't affect you, too. Of course you might not care at all. You've been gone so long . . ."

"This is the speech you rehearsed?"

"Don't tease me, this is too important. I'm selling the house."

His immediate reaction was that it didn't matter and that she'd been foolish to let something so insignificant get her this upset. But then as snatches of memories of the years he'd lived in the house came back to him, he realized it wasn't a house she was selling, it was the only real home he'd ever known.

"Why?" It was an unfair question. "Never mind. It isn't important."

"It wasn't an easy decision, Adam. I know what losing that house will mean to you—what it means to me. But it's time for me to move on." Her voice had grown softer, until in the end, it was little more than a whisper. "Please tell me you understand."

"Of course I do." Somehow he had to convince her that his feeling of loss wasn't her responsibility. "You and Michael need to build something together." How could it be so hard to say something he truly believed? "It would be nice, of course, if you picked a house with a guest bedroom for your wandering son."

She blinked, hard, and then held her eyes closed for several seconds. When she looked at him again, she said simply, "I love you."

Adam put his feet back on the floor and sat forward in his chair. "I love you, too." He needed time to think, to absorb this new piece of news. "Now, how about that lunch?"

Later, over cheesecake, Mary said, "It's a guest wing."

It took him a second to figure out what she was talking about. "You've already found a new place, I take it?"

"The decorators are at work as we speak. It's a spectacular house, Adam, big and roomy, perfect for children—or grandchildren."

Adam laughed. "I knew it had to come some day."

"I'm not putting any pressure on you. I just wanted you to know that I'm not the kind of woman who thinks having grandchildren around makes her look old."

"Thanks, Mom. I'll keep that in mind."

"One more thing and then I'll let it go."

"Yes?" He got up to pour them each another cup of coffee.

"I'm not going to put the house on the market right away. You might decide you'd like to live there yourself."

Suddenly they weren't talking about the stuffy attic he'd explored as a child or the banister he'd fallen off and broken his arm or even the two story living room where they'd put up the tallest Christmas tree they could find every year. They were talking about a seventy-five-year-old, ten-thousand-square-foot building on two acres of landscaped ground. The maintenance and upkeep were full-time jobs, the taxes were more than he would make as a handyman that year.

"Not a chance," he said. "I could never afford it."

Her hand curled around the fork she was holding as if it were about to use it as a weapon. "You could take care of ten houses just like that one with the interest you get on your trust fund every quarter."

"I never think of that money as mine." He knew she had trouble believing him. Why wouldn't she? He often wondered how he could forget something like that himself.

"I love you dearly, Adam, but there are times you annoy the hell out of me. Why are you so afraid of that money? What do you think it will do to you?"

"The reasons change with the weather," he admitted as much to himself as to her. "Right now, I worry that it could change the way people see me. I want to be liked for who I am, not what I have."

He might as well have waved a red flag in front of her. "Something tells me you're not talking in the abstract." She studied him through narrowed eyes. "It isn't *people* you're worried about as much as a person—namely one Miranda Dolan?"

"I don't want to talk about it."

"Fair enough." It was accompanied by a satisfied grin.

"You're making more out of it than there is." Adam gathered the remaining crumbs from his cheesecake with his fork. "There are problems. A lot of them."

"I thought you liked challenges. At least you used to."

Adam chuckled. "You don't know anything about Miranda and you're cheerleading for her."

"If she weren't special, you wouldn't be involved with her. Even more telling, you wouldn't be reluctant to talk about her."

"Interesting piece of logic."

"And true?"

"You're fishing."

"So I am," she acknowledged.

The only way he was going to get her off Miranda was to move on to something else. "You said you brought some papers for me to sign."

"They're in my briefcase." She got up and went into the living room.

While she was gone, Adam cleared the dishes. As inopportune as his mother's visit was, he was grateful for the distraction. He would be going out of his mind if all he had to do was sit and think about Miranda alone with Clifford. What was with the kiss? Was it something new or kindling brought to an old fire? For the first time in his life, Adam understood jealousy. He didn't like the way it made him feel.

Mary returned and laid a stack of papers on the table. "You want me to stick around while you read them in case you have questions?"

"I assume you've gone over them with Felix and you're satisfied?"

She handed him a pen and a look of resignation. "You know you should never sign anything you haven't read yourself."

"What am I going to find, that you discovered a way to make me take the money after all?"

"You never know," she said.

Adam ignored the implied warning and flipped through the legal documents looking for lines awaiting his signature. "If you can't trust your own mother, who can you trust?"

Mary glanced at the ceiling as a small, guilty smile formed.

Eighteen

Miranda took a shortcut to Adam's house, cutting through the woods instead of following the road. The leaves on the rhododendrons were heavy with morning dew, the ferns soaked her tennis shoes and pants legs. She should have been cold, but a pervasive numbness shielded her.

She'd started to drive over, but hesitated when she saw the sun was barely up. Just because she'd lain awake all night didn't mean Adam had. What she had to say wasn't something he should hear half awake. Walking would kill time and might even help put her thoughts in order.

Everything would have been so much simpler and cleaner if Adam had just come in five minutes sooner or later. She wouldn't have had to explain that God damned kiss and he would never have needed to know the ugly details of her and Clifford's relationship.

Could the tenderness and sympathy and understanding he'd shown the past few days withstand knowing how it had been between her and Clifford?

The memory made her physically sick. Until now the shame she'd felt when she thought of Keith had centered on her neglect, that she'd been on the verge of betraying him spoke volumes about the person she was under the facade. She could understand, even forgive, that she'd convinced herself she no longer loved Keith, but she would be a long time absolving the woman who had been on the verge of destroying his trust.

What had happened to her? How had she become that woman?

Miranda neared Adam's house and saw smoke drifting from the stovepipe chimney. He was up. She walked a little farther so that she could see behind the house, the coward in her hoping he'd already left for work and she would have a few more hours to come up with a way to tell him . . . What? That she wasn't a person he would like if he really knew her? That Clifford's coming had snapped her out of the trance she'd been living in and made her realize Mendocino was only a stopping off point in her life?

A movement at the house caught her attention. The door opened and Adam came out carrying a small, designer suitcase. He looked as if he'd just gotten out of the shower, his hair wet and slicked back, wearing only jeans and tennis shoes. His destination was a small green car half hidden by several pine saplings. Curious, she moved closer and saw that it was a Mercedes, one of the most expensive they made.

Adam opened the trunk, put the suitcase inside and headed back to the house. Before he got there, a woman came outside. He stopped to wait for her. When she came up to him he put his arm around her and walked her to the car. They talked for several seconds, hugged with obvious, deep affection and kissed good-bye. Adam stood in the yard and watched until she was gone, then went back inside.

Miranda felt as if she were trapped in a child's spinning top where someone had just pushed the plunger. She'd thought she knew how Adam must have felt when he saw Clifford kissing her, it hadn't been close.

She had to see him, to explain, to be explained to.

Adam answered her knock fully clothed. He glanced past her into the yard. "You walked over?"

"I needed time to think."

"Yeah, I can understand that."

"Can I come in?"

"Sorry—" He stepped from the doorway. "You want coffee?"

She could smell breakfast; he'd been up for a while. She desperately wanted the coffee, she was cold and needed something to hold onto, but she didn't want to go into the kitchen to be faced with something, anything the other woman might have left behind, not even dirty dishes. "No thanks."

"How's Clifford?"

He didn't give a damn *how* Clifford was, he wanted to know where he was. She moved past him into the living room, dropped her coat on the sofa, and then went over to the stove. The cast iron doors were open; she held her hands out to the flame. With her back to Adam, she said, "I sent him away—not long after you left."

"Not on my account, I hope. I would hate to have you cut your visit with an old friend short because of me."

This was not the Adam she knew. Sarcasm was as alien to him as subterfuge. She moved closer to the stove knowing all the while it could do nothing to warm her. The cold she was feeling came from a place too deep.

"You said 'away,'" Adam prompted. "As in back to Denver, or one of the local motels?"

"Denver."

"Why was he here?"

She turned. "I didn't ask him to come, Adam. I was as surprised to see him here as you were."

He gave her a withering look. "Somehow I doubt that."

She couldn't tell whether it was anger or hurt or a combination that fueled him. Whatever his feelings they had been strong enough to make him reach out to someone else. "Who was that woman?" She tried hard not to make it sound like an accusation, but the words themselves carried their own message.

Adam frowned. "What woman?"

"The one I saw leaving here this morning."

He looked at her for a long time before he sighed and wiped his hands across his face. But the weariness couldn't be erased so easily. "How long were you outside?"

The question scared her. Was there more she hadn't seen? The woman was attractive, somewhere around Miranda's own age and obviously wealthy. Typical for him? A pattern? One she had fallen into? Dear God, could it be? "I saw her leave."

He didn't say anything right away, as if he were replaying the moment in his mind, searching the details. "You should have let me know you were there."

"Why? Would you have done something differently?" Would he have tried to protect her or taken the opportunity to flaunt his actions?

"I could have introduced you—to my mother."

"Your mother?" she repeated slowly, feeling incredibly foolish.

"You would have met her before now. She usually comes up a couple of times a month, but she's been busy lately."

Miranda almost laughed out loud. The sense of relief made her feel light headed. She fought to keep it from showing. He could know she cared, just not how much or she would never be able to protect herself. "I . . . I didn't want to interfere."

"Nice try, Miranda, but we both know what you thought. Jesus, is that what your life was like before you came here? I catch you with some guy and you automatically think I'm going to retaliate by bringing someone home with me?"

"Catch me?" His accusation was no more than she'd expected, his conclusion obvious. How then could there be this much pain? "How dare you?"

"Then you tell me the words I should use."

"He surprised me. We were—"

"Wait a minute. Are you asking me to believe there has never been anything between you and Clifford, that he came all this way after all this time because it finally occurred to him he couldn't go on without you?"

"Don't play games with me, Adam. You know that's not the way it was."

He folded his arms across his chest. "Just how was it, Miranda? Tell me so I don't make rash assumptions."

Her mouth opened, but there was no way she could say aloud something she'd kept hidden all these months, even from herself. "I can't."

"Were you lovers?"

She couldn't look at him anymore and turned back to the fire. "No."

"But you would have been, given a little more time."

"Yes."

"Did Keith know?"

A sharp pain sliced her chest. She closed her eyes and struggled to draw a breath. "Please, Adam . . . no more."

He came up behind her, put his hands on her arms and drew her against his chest. She held herself stiffly, afraid of the comfort he offered. To give in would make her vulnerable. She couldn't let herself need something that could be taken away.

"Why did you tell me about Keith and Jenny and not Clifford?" Adam asked.

How could she explain something she didn't understand herself? "I forgot . . . or I just didn't want to remember."

The answer seemed to satisfy him. "Do you still love Clifford?"

"I never loved Clifford." She knew that now, she hadn't then.

"Then why would you have an affair with him?"

Adam was the consummate romantic. He might sleep with someone he didn't love, but he would never betray someone he did. "It seemed the right thing to do at the time."

"And now?" he asked carefully.

She turned and looked up at him. "How could you ask me something like that?"

"I have to know how you feel about him."

"Why?"

"Because . . . " Confusion, fear, doubt emanated from him. "I love you."

Tears burned the backs of her eyes, her throat knotted at the effort to contain them. She touched his face. "Oh, Adam—what have I done to you?"

He brought her into his arms. "Turned my world upside down."

"I never meant for this to happen." She laid her head against his chest.

"God—me neither," he admitted.

"If I could, if it were another time, a long time from now, I think I would love you, too."

He lowered his head and whispered in her ear, "But you do, Miranda. You just haven't realized it yet."

She squeezed her eyes tight, but not before a tear had escaped. She would give anything to believe him. "You're wrong, Adam. That part of me died with Jenny and Keith."

Adam brought her closer. Her grief had become her protection, her guilt the punishment that put reason to something that had none. Miranda could no more believe in fortuity than aliens. Her life, her beliefs were grounded in pragmatism. "What if I were to die, Miranda? Would you grieve for me?"

"Don't say that."

"Would you?" He made her look at him.

"Of course."

"Why?"

She struggled with the answer. "You're my friend."

He touched his lips to hers in an infinitely tender kiss. "It's enough for now."

"I can't love you, Adam."

She wouldn't let go until she'd convinced him—or he convinced her. "If I left tomorrow and never came back, would you miss me?"

"That doesn't prove anything. You can miss friends."

He kissed the hollow behind her ear. When she brought her hand up to stop him, he held it and touched his tongue to her palm. Slowly, purposefully, he took a finger into his mouth. He stared deeply into her eyes daring her to deny the hunger he saw building.

"Sex isn't love," she said.

He untucked her sweater and cupped her breast through the flimsy barrier of her bra, letting the yielding flesh fill his hand, the nipple grow hard at the demanding stroke of his thumb. "What is sex with a friend?"

She caught her breath. "It still isn't love," she insisted. "It can't be."

"Do you want me?"

"No—" He kissed her, deep and without restraint. "*Yes.*"

"Do you need me?"

"Why are you doing this?"

"*Do you need me, Miranda?*"

It scared her how much. "Yes," she finally admitted.

"Do you love me?"

With all her heart she wished she could give him the answer he wanted. "No." It was as if the word had been ripped from her.

A slow, gentle smile formed. "The hell you don't," he said softly.

She put her arms around his neck, her determination to convince him she didn't love him overpowered by her need to be made love to. The only time she escaped her demons was when she was with him, when he stole her reason and restraint. Just once more, that was all she asked. Then she would let him go.

Adam tried to slow her urgency, to make the ride long and tender, but as always, once aroused, she would not be stayed. She moved against him, her fingers releasing the buttons on his jeans, her hands working his erection in a mind-blowing combination of strength and gentleness.

He lifted the hem of her sweater and pulled it over her head. The scrap of lace that covered her breasts yielded without effort. She arched her back in invitation; he lowered his head and drew a nipple into his mouth.

Miranda whispered, "Yes . . . " She put her head back and repeated the word. It was a sigh, a cry of yearning, a release. "Yes . . . "

Adam hooked his thumbs under the waistband of her sweats and bikini panties and stripped them from her. She kicked off her shoes. He started to pick her up.

"No—take me here. Now."

He caught her hands and stilled them. So that she could not mistake his intent, he waited until she looked at him before he said, "We do it my way this time."

A panicked, cornered-animal expression crossed her face. She started to pull away. He didn't fight her, but he didn't let go either. Slowly, understanding replaced the panic. "It won't make any difference."

"I don't care."

She hesitated. Her body throbbed with unre-leased tension. She willed him to finish what she'd started, but he didn't touch her except to hold her still. All the while he looked at her, his eyes filled with the promise of wild, erotic pleasure. Had she not known the heights he could take her, were she not already halfway there, she could have resisted him. At least that was what she told herself. She swallowed and touched her tongue to her lips. "Where?"

Without a word of reply, he took her hand and led her to the bedroom.

Nineteen

Miranda lay with her back to Adam, his arm across her waist, his hand tucked between her breasts. They had been that way for a long time, the only movement when Adam brushed a strand of hair from her neck before settling his chin into her shoulder. Her body still flushed and sensitive from their lovemaking, she was as aware of the tips of her fingers as the curve of her spine. The sore places—her thighs where she'd cradled his hips, where she'd taken him into her body and urged him to come harder and deeper, her breasts, her lips—would remain tender for days, constant reminders of this, her last morning with Adam. But there was more. They'd never made love with more intensity, never given or taken more completely. Adam had an intimate knowledge of her body she'd never allowed anyone, not even Keith. He took without asking and she gave without thought of denial. She'd been left sated in a way that was an awakening, had acquired an insight into herself that would become more curse than gift when they were no longer together.

It was masochistic to go on pretending. In a flat, emotionless voice that gave no clue to the heartache behind the words, she said, "I have to leave, Adam."

"I'll take you." He opened his hand and possessively captured her breast. She'd scared the hell out of him before and touching her was the only way he'd been able to settle the fear.

"That's not what I meant—I have to go home, to Denver."

She might as well have gut punched him. "Home?" he said carefully. "When did you start thinking of Denver as home again?"

"I never stopped. Everything I own is there, my house, my paintings, Keith's car, all of Jenny's things. I just walked away when I left. It's time I went back and faced what I couldn't face then."

Adam rolled to his back and tucked his hands under his head to keep them still. "When?"

"Tomorrow."

He forced himself to take a deep breath before asking, "Why so soon?"

"It isn't soon. I should have gone a long time ago."

"I'll go with you."

"No . . . this is something I have to do alone. I ran away when I left. There's a lot of unfinished business waiting for me."

He didn't like the direction their conversation was headed, but couldn't keep from asking, "Does that mean you're coming back when it's done?"

A sudden, deep chill made her shudder. She reached for the blanket and pulled it over her shoulders then tucked it tight under her chin. "I don't know." She paused. "Yes I do . . . I'm not coming back, Adam."

"How do I fit in to these plans of yours?"

She didn't say anything for a long time, just lay there with her back to him. When he'd begun to think she wasn't going to answer him, she said softly, "You don't."

His reaction was swift and physical. He grabbed her arm and turned her to face him. "How can you just walk away from me like that?"

She kept her eyes downcast, refusing to look at him. "Because you were right. I do love you."

"Jesus Christ—would you listen to what you're saying? You're not making any sense."

"Anything beyond what we've had these past two months would never work for us, Adam. I can see that now. We're too different."

"That's bullshit."

"Please, listen to me." Now she had to look into his eyes if she had any hope of convincing him. "Do you remember when I told you how alike you and Keith were? If you came with me, I would wind up doing the same thing to you that I did to him. I couldn't stand that. It would destroy me right along with you."

"I can take care of myself, Miranda. I would have thought you'd learned that by now. Besides, you've changed. You're not the woman you've tried to convince me you were back then."

She prayed he was right, but she couldn't take the chance. "Maybe."

"Is it Clifford?"

"No—yes, in a way, but not the way you think. Seeing him made me remember the good that was in my life back then—how much I used to love the law. I think I still do. It's one of the things I have to find out."

"What you're saying is that I wouldn't fit into that world?"

"It isn't that you wouldn't fit. Those people wouldn't understand you. They're incapable of seeing how special you are, and what they don't understand, they attack. They would eat you alive, Adam. I can't let that happen. I won't."

"And this is what you miss?"

"What I miss is making a difference. The other is an ugly by-product I can't control or change so I have to accept. I know now that if I'm ever going to really recover from what happened and get on with my life, I have to do it someplace where I can practice law. It's who I am, Adam. That's the real me, not the woman you pulled out of the water and fell in love with."

"How can you be so sure that what you left is what's right for you? Two days ago you were—"

"I may be wrong about going back," she admitted. "But the only way I'll know for sure is to go there and see for myself."

"And if it doesn't work out?"

"I'll deal with it."

"And where will I fit in then?"

"You won't." How long could she go on hurting him? Why wouldn't he let it go? "It doesn't matter whether I practice law in Denver or New York, we can't be together."

"Let me get this straight. You're dumping me because you think I'm incapable of fitting into the elite lawyer crowd you run with?" He'd grown up around people like that. They were the reason he left, the reason he never told anyone who he was or where he'd come from. How could he have been so wrong about Miranda? Hadn't she told him over and over again what she was really like? Why didn't he believe her?

"It's more than that."

"Am I supposed to guess?"

"It's your age—or my age, however you want to look at it. I've never hidden how I feel about it, Adam. Every time we go somewhere I wonder what people are thinking. Your mother looks more my contemporary than you do."

"Why do you care what other people think?"

"I wish I didn't . . . I tried to stop, I really did. But the pattern is too deeply ingrained. I am who I am, Adam. The only way I can be happy again is to stop beating myself up for something I can't change."

Adam sat up and leaned forward. Pain and anger twisted his thoughts and made him want to strike out. "If this is really the way you feel, what the fuck have we been doing together all this time?"

She brought the sheet up to cover her breasts, feeling a shame that went beyond words. "I think you answered your own question."

"If I thought you really believed that . . . "

"What?" she asked, terrified of the answer.

"You've said you loved me a dozen times in a dozen ways."

She'd been wrong to reveal her feelings; it only made what she had to do harder. But she couldn't back down. She'd never been more sure of anything in her life. If she stayed with Adam, if she let him come with her, eventually, being with her would destroy everything that made him special. "I lied."

If she had put a knife in his back it would have hurt less. "I didn't," he said.

Miranda knew she had to get out of there before

she broke down and admitted how much she cared. "I'll write and let you know how I'm doing."

"Why? Am I supposed to care?"

For all her conviction she was doing the right thing, there was a part of her that recognized she was walking away from the only chance she would ever have at real love again. Nobility wasn't all it was cracked up to be. It hurt like hell.

"If you'd rather I didn't," she said, "I would understand."

"I'd rather you didn't."

"If I send you my address will you at least let me know how Jason is doing?"

"What kind of game are you playing now, Miranda?"

"You're right. I'm sorry. I should never have asked that of you."

"I think you should go."

She sat up and laid her hand on his back.

He shrugged her away. "Don't—it's not something I need, and it sure as hell isn't something I want."

"I can't leave you like this. Not after everything you've done for me. I owe you so much."

He turned to look at her. "What did you have in mind?"

She recoiled at the pain in his eyes. "You're special, Adam, more caring than anyone I've ever known. You deserve someone who—"

He got up and walked to the door. "I would have thought you could come up with something better, Miranda, what with all the training in rhetoric they give you in law school."

"I suppose I deserve that. You have every right to be mad at me."

"Oh, please, this is turning into a cliché." He grabbed his jeans, put them on and left. He was back seconds later carrying her clothes. "Right now, all I want is to be left alone.

"You've worn me down, Miranda. I need time to think." He tossed her clothes on the bed. "My keys are in the truck. Take it. I'll pick it up after you're gone."

"This is exactly what I'm talking about," she yelled as she came up on her knees. "What is this frigging compulsion you have to be the nice guy? By your own admission, I've turned your life inside out and still you want to give me your truck so I don't have to walk home." The last was said in a singsong voice designed to make him angry. "What's wrong with you? Why don't you ever fight back?"

"There isn't anything wrong with me, Miranda— you're the one with the problem. You're like those women who go from one abusive relationship to another because it confirms their own feelings of worthlessness."

"You don't know what you're talking about."

"Then why are you so determined to prove how terrible you are? Why this self-sacrificing attempt to save me?"

"I told you once before you weren't qualified to play psychiatrist, so give it up, I'm not listening."

"Afraid of what I might discover?"

"Go to hell, Adam."

"Was that the best you could do?" He held his arms out wide. "Look, I'm not bleeding. Doesn't this prove you don't have to protect me, that I can take care of myself?"

She stood and yanked her sweater over her head.

"I suppose I should thank you. I was worried you might be hurt by my leaving. Now I can see if you are, you'll snap back in no time, probably before my plane lands in Denver."

"*But will you?*"

Her head jerked up. "I don't need you." The fire left her eyes. "I did once, but not anymore."

Adam's hands dropped to his sides. "What if I need you?"

Tears welled in her eyes. *Oh, Adam, why can't you understand I'm leaving because I love you?* "You're young. Someday you'll—"

"Jesus, spare me." He backed out the door. "Don't lock up when you leave."

"That's it? No good-bye?" What was wrong with her? Why was she trying to keep him there?

"You've got to be kidding."

"After everything . . ." Her throat tightened convulsively. "It just seems wrong for it to end this way."

"Your choice, Miranda."

"I'll never forget you."

"That's supposed to make me feel better?"

"Good-bye, Adam."

He shook his head, turned and left.

Miranda sank to the bed. To keep from going after him she told herself that in giving him his freedom she had given him a gift. Never mind what it cost her. Never mind that he didn't know the value. Someday he would realize how much she had loved him. It was enough. It had to be.

Adam climbed the hill behind his house, taking the steep route with long, determined strides. When he was sure he could see and not be seen, he stood with his back against a redwood and waited for

Miranda to leave. A short time later she came out of the house, walked past his truck and into the forest.

Just that quickly, it was over.

It didn't seem right. A storm should have marked the occasion, with lightning and thunder and a roaring wind to tear branches from trees. At the very least there should have been fog, thick and heavy and dark.

He looked up at the cloudless sky, at the sunlight piercing the shadows on the forest floor and at the thin ribbon of smoke lazily drifting upward from the stovepipe on the roof of his house.

He didn't want to see, even tried closing his eyes, but the beauty was as tenacious as the grief. For him, it would always be that way.

Twenty

Miranda arrived home mid afternoon, three days after she left Mendocino. She sat outside in her car, staring at the brick colonial house with the white shutters, trying to remember what it had been like when she had come there every night after work. Had she ever stopped to notice how the setting sun reflected gold off the upstairs bedroom windows? Had there been as many birds then? Had she loved the house because it was home, or because it was big and impressive and in Cherry Hill?

She sat in the car until the sun disappeared and the cold penetrated her down jacket. The automatic lights came on as she stepped on the porch, making it seem as if someone had come to the front door to greet her. Stephen Kastner, a friend of hers and Keith's, as well as their accountant, had taken over the care of the house while she was away.

In monthly letters that were forwarded to her in Mendocino, Stephen detailed the bills he'd paid, told her when he hired a painter to spruce up the trim, and when he fired and hired a new gardener. Periodically he would mention going inside the house to make sure everything was all right. Depending on the season—because of the need to maintain temperature for the computers and her art work—he would check that the heater or air conditioner were working and whether the automatic lights needed replacing.

By Stephen's own admission, he stayed no longer than absolutely necessary, which was understandable. Stephen and Keith had become friends because of their daughters. Jenny and Lynne found each other the first day of school. The bond they formed lasted through moves, separate classes, and even different grades when Jenny skipped ahead. For Stephen the house would be an inescapable reminder that life, even for the young and innocent, could be brutally transitory.

Miranda slipped her key in the brass lock and turned the handle. Air swirled around her as she stepped inside, warm, but lifeless. There were no cooking odors, no smells of furniture polish or clothes fresh from the dryer. Worst of all, no sounds disturbed the silence, no stereo in the background, no Nickelodeon on the television, no reason to call out that she was home.

She crossed the entrance hall to the closet to hang up her jacket. Her movements were quick, her gaze focused on her actions, careful not to drift to the garments she pushed aside as she made room for her own. The door was halfway closed when it struck her what she'd done. There could be no more running away, no more denial, not if she was ever going to move forward again. Steeling herself, she purposely looked inside. Her gaze landed on Jenny's bright red parka, the one she'd found and fallen in love with on a trip to Aspen. Miranda had surprised her with it that Christmas, Jenny's last.

Keith's old blue raincoat hung beside the parka. Miranda had given him a Burberry one year, hoping he would give the other one to Goodwill. He wore her gift whenever they went out together and looked elegant, if not comfortable. His denim jacket hung next to the raincoat and next to that a wool sweater of Jenny's . . . and on and on and on. Miranda ran her hand along one sleeve after another freeing long-denied memories, letting them take her wherever they would. She only realized there were tears on her cheeks when she smiled at something that released her—the closet might be a treasure of happy times, but it was also in desperate need of a good cleaning. Keith's housekeeping stopped short of closet doors, a trait reinforced by a daughter whose clothing rarely found hangers without prompting.

Miranda went into the family room. Eerily, it was exactly as she'd left it—the hand knit afghan tossed on the end of the sofa, the empty glass on the coffee table, the stack of folded, unread newspapers in the basket beside the fireplace. Nothing, save a thicker layer of dust, marked the passage of time.

As she looked around the room she could see herself the way she'd been all those months ago. The image was both disturbing and reassuring. She wasn't the same woman who'd lived here then, who had closed herself off from life. The distance she'd traveled had nothing to do with miles, but was in the mind. Her vision of the woman she'd become during her self-enforced isolation was a clarity of thought that could only come in hindsight.

Miranda went to the sofa and picked up the

afghan. It had been a birthday gift from Keith, a private joke because he was always teasing her about her cold feet. The afghan had become her constant companion after he was gone. She'd either had it tucked around her legs when she was burrowed into the corner of the sofa or worn it wrapped around her shoulders, shawl fashion. With purposeful movements, she folded the blanket and put it in the hall linen cupboard. That done, she went back to the family room, picked up the empty glass and took it to the kitchen.

Someone had gone through this room. The counters and floor were scrubbed and glistening; the refrigerator had been emptied and cleaned. She saw Stephen's wise hand in the work and mentally added to her list of reasons to thank him.

She rounded the cooking island to the sink. Her hand was on the faucet when the telephone rang. The sound ripped the silence and set her heart racing. She snatched the receiver off its hook, unreasonably upset at the intrusion.

"Hello."

"Miranda—you're home. I've been calling since yesterday. When did you get in?"

It was Clifford. She should have known. "Just a few minutes ago."

"Have you had anything to eat?"

"No . . . " When it hit her why he was asking, she quickly added, "I mean, yes. Actually, I'm not hungry."

He laughed. "What was that, a multiple choice answer?"

"I'm too tired to think about food, Clifford. I'll probably have a cup of tea and go to bed."

"Breakfast then. I'll come by to pick you up. Seven-thirty okay?"

"I appreciate the offer, but—"

"I've told everyone at the office I'd be bringing you in as soon as you arrived. They can't wait to see you, Miranda. You wouldn't believe how excited they all are that you're coming back to work. You wouldn't want to disappoint them."

Had she always been so easy to manipulate? "Then it would probably be best if you put off telling anyone that I'm back for a couple of days. I have some things I have to get done before I even think about going into the office."

"I didn't mean to pressure you. To be honest, it's more for myself that I'm asking. I've missed you, honey." He chuckled. "I had no idea how much until I saw you last week."

Honey? Where in the hell had that come from? Clifford was not the type to use endearments. "I think we should take this slow, Clifford. I'm not ready for—"

"I didn't mean you had to start work right away. You can ease into things, pick your own pace until you feel ready to jump back into the thick of it."

She couldn't tell whether he'd deliberately misinterpreted her or automatically assumed she couldn't be talking about him. When he'd come to her house in Mendocino, he'd given every indication he was ready to pick up where they'd left off. But the memory of how it had been between them was still too new, too disconcerting for her to feel anything but sickened at her behavior. It would be a blessing to be able to forget again.

"Why don't you call me in a couple of days?" she said. "I should have a better idea then when I'll feel like going in to see everyone."

"What's on your schedule for tomorrow?"

He wasn't going to let it go. "I have an appointment with Stephen Kastner."

"Wasn't he your accountant?"

"He still is."

"As I recall, his office was here in the city. I assume it still is?"

She could see where he was leading but didn't know how to cut him off. "Yes."

"When are you meeting him?"

"Early."

"You have to eat, Miranda. Meet me for breakfast."

He'd always been able to wear her down, no matter how determined she'd been to resist. She was better off giving in than fighting, especially over something this inconsequential. She'd save her energy for the battles sure to come when he found out she had no intention of renewing their relationship. She closed her eyes and leaned her head against the cupboard. "Where?"

"My place is as good as any. I didn't get a chance to tell you before, but I have an apartment near downtown now."

That far she wouldn't go. "It just occurred to me that lunch would be better, Clifford. Why don't you meet me at Woodward's? Say around one? That should give me plenty of time with Stephen."

After a long pause, he said, "Lunch it is. I'll have Vicki make the reservations."

Miranda smiled at the mention of Clifford's secretary. She liked Vicki. It would be good to see her again. Despite her fatigue and the emotional tightrope she was walking, Miranda felt the beginning of a sense of excitement about returning to work. "I'll see you tomorrow, Clifford."

"Wear something special. I want to show you off."

She was too stunned to answer right away. Had he said things like this to her before? She couldn't remember. "I'll give it some thought."

"God, I've missed you, Miranda. I can't tell you what it means to me that you're finally back."

If he'd missed her so much, why had it taken so long to get in touch with her? Where had he been when she was alone and desperate for a friend? She was almost tired enough, almost indignant enough, to ask the questions aloud, but the rational side of her brain insisted she wait for calmer waters. This was the man who would ease her way back into practicing law. If there was to be an argument about such things, it wasn't one she wanted to lose.

And, like it or not, she owed him. He'd not only held her position at the firm all these months, he'd kept her on the payroll. She was back in the real world, the world of compromise and game playing. It was time she acted accordingly.

Adam would never approve.

The thought created a lump in her throat. She hadn't expected to doubt her decision to leave him so soon. She'd known it would come eventually, when the glow from self-sacrifice was replaced by the reality of being without him. But she'd hoped for more time.

"It's good to be back," she said without conviction.

"Are you sure you're all right? You know you don't have to stay there alone tonight. I could be with you in no time."

"I'm fine—just tired. I'll see you tomorrow, Clifford."

"If you're sure."

"I'm sure."

"Miranda . . . never mind. I'll save it for another day. When you're not so tired."

She hung up and thought about what it might be that Clifford wanted to say to her. He believed there was still something between them. For a moment she let herself consider the possibility. She imagined them making love. In the courtroom he came across aggressive and domineering. Were they the traits that would carry through to the bedroom?

How could Clifford be the kind of man she'd once convinced herself she belonged beside, yet when she fell in love again, it had been with Adam?

The next morning Miranda left for downtown early to avoid rush hour traffic. After realizing she'd gone blocks out of her way to keep from passing the Morris building and the law offices of Coker/Standish, she purposely turned around and drove by, twice.

When she arrived at Stephen Kastner's office she found him pacing the reception area. He denied he'd been waiting for her, but greeted her with a bear hug, a warm smile and a look of concern. He looked pretty much the same except he was wearing his hair in a new style, shorter and to the side instead of combed straight back, and touches of gray now mixed with the black—evidence of his foray into his forties. She had a hard time thinking of Stephen as aging. In her mind he would forever be Keith's contemporary and Keith would forever be thirty-nine.

Stephen took her into his office and guided her to a chair opposite his desk. "How are you doing—really?"

"Last night was hard," she admitted. For the first time since the shooting, she'd slept in her and Keith's old bed. She had no idea what time she'd actually fallen asleep, only that when the alarm went off it seemed too soon.

"You look good. A lot better than I expected."

"Considering the last time you saw me, I hate to think what you were expecting." She hooked her purse over the back of the chair. "How's Carol?"

"Great—anxious to see you. I promised her I'd talk you into coming to dinner sometime soon."

The next was difficult. "And Lynne?"

He picked up on either her forced enthusiasm or the way her hands gripped the chair, because he gently said, "You don't have to do this all in one day, Miranda. Some of it will keep."

"I've been running away too long. I can't do it anymore. Besides, I really do want to hear about Lynne." Only then did she realize she was telling the truth.

"She's growing like a weed. I'd started thinking I should be looking into basketball scholarships, but the doctor assured us she was only going through a normal growth cycle."

"Jenny would have been jealous. She hated being the shortest girl in fourth grade. I kept telling her it was because she was also the youngest, but you know how girls are."

Stephen went to the window and adjusted the blinds before he sat down. "California was good for you then?"

She appreciated the change of subject. "Yes . . ."

"I've heard the Mendocino coast is beautiful."

There were no words to convey the beauty, at least none she knew. "Yes, it is."

"Would you rather not talk about your time there?"

She considered his question. "I don't know how."

At first he seemed confused by her answer. "I've never known you to be at a loss for words." But even as he spoke, a look of understanding hit. "You met someone."

She didn't want to talk about Adam, not to Stephen, not to anyone.

"It's all right, you know," Stephen told her. "The last thing Keith would have wanted was for you to spend your life alone."

"You sound so sure."

Her question threw him. "Come on, Miranda, you knew Keith better than any of us. When you love someone as much as he loved you, all you care about is their happiness."

His answer didn't have the effect he'd intended. She didn't want to hear how much Keith had loved her, it still hurt too much. "It's a moot point, Stephen. I met someone, but it's over."

"I'm sorry—maybe it was for the best. You don't want to get tied down with the first guy who comes along."

"Can we talk about something else?"

"Sure—now that you're back we'll have lots of time to catch up on things."

"I've been thinking about selling the house and Keith's car."

He rocked back in his chair. "The thought hadn't even occurred to me, but it makes sense. You don't need all that room, or the financial drain, and you sure as hell don't need two cars."

"Speaking of finances, how am I doing?"

His demeanor changed as he opened the drawer beside him and brought out a thick file. The friend was still there, but the accountant took precedence. "You're aware the firm kept you on the payroll this past year?"

She nodded.

"As I understand it, they kept you at your class draw."

"I don't know, Stephen. I wasn't in touch with anyone at the office to know what the draw was for my class this year. I do know that they were very generous."

"After I paid the bills, I put the excess in short term CDs. We haven't kept up with inflation, but I didn't want to go with anything riskier without your being involved in the decision."

With sudden, embarrassing clarity she realized Stephen had spent an enormous number of hours on her business. What time he hadn't taken from other clients, he'd taken from his family. "How much do I owe you?"

Instantly his gaze dropped to the papers in front of him. "I don't know what you're talking about."

"Come on, Stephen, you don't have to coddle me anymore. I'm back now, and ready to take on my responsibilities."

He looked at her. "Whatever I did for you, I did because I wanted to. You don't owe me anything."

She shook her head. "Didn't anyone ever tell you never to get emotionally involved with your clients?"

"Seems to me I knew an attorney once who said things along those lines."

"Well, from now on, I want you to start listening to her." She smiled, no longer able to maintain the forced sternness. "At least where your other clients are concerned."

"Is that free legal advice I'm hearing?"

"My God, it is. Don't tell anyone."

Stephen returned her smile. "It's good to have you back, Miranda."

"Thanks."

"Now, about the house. Do you want me to find a real estate agent for you, or did you have someone in mind?"

"I don't know." The decision to sell was still too new, too tentative, to have thought that far ahead.

"Have you considered where you'd like to live?"

"I think an apartment would be a good idea. At least for a while."

"Tax wise, you have two years."

"That should be more than enough time."

"What about the . . . furniture?"

It wasn't the furniture he was asking about, it was everything that had belonged to Jenny and Keith. She struggled with the answer, no closer to a decision than she'd been when she left.

"Do you want some help?" Stephen asked. "I could ask around about the different agencies in town. There are a number that could use whatever you wanted to give them."

"Would you mind?"

"I'll put Carol on it. She's asked a hundred times what she could do to help."

"I should have called her." Her list of "should haves" kept growing.

"Would you stop beating yourself up?"

She came forward in her chair. "Back to my finances."

With the conversation focused on business, the morning passed quickly. Not until Miranda felt her stomach rumbling did she look at her watch.

"My God," she said. "I've got to get out of here. I'm supposed to meet Clifford in five minutes."

"When do you plan to go back to work?" Stephen asked.

She liked that he hadn't said "try" to go back to work. "Probably next week. I need some time to get things in order at the house."

He walked her out to her car. "I'll get back to you after I check with Carol, but how does Saturday dinner sound?"

"Great." She gave him a quick kiss on the cheek and got in her car. "Just let me know the time, and what I can bring. How about dessert—lemon pie?"

"You've learned how to bake?"

She laughed at his surprise. "I know how to do something even more important—support my local bakery."

"Have a nice lunch," he said as she backed out of her parking space.

She waved. "I will."

At the restaurant Clifford stood to greet her when he saw her arrive. Through the smile, she saw a quick flash of irritation at her lateness. Clifford Chambers was not used to being kept waiting.

"You look incredible," he said as he took her hand and gave it an intimate squeeze.

She'd known he wouldn't try to kiss her, not in a public place. "I feel good, too. Stephen and I got a lot accomplished this morning."

"Anything I should know about?"

The question threw her. "Like?"

He had the good graces to look discomfited. "I don't want it to seem like I'm prying, but I assume Keith didn't carry a great deal of insurance. If you need help with anything, I just want you to know you can come to me."

She'd never tell him, but he was the last person she would go to. Once there, she would never be able to extricate herself. "I appreciate the offer, but it isn't necessary. I'm doing fine."

She opened her napkin and laid it across her lap. "Allowing me to continue at my usual draw was very generous, Clifford. I owe all of the partners a great deal of gratitude."

"Having you back and ready to go to work is all the thanks any of us needs."

Miranda reached for her menu. "I'm glad you feel that way. It makes my return a lot easier."

He dipped his head, lowered his glasses, and looked at her over the top. "I'm not sure I understand what you mean."

She met his gaze. "You can imagine how hard it would be if I thought there were any strings attached to my being here with you today."

He pulled his glasses off and flung them on the table. "I can see we need to talk, Miranda."

"Yes, Clifford," she said, "we do."

Twenty-one

Miranda had been home over a week and back to work three days when she heard a knock on her office door. Assuming it was her temporary secretary, she waited for her to come inside, then glanced at the clock and realized the woman would still be on her lunch break.

"Come in," Miranda called.

The door opened slowly, and then with a push, swung wide. A wheelchair appeared. A young, pretty woman with dark hair and enormous blue eyes maneuvered the chair into the doorway. "Hi, Ms. Dolan. I've been wanting to stop by and welcome you back. Mind if I come in?"

Miranda's jaw dropped in surprise. Her heart skipped a beat. This was the first time since returning from California that she'd come face to face with anyone who had actually been in the conference room that day. "*Margaret*—no one told me you were coming."

"I see you're working on something. If this is a bad time, I can come back later."

"You'll do no such thing." Miranda got up and

came around her desk to hold the door while Margaret wheeled through. "Did you come downtown just to see me? You should have called. We could have gone to lunch. Next time we'll make a day of it." God, she was babbling. She had to get herself under control before she made Margaret think she was unstable. "Come in. Would you like something to drink? I can have someone bring us coffee. Anything you want."

"Please—I know I make you nervous. It's okay," Margaret said. "I seem to have that effect on everyone around here."

The statement put a tail on Miranda's wildly flying kite. "I'm sorry. It's just that . . . "

"That it's hard to see me like this?"

Miranda went around the wheelchair and leaned against the corner of her desk. Margaret's need to be treated with a degree of normalcy struck a responding cord. "God, you must get tired of hearing that."

"Finally—someone who understands." Margaret leaned her head back and looked up at the ceiling as if engaged in a silent prayer of gratitude. "No one around here can seem to get it through their head that I don't want to be pitied, I just want to do my job."

"You work here? Why haven't I seen you?"

"You haven't been to the library yet. It's my new office."

"What in God's name are you doing there?" Margaret had been the kind of secretary junior partners hoped to attain one day, a status symbol of sorts, efficient, savvy, and loyal. The libraries were located in the internal core of each floor, surrounded by copying, lunch and bathrooms. They were depressing areas, without windows or charm.

"Keeping track of the books, looking things up, putting books away, that kind of thing."

What Margaret said didn't make sense. She was doing something interns from local high schools could do. "Is this what you want?" Miranda asked, too surprised by the news to guard her reaction.

"I don't have much choice. If I give up this job, I'll never get insurance again." She immediately seemed to regret saying what she had. "But that doesn't make me any different than hundreds of other people." She forced a smile.

"I can understand about the insurance, it's working in the library that's—"

"I came in here to welcome you back, not to talk about me." Again, there was the artificial smile. "I should be going now. You have work to do and so do I." Margaret moved to turn the wheelchair around.

"Wait a minute," Miranda said. "First tell me why you gave up your secretary job."

The question clearly made Margaret uncomfortable. She glanced behind her at the open door before saying anything. "Everyone thought it was for the best," she said, her voice lowered.

"Everyone?"

There was another quick glance backward. "Actually, it was Mr. Chambers who talked to me, but he was only the messenger. I guess the senior partners had a meeting—"

Miranda got up and closed the door.

"—and they decided it would be best if I weren't so visible for a while."

"I don't think I'm following you." She was, but she didn't like where her thoughts were leading and hoped Margaret would prove her wrong. She pulled a chair over and sat down so that she would be at eye level with Margaret and not looming over her.

"I'm sure you noticed a lot of money was spent changing everything on this floor. Mr. Chambers said it was important that clients not be able to come here and see something that would remind them of the shooting."

The changes were dramatic and comprehensive. It had taken Miranda most of her first day to orient herself. The conference room was gone, broken up and replaced by offices. "Are you telling me Clifford included you in that statement?"

"Not openly, it was more implied. You have to admit, someone in a wheelchair draws attention."

There was one sure way to find out if Margaret's imagination was working overtime or if there really was a calculated effort to shut her out of the mainstream. "I haven't hired a secretary yet. Would you consider the position?"

"I can't." She shook her head at the same time, reinforcing the words with action. "It isn't that I don't want to, but like I said before, I need this job. I could really screw things up for myself if I made the wrong people mad."

"No one is going to give me flak about this," Miranda said. "I've been given carte blanche to set up my office anyway I like and that includes who I hire for my secretary."

This time, Margaret wasn't as quick to answer. "What if you decide working here wasn't what you wanted after all and leave again?"

"I can't promise that won't happen," Miranda said. "But I wouldn't have come back if I didn't intend to stay. I gave up a hell of a lot to be here."

"We all thought you were gone for good."

"For a while, so did I," Miranda said. "Then I realized this is my home. It's where I belong."

"Even without Mr. Dolan and Jennifer?"

The question was so unexpected, Miranda was left speechless. Until then, everyone except Stephen and Carol had studiously avoided any mention of Keith or Jenny. At a meeting that morning she'd asked if anyone had a favorite charity that could use Keith's or Jenny's belongings. An awkward silence was followed by a change of subject. Everyone joined in and it was as if she'd never said anything at all.

Since coming home, Miranda found she wanted to talk about Keith and Jenny. She'd tried to "get over" their deaths by locking them inside. It hadn't worked. The attempt took enormous energy and left her exhausted. Keith and Jenny were a part of her and always would be. They belonged in her every day life.

If not for Adam, she might never have known this.

"You asked that on purpose, didn't you?" Miranda said.

"I thought you might want to talk about them. If everyone treats you the same way they do me, you don't get an opportunity very often. I worked for Mr. Richards right here on this floor for over six years and now I'm supposed to pretend he didn't exist. I can't even bring *his* name up around here without everyone instantly having something else they have to do. It's as if we're supposed to forget the people who died ever existed."

"Even your parents close you off?" She suddenly remembered Margaret had been engaged. With a surreptitious glance, she looked for a ring. She was inordinately pleased to see the small diamond was still on Margaret's finger. "What about your boyfriend?"

"In the beginning he was uncomfortable when I would talk about it, now he gets up and leaves the room. My parents think I'm dwelling on the past if I say something. I have so many feelings bottled up inside of me there are times I think I'll go crazy if I don't get them out. But no one wants to listen."

"I will," Miranda said. After a while she smiled. "But that means you have to listen to me, too." She told herself that the threads that tied her to this young woman were strands of guilt, not friendship, that lawyers at Coker/Standish did not fraternize with secretaries. It made no difference. She and Margaret might never be real friends, but they would forever be soulmates.

"It's a deal."

"You know, if you were my secretary, it would be a lot easier for us to have these talks."

"It isn't that I don't want—"

"How about if I mention the idea to Clifford and see how he reacts? I won't tell him I've talked to you already. That way he won't be afraid to say what he thinks and nothing will come back on you."

"Are you sure you really want to do this?"

The hope, the guarded excitement in Margaret's voice was enough to convince Miranda she was doing the right thing. "It's completely self-serving, Margaret. Everyone knows what a good secretary you are. I'd be crazy not to take advantage of your availability."

"When do you think you'll be talking to Mr. Chambers?"

"Today."

She looked frightened and excited at the same time. "Let me know."

"If you change your mind, I'll understand," Miranda said.

"No—I want to do this. I'm sick to death of coming to work and being stuck in that room."

Miranda went to the door with her. She watched as Margaret maneuvered down a too narrow hallway on her way back to the library. How had the remodeling contractor gotten something like that past the inspectors? Weren't there codes to cover such things?

She started back inside her office then decided she was too anxious to speak to Clifford to get any work done. There was nothing to be gained by putting it off. She headed for the stairs, climbed three floors and headed for the corner suite.

Clifford's secretary informed him that Miranda was there, then reached under her desk to press a button that unlocked the door. The security system was something new and reserved for the senior partners in their corner offices.

Clifford looked up when she came inside. He was on the phone and put his hand over the mouthpiece before greeting her. "I'll be with you in a minute." He motioned to a chair. "Have a seat."

The first time Miranda had been in Clifford's office she'd vowed that she would have one just like it someday. It wasn't that she needed more space, she had a tendency to nest when she was working, settling in one part of a room and staying there. What she'd wanted was the position in the firm that came with the corner office. And she didn't want the east side, only the west would do.

Remembering how she'd been before the shooting was what she imagined an out of body experience might be like. Only, to her surprise, she'd discovered she didn't always recognize the woman she visited.

Clifford hung up the phone and came around the desk to sit in the chair next to hers. "You look wonderful. But then I've always loved you in that suit."

So that he didn't think she'd dressed to please him, she said, "This is about the only thing I have that doesn't hang on me. I've either got to put on some weight, or break down and go shopping."

"Forget the weight. You look perfect the way you are now."

Just what she needed to hear, especially after Adam had reawakened her love of Brie and crackers and all things chocolate.

"I have a great idea," he went on. "Let me go shopping with you. You know I have an eye for clothes—and I can't think of a better way to spend this Saturday."

"I appreciate the offer," she said with what she hoped was enough enthusiasm to maintain his good mood, "but I've decided I'm not going anyplace or doing anything until I get the house in order."

"Why don't you just hire someone? It's crazy for you to be cleaning that place yourself."

"I'm not cleaning, Clifford. I'm going through Keith's and Jenny's things trying to decide what I should keep and what I should give away."

"I would have thought you'd taken care of that a long time ago."

"I wasn't ready then. I am now." She'd forgotten he hadn't been at the meeting where she'd asked about charities.

He put his hand on her arm. "I can't tell you what a delight it is to see you finally moving forward again. At the rate you're going, you'll be back in the courtroom in no time."

"It feels good to be back, too. Even better than I'd anticipated." He'd given her the perfect opening. "Which is why I wanted to see you." She didn't want to have this discussion with his hand on her arm, so she reached down to adjust her shoe to dislodge him.

"You know I'm always available to you, Miranda. Anything you want, just ask and it's yours."

"All right—a secretary. Margaret Kinnion to be precise."

There was no reaction, but then she hadn't expected any. Clifford was a master of the blank expression. "Margaret already has a job. As I understand it, one she likes very much."

He was baiting her. "Even if she does, her talents are wasted taking care of the library. The firm would be far better served with her as my secretary."

"Is that your opinion or hers?"

Now it was time for Miranda to exhibit her blank look. "I don't understand what you're asking."

"Did she come to you, or did you go to her with this idea?"

She answered the question precisely as it was asked. "Neither."

He leaned back in his chair. "Then there's no harm done. I would hate to get Margaret's hopes up over something like this."

"You've lost me, Clifford."

"I'm afraid Margaret is one of those unfortunate people who suffers from post shock syndrome. She can't seem to put what happened behind her, at least not the way you have. Can you imagine the repercussions if she broke down and said something in front of a client?"

"What makes you think that would happen?"

"It doesn't matter, we just can't take the chance."

He almost had her. She was leaning his direction and might have been persuaded, if he hadn't decided to take it one step farther.

"I feel terrible about it, but even if Margaret were perfectly stable, there's the wheelchair thing we'd have to consider." He'd adopted his reasonable, understanding pose, the kindly father explaining something discomforting to a beloved child. "If she'd come to us like that, we could put her out front and everyone would applaud our progressive hiring practice. The way it is now, she's become a constant reminder of something we've all fought to put behind us. I'm afraid we'd have a real morale problem if we moved Margaret out of the library."

"If you feel this way," she said carefully, "why don't you let her go?" Miranda said a silent prayer that he would come up with something to redeem himself.

"Don't think the idea hasn't occurred to us. But how would it look? If the newspapers ever got hold of it, we'd have a PR nightmare on our hands."

"Maybe when the settlement comes in she'll leave voluntarily."

Clifford was suddenly, intensely interested. "She has a settlement coming in?"

"Sorry, I just assumed the firm would be handling it for her."

"Handling what?"

"A suit against Trout's estate."

The interest turned to alarm and then anger. "For Christ's sake, Miranda, would you get your head out of your ass?" He got up and moved to his desk. "I hope for your sake you haven't said anything to Margaret about this."

She was so stunned by the attack it took several seconds to set her mind working on the possible motivation behind it. "Are you telling me we're still handling Trout's business?"

"You're damned right we are. It took us weeks of negotiating to keep the family from moving to another firm."

"You don't think that sets up a conflict of interest?"

"No, I don't. Why should it?"

"None of the people who were involved are suing?"

"We took care of our own, Miranda. With the money the Trout family supplied, we set up over twenty college funds, and as long as they don't get married again, the surviving spouses will continue to receive a monthly draw. All of this was done regardless of whatever other insurance any of them might have had."

So much for feeling grateful for being kept on the payroll while she was gone. "And what did you get in return, a promise they wouldn't sue? Was that part of the deal you made with Trout's family?"

"You know it wouldn't be ethical for the firm to do something like that. There was a simple, handshake agreement that we agreed was in the best interest of all concerned. No one wanted to see this thing dragged through the courts, least of all the families. Everyone came out winners, both financially and emotionally."

Funny, she didn't feel like a winner. Somehow she doubted any of the others did either. "What about Margaret? What kind of deal was she offered?"

"We offered her the same terms as everyone else—she could stay home and receive a monthly check for the rest of her life, but that didn't interest her. She wanted to come back to work. We let her." He sent her a damning look. "Save the outrage, Miranda. A year ago you would have begged me to be the one doing the negotiating."

It was no wonder Margaret wouldn't agree. A settlement would have to be enormous to take the place of medical insurance.

Miranda had to get out of there or she was going to say something stupid. She needed time to think before she reacted. And she needed time to plan her next move.

She'd been right to come back. She could see that now.

Twenty-two

The afternoon of the wedding, the house on Nob Hill stood
poised for celebration. A garland of glossy leaves and
white roses had been draped in graceful arcs across
the second floor landing and down the banister on
the stairs where Mary would descend to meet Adam.
The ceremony would take place in the living room
where chairs were set in rows for the eighty select
guests. The green and white theme had been carried
through here with catatleya, cymbidium, and phalaneopsis orchids. A hundred candles stood at the
ready, to be lit just before the guests arrived. Another
two hundred were in reserve to replace the others as
they burned down. The caterers had been at work in
the kitchen since dawn. The cake—chocolate with
cream cheese swirls—the frosting, a deep, rich
ganache with white buttercream design, had arrived
and been set up an hour before.

Adam had come to his mother's room to see if
there were any last minute instructions. "You've
made this place your own," he said. "The house looks
spectacular."

She glanced at herself in the full-length mirror. With an impatient gesture, she tucked the strand of hair behind her ear that the stylist had spent a full five minutes coaxing into a curl. "Shows you what a modicum of talent and a ton of money can do."

"Nervous?"

"I'm beyond nervous." She started to sit down in the brocade chair beside her, then quickly straightened and brushed wrinkles that hadn't had a chance to form from her skirt. "I don't know what I was thinking when I picked the material for this suit."

"Maybe that it looked fantastic on you?"

She came up to him and touched his cheek. "Thank you, darling. I can always count on you to fling a little bull in my direction." Again she ran her hand down her skirt. "I can't sit, I can't eat, I can't do anything but stand around and hope I look half as good as I want to think I do."

He smiled indulgently. "Settle down. You could walk out there in your bathrobe and slippers and Michael wouldn't care. He's swallowed the hook, Mom. There's no way he's going to let you turn him loose."

"I don't know what's got me so nervous. I haven't been this sure of anything in a long, long time and today still scares the hell out of me." She went to the bed and fluffed the tulle on the headpiece she would put on just before she went down.

This was a side to Mary that Adam had never seen. Today she wasn't his stalwart, always-there-for-him mother—she was more a charming, beautiful friend who looked to him for reassurance. "Michael's lucky to have you." He gave her a sly wink. "But I've got to admit, the better I know him, the more I've started thinking you're pretty lucky to have him, too."

"Oh, Adam, that's the nicest present you could have given me." She hugged him.

He gently cradled her, careful not to disturb her hair or hold her so tight it would create one of her dreaded wrinkles. "You're not going to cry, are you?"

She looked up at him. "I wouldn't dream of it—it's so clichéd."

He laughed. "I know you have your standards, but I think you're entitled today."

Her expression grew serious. "I want this kind of happiness for you, Adam."

"Someday." He didn't believe it, not anymore, but the reassurance was what she wanted to hear and on this day he would do anything for her.

"Are you ever going to tell me what happened between you and Miranda?"

"It's in the past, Mom. Let it be."

"If it were in the past, the mention of her name wouldn't still eat at you the way it does. Have you heard anything at all from her?"

"I didn't expect to." He didn't want to talk about Miranda. Since she left, the emptiness and pain he'd felt had undergone a metamorphosis. Now, he was as angry as he was hurt, as likely to think of her with resentment as with longing. He pressed a quick kiss to his mother's forehead. "Can we talk about something else?"

The doorbell rang. A panicked look widened Mary's eyes to saucers. "That can't be one of the guests. Not yet. It's too early. There's no one to greet them. No one told Elizabeth to light the candles."

"If you don't settle down, I'm going to have to

scrape you off the ceiling." Adam set her aside and went to the window. "It's the florist." He started to turn away. "Wait a minute, I can see someone coming . . . "

Mary came up behind him. "Where?" And then after looking in the direction he pointed, asked, "Can you tell who it is?"

Adam smiled. "It looks like Jason and Tony to me."

"You're right." She put her hand on his arm. "How wonderful. I was afraid they wouldn't come."

As glad as Adam was that Jason had decided not to let the possibility he might run into his parents keep him away from the wedding, he couldn't help being concerned what would happen when they did see each other. "I did hear you say that Barbara and Fred were going to be here today, didn't I?"

"They postponed their cruise so they could be here."

"And they know you invited Jason?"

As the two men turned into the gate, Mary opened the window, stuck her hand out and waved. "Jason is my friend," she said to Adam.

"That's not what I asked."

"Barbara and Fred are smart people. I'm sure they figured it out for themselves." Jason saw her and waved back.

Adam groaned. "I'll do what I can to keep them apart, but I'm not making any guarantees."

"Jason is such a handsome young man. And that Tony—he always looks as if he's on a camera shoot for *GQ*." She turned to Adam. "Do you suppose it's something in the genes that the really drop-dead gorgeous men are always gay?"

He shook his head in mock disapproval. "Clichés

and stereotypes in one day? I wouldn't have thought it of you."

"Stop picking on me. You know very well what I mean."

He bussed her cheek. "I'm going to go downstairs now. When I see Jason and Tony I'll ask them what they think of your theory."

She gave him a threatening look. "Don't you dare."

"Tony won't mind. He likes hearing that people think he's good looking."

"You seem to have accepted Tony being back. Have you, or is it something I'm imagining?"

"I don't know that I'll ever be able to forget and forgive the way Jason has, but I have to admit, he seems happier now than I've seen him in a long time. If Tony's responsible, who am I to say he has no business being there?"

"If he's back and taking care of Jason, where do you fit in? I know his being there doesn't automatically exclude you, but—"

"I've been doing some thinking along the same lines lately, but let's talk about it later. I should get downstairs just in case Barbara and Fred get here early."

"Trust me, they won't. You can't make an entrance if there isn't anyone to see you. Now tell me what you've been thinking."

He could see that she was concerned, but there was something more behind the questioning. "All I know for sure is that Jason and Tony are a couple. I have about as much business hanging around them as I do tagging along on your honeymoon."

"So what are you saying?"

"It's time for me to move on." That much he knew. He'd come to the decision on his trip down but hadn't told anyone yet. "I still have a couple of jobs to finish. As soon as they're out of the way, I'll probably close up shop and hit the road again."

"Where will you go?"

"I don't know." A year ago the prospect of exploring unknown territory, of meeting new people and learning new lifestyles, would have kept him awake at night in anticipation. But his need to be on the move wasn't the compelling force it had once been. Instead of looking forward to the unknown, he found himself thinking about the towns and cities he'd already seen, the friends he'd left behind.

"You're not planning to leave before Christmas, are you?"

"Of course not." There was something in the way she asked the question that told him she wanted more than a chance to say good-bye. "What's going on?"

"Nothing," she said, too quickly to be convincing. "It's just that I've been spoiled having you so close all these months. I'm going to miss you when you're gone."

He wasn't buying it but knew it would do no good to push. She'd tell him when she was ready. "I'm going to miss seeing you, too."

"You don't have to go, Adam."

"I might agree with you if I had some idea what I would do with myself if I stayed."

She started to say something more and stopped. "Tell Jason how happy I am that he came and that I'll talk to him later." She took his arm and walked him to the door. "And if you see Michael, would you send him up?"

Adam met Michael in the foyer and passed on his mother's message. He found Jason and Tony in the den studying the painting over the fireplace. "So, what do you think?"

Jason turned. "Fragonard has never been one of my favorites, but this isn't bad."

Adam laughed. "About the house, you idiot."

He looked around the room. "What's not to like? I think I could live here and adjust to the change without too much strain."

"Yeah, me, too," Tony said. "I miss being in a city where there's a little action."

A flash of anger coursed through Adam. Tony had the good time, Jason paid the price. Not even knowing Tony would also pay the price one day mitigated Adam's feelings about him.

Almost as if he could read Adam's thoughts, Jason said, "Tony was working with the AIDS hospice program in Seattle before he came back to Mendocino."

"I've been trying to talk Jason into coming down here and working in the program with me."

They exchanged looks before Jason said to Adam, "I've been giving it some thought, but I'm not sure I'm up to seeing first-hand on a day-to-day basis what's in store for me. At least where I am now I'm able to forget once in a while. Makes me sound like a coward, huh?"

Tony touched Jason's arm and said softly, "I told you we wouldn't make the move until you're ready."

Adam heard the doorbell ring. More guests were arriving. "I thought I should warn you, Jason. Your folks are going to be here."

"For sure?" In an obvious attempt to appear

unruffled at the news, he opened his jacket and stuffed his hands in his slack pockets.

"I'm afraid so. They postponed their vacation rather than miss the big day."

"Maybe we should leave, Jason," Tony said. "You've put up with enough shit from them, you don't need anymore. They aren't worth it."

The comment led Adam to believe Tony knew what had caused the split between Jason and his parents. As far as he knew Jason had never told anyone. "Maybe they've come around," Adam said. "It's been almost two years." He didn't believe it any more than he believed Miranda would walk through the door and tell him she'd made a mistake when she left. There were some things so impossible you didn't let yourself imagine them.

"They won't be happy until Jason is dead," Tony said with barely suppressed anger.

There was a long, terrible silence. "What's that supposed to mean?" Adam finally asked.

Tony started to answer, Jason stopped him. "They've told me it doesn't matter how sick I get, they won't have anything to do with me. They feel I betrayed them and everything they stand for when I 'let' myself get AIDS. As far as they're concerned, they no longer have a son."

That much Adam knew, even if he couldn't comprehend the reasoning. Barbara and Fred hadn't been thrilled when they found out their only child was gay, but at least they hadn't tried to haul him off to psychiatrists or take him to their minister to get counseling.

"All of this thanks to me," Tony added in a pained voice.

Jason leaned his elbow on the mantel and rubbed

his hand across his forehead. "It was all right that I was gay. After all, some of the most famous and talented people in the world are gay. But having AIDS was something else entirely. It was utterly déclassé, an impossible thing to admit to their friends. AIDS is a disease of drug users, prostitutes, and lowlifes, none of which they want associated with the name Delponte."

"Son of a bitch," Adam said softly, stunned by the revelation. After several seconds, he told Jason, "I'm sorry. I had no idea."

"It threw me for a while, too. They actually had me believing it was my familial duty to stay hidden up in Mendocino. But that's in the past. I'm not going to let it keep me from things I want to do anymore."

Adam nodded. Before he had a chance to say anything else, the doorbell rang again. "I'm supposed to be helping with that." It was a lie, but he needed a quick, clean exit line. "We'll finish this later."

"Adam?" Jason lowered his arm and nervously adjusted his jacket by rolling his shoulders. "I don't want anyone else to know about this."

If it were up to him, Adam would have taken an ad out in the *Chronicle* to expose Barbara and Fred for the bigots they were. "If that's the way you want it," he said reluctantly.

"Thanks."

Adam looked at Tony. He was staring at Jason. They weren't touching, they weren't even close, yet the moment was one of the most intimate Adam had ever witnessed. Only at that moment did Adam believe Tony had truly returned. He would not run away again. The love he felt for Jason would sustain him through the horror that lay ahead for them both.

Adam's greatest fear was laid to rest. Jason would not die alone.

On his way upstairs again, Adam passed Michael coming down.

"Do you have a minute?" Michael asked.

"Sure—what can I do for you?"

"Mary and I would like to talk to you . . . "

"Now?" The ceremony was due to start in less than half an hour.

"I know, it doesn't make sense to me either, but she's afraid we won't get a chance during the reception. And since we're leaving for the airport tonight she thinks it's now or never." His eyebrow rose in a questioning expression. "Did you say something to her about leaving Mendocino?"

"Yeah, but not right away."

"Well, she's got it in her head that you'll change your mind and be gone by the time we get back and that it will be too late."

"Too late for what?"

"You'll understand once she tells you." Michael put his hand in the middle of Adam's back and gently guided him upstairs.

When they were inside Mary's room, the door closed behind them, Adam turned to his mother. "Whatever you have to tell me couldn't possibly be as good as the buildup."

A nervous smile came and went. "I'm not sure how to start." She looked at Michael. "Feel free to jump in at any time." When he didn't say anything, she prompted, "Like now."

Michael unbuttoned his jacket and sat on the edge of the bed. "You two are a mystery to me. If I didn't know better, I'd be suspicious the money coming in from the sale of Kirkpatric Ltd. was tainted. How anyone can—"

"I asked for your help," Mary said, "not a lecture."

Michael nodded, folded his arms across his chest and met Adam's curious stare. "Basically, what we want you to know is how the money from the sale is going to be handled. Your mother is setting up the Gerald F. Kirkpatric Foundation." He paused, as if waiting for the information to settle in before adding anything more. "Of course the ideal situation would be to have someone in the family as administrator, but it isn't essential. There are several people I know who would do an excellent job. Frankly, I don't think anyone who's had their training in the corporate world could bring the same level of understanding to the position that you could, not with your experiences with charitable organizations, but your mother and I don't want you to feel you're being coerced into taking the job."

"As if that could happen," Mary said.

Adam glanced from Michael to his mother and then back again. As relaxed as Michael appeared, there were telltale signs to his nervousness. His hands didn't just rest on his arms, but gripped them, a muscle twitched between his jaw and ear and he was talking faster than normal. Mary was nearing the point of hyperventilating. "Just out of curiosity, what were the two of you thinking would happen when you told me?"

Mary made a face and smoothed her jacket before dropping her arms to her sides. "I was afraid you'd see the foundation as just another way to try to control your life. But it wasn't meant as that, Adam. I wanted to find *something* to do with the money besides letting it sit around making more money. The foundation was Michael's suggestion. And I thought it was a damn good one."

He was surprised how much and how quickly the idea appealed to him. Like it or not, he'd learned there were times when helping someone came down to having the money to do so. Good intentions and a willingness to work didn't put food in the stomachs of starving children. What he didn't like was having everything laid out for him. The cage they'd presented might be dressed up in altruistic gilt, but should he take on the position, the door would close just as tightly behind him as if it were the presidency of Kirkpatric Ltd. "I don't understand why it was so important to tell me now."

"I was afraid once you took off, it might be years before you came back again," Mary said. "Right now we have a narrow window of opportunity for all of us. Once someone else is in the director's position, I know you would never agree to taking it away."

"And there's still time for your input," Michael said. "If you decide you're interested, Felix will explain the laws that govern charitable foundations and how you can set this one up to operate under your own guidelines within those restrictions."

Adam ran his hand through his hair. "I think the foundation is a great idea," he said slowly, his thoughts forming as he spoke, "but I'm not convinced I'm the right person to run it." He was no more qualified to take on something like this than to take over Kirkpatric Ltd.

"Obviously your mother and I disagree with you," Michael said. "We happen to think the years you've spent with different volunteer organizations have left you uniquely qualified. But you can't do this for us, it has to be something you want for yourself."

"Whether you take the job or not," Mary said, "the foundation will still be there. In the beginning I thought Michael's idea was the perfect compromise. You wouldn't have to take over the business, but you wouldn't completely abandon your inheritance either. Since then the project has grown beyond my original self-centered motives. I know we don't have enough money to change the world, but properly administered, there are a lot of dark corners we can light. And the idea makes me feel good. I know it would please your father, too."

Only in the past few months had Adam come to realize how narrowly focused his view of his father had been. Their relationship had been a child to a parent. After his father's death, Adam had tried to imagine how he would react to given situations, and for years had convinced himself supposition was fact. But in reality, Adam had no idea what Gerald Kirkpatric might think or do about anything—not about the prospect of the profit from the sale of his business being given to strangers or a son who couldn't seem to figure out what to do with the rest of his life.

But then it really didn't matter. His father was gone. Whatever dreams or wishes or ambitions had sustained and driven him throughout his life were gone, too. The money from the sale of Kirkpatric Ltd. wasn't his father's. It was his mother's both through rightful inheritance and labor. The decision of what to do with that money was also hers.

"I'm proud of you, Mom," Adam said. "The foundation was a terrific idea. I just don't know about—"

"Don't say anything now," Michael said before Mary had a chance to answer. "Give yourself time to think it over." He got up, put his hand on Adam's shoulder. "Whatever you decide, do it for you." He looked at Mary. "The doorbell's stopped ringing. Everyone must be here. Are you ready to get this show on the road?"

She smiled and winked. "You bet I am."

"Give me a couple of minutes." Adam said to Michael then turned to his mother. "There's something I think you should know first."

Michael started for the door. "Send word when you're ready."

Ten minutes later the pianist struck the opening cords of Mendelsohn's Wedding March. Mary walked onto the landing carrying a bouquet of phalaneopsis and stephanotis and descended the stairs. For this moment she was a young woman again. The promise of happiness in the life ahead was a mantle she wore as confidently as a queen her crown and robes. She smiled at the two men waiting for her, unshed tears shining from her eyes.

Adam put his hand out as she reached the final steps. She mouthed the words, "I love you." She then turned to the man next to him. "I love you, too, Jason." She stood on tiptoe and kissed one and then the other. "From today on, I have two sons."

Together, arm in arm, the three of them walked down the aisle to an awaiting, smiling, Michael.

Twenty-three

Adam sat in the executive lounge at the Denver airport staring at a half-empty glass of gin and tonic left by a man who'd just made two phone calls to two women he'd called darling. Normally Adam didn't mind delays, considering them part of the process of getting from one part of the world to the other. Any unanticipated time in Denver, however, was the exception. Intellectually, he knew the chances of running into Miranda were on a level with winning the lottery, but there was a voice inside him insisting that, despite the odds, someone always held the winning ticket. Only in his case, running into her would be more like holding the losing ticket.

Earlier, when he'd taken out his wallet to pay for a sandwich, he'd found the folded postcard that had been in there for months. On impulse, he'd stuffed it in his pocket. Now, with nothing to do while he waited for an update on his flight, he took the dog-eared missive out and passed it between his fingers, the way a magician did a coin. It wasn't necessary to unfold the paper to know what was inside. Without trying, he'd memorized the three lines on first reading. Not that it had been all that hard. There was only a name and address printed in tight block letters. Of course it helped that it had been Miranda's name and address.

For weeks he'd tried to figure out what the cryptic message meant. Did she want him to write back? Was it an overture or simply a way to let him know she was all right? Did she think that if she'd actually written something or sent a Christmas or birthday card, he might believe she still cared and do something foolish like going to see her?

Whenever he felt himself weakening, whenever the nights became so achingly lonely he broke down and allowed himself to imagine she was there with him, whenever he failed to convince himself someday there would be someone else for him, he forced himself to remember the day she left. Her decision to abandon their relationship might have been difficult for her, but she'd made it and followed through without a backward glance. If she truly wanted to see him again, she would find a way.

And it wouldn't be through some damned postcard.

His antidote to missing her had been to keep busy. Setting up the foundation and getting it going had turned out to be a far bigger job than any of them had envisioned. To Adam's surprise, he'd discovered he had strong opinions about how things should be run, and once tapped, ideas that came like a free-flowing stream, spilling over in every direction. Once things were up and running, he kept the quiet moments at bay by working late into the night. On weekends he either took work home, visited Jason and Tony in Mendocino, or sailed Michael's ketch on the bay. Sometimes the therapy worked. Most of the time, especially when he went north and saw the places he'd been with Miranda, it didn't.

A woman in a blue uniform approached Adam. "Mr. Kirkpatric?"

Startled, he dropped the folded postcard and leaned forward to pick it up from the floor. "Yes?"

"Your plane has arrived and will begin boarding in a few minutes."

"Thank you." He retrieved his briefcase and garment bag from the hanger and went to the gate to wait for the first class passengers to be called. After logging over a hundred thousand miles in less than four months, flying first class had become more necessity than indulgence. He now accomplished almost as much work in the air as he did on the ground. At first he'd used the frequent flyer miles for upgrades then he'd finally broken down and used the money from his trust fund, discovering it spent as easily and unremarkably as the money he'd earned repairing people's houses.

An attendant opened the door to the gate and stood to the side to take tickets. The call went out for first class passengers and anyone who needed assistance. As Adam waited for a young man in a wheelchair and then a woman with two small children to board, he set his garment bag beside his briefcase and stuck his free hand in his pocket. Automatically, his fingers wrapped around the postcard.

He was still there when they began boarding the rest of the plane. He told himself he was waiting for the crowd to clear. But ten minutes later when there was no one at the door and a warning came over the loudspeaker that it was the last call for passengers on flight 384 to San Francisco, something kept him from moving.

The attendant gave him a questioning look. "Sir? Isn't this your flight?"

Slowly, with a sigh of resignation, Adam shook his head. "It seems I have some unfinished business I need to take care of before I leave Denver."

Miranda leaned back in her chair, stared up at the ceiling and immediately wished she hadn't. Even in the dim light of a sixty-watt bulb, she had no trouble seeing a brown spot on the plaster the size of a dinner plate. She was positive it hadn't been there that morning before the storm hit. The contractor she'd hired to replace the gutters had warned her she needed a new roof. She'd tried to talk him into repairing what he could, but he'd insisted that patching would only make the places he didn't fix more prone to leakage.

The worst part was that her office was on the first floor, which meant the water was running down the attic through the second story walls and halfway across her ceiling before it reached a low point and began to drip on the plaster.

Everyone, from Stephen to Margaret to the law clerks who had left Coker/Standish to join the new firm, had tried to warn her about buying the old Victorian. But no one could come up with a way to get as much office space at anywhere near the same price per square foot. And then there was the money she saved on a place to live. The upstairs apartment, originally the maid's quarters, wasn't exactly palatial, but it was big enough for her needs. As an added bonus, it took less than a minute to get to work. She could be at her desk as late as necessary at night and actually sleep in until seven-thirty the next morning.

She pulled a chair under the stain and started to climb up to give it a closer inspection when the warning buzzer sounded in the entry. She glanced at the clock as she waited for the "all clear" signal. It was dark outside, and too late for a casual visitor or delivery.

For all of the benefits of living and working in the same place there was one undeniable drawback—she was never able to escape the constant tension of waiting for the day the all clear signal didn't sound. She hated being afraid almost as much as she hated the feeling that came when she saw someone sitting across the street in a car she didn't recognize or when someone stayed behind her for more than a block on her afternoon runs. Even now, she was angry at how easily the buzzer sent her heart racing and knotted her stomach.

Finally, the all clear signal came, followed by a knock on the front door. Miranda left her office, turning on lights as she moved through the outer rooms to the reception area. She called to the guard and waited for him to answer with that day's code before she threw the two dead bolts, pulled the brace from the floor, and opened the door.

"What in the hell is going on around here?" Adam demanded.

Miranda's jaw dropped. The impact of seeing Adam again was as physical as mental. A wave of pleasure left her skin flushed; her mind raced with possibilities and questions. "Adam—my God, you're the last person I expected."

"Then I shouldn't think this,"—he waved his arm wide, indicating the security fence, the uniformed guard, and the dog— "was meant for me? I shouldn't take the frisking personally?"

She was too glad to see him to be offended by his sarcasm. "What are you doing here?"

"Excuse me, Miz Dolan," the guard said. "But could you please move this inside?"

"Of course." She stepped out of the doorway.

Adam reached for his briefcase and garment bag.

The dog stood and bared its teeth. "I'm sorry, sir," the guard said, "you can't take that with you."

"It's all right," Miranda told him. "Adam's an old friend."

The man refused to back down. "These things stay with me until I've checked them out."

"It's his job," Miranda explained to Adam.

"There are important papers in the briefcase," Adam said. "I'd appreciate it if you—"

"I'll make sure nothing happens to them."

Adam nodded and went inside. He waited until Miranda had secured all the locks before he asked, "You want to tell me what this is all about?"

She tried to act as if having him there was nothing out of the ordinary, that her heart wasn't pounding so hard she could feel it in her throat, that her skin hadn't gone from mere warm to feeling on fire. "It's a long story."

"Is that supposed to put me off?"

Her gaze feasted on him, taking in every detail from his hair, damp and shiny from the rain, to the look in his eyes, guarded and full of challenge. How could he be more handsome than she remembered, when even her memories took her breath away?

He was wearing a charcoal gray suit with fine pin stripes that fit as if it had been custom made for him. She was sure she recognized his tie as Hermés. This new look was so different, so unfamiliar, it was almost off putting. His jeans and T-shirts had given him an approachability that was missing now. In a strange way the suit seemed to create a barrier between them.

As if he had read her thoughts, Adam removed his jacket and tossed it in a nearby chair. "I'm waiting."

"I'm in the middle of a lawsuit against some people who aren't very happy about the prospect of losing." She had to fight a powerful impulse to remove his tie for him, too. He hadn't said why he'd come, but it didn't matter. He was staying, at least for a while. She felt lightheaded with relief.

"What people?"

"The names wouldn't mean anything to you."

He pinned her with a dark stare. *"Then tell me what would."*

She didn't want to talk about guards and lawsuits and the constant, vitriolic threats on her life. She wanted to talk about him, about them. "Primarily they're the radical arm of the gun groups and several militia organizations that have branches in Colorado."

"I assume you're talking about the lunatic fringe that thinks anyone who doesn't look, act or think like them is the enemy."

"They got hold of Tobias Trout about ten years ago and it turned out to be a match made in hell."

"These are the people you're suing?"

She nodded.

"On what basis?"

"Denial of civil rights to the men and women— and child—who were injured or killed when Tobias Trout followed the preaching of the leaders of those organizations."

"So, you've found a cause," Adam said.

"I think it's more that the cause found me. Being the victim of violence is frequently an activist birthing process. I didn't understand until I was there myself."

Adam didn't say anything right away as he worked to fill in the blanks left by her economical telling of something with such enormous, far-reaching consequences. "It's the members of these fringe groups that have threatened you, I take it?"

"On a daily basis. But then lately even some of the mainstream organizations have started making noises against us. Far more subtly of course, but then they've been at it longer." Their methods of intimidation ran more to campaigns to discredit the suit and those behind it as misguided victims caught up in their need to find someone to blame for their misfortune. The strategy was carefully orchestrated and better financed. "I don't think they took us seriously in the beginning. Now that they know we're in it for the long haul, they're afraid if we win, the result will lead to legislated gun control."

"The mainstream gun people have pretty deep pockets. If they decide to funnel money to these fringe groups, they could keep you tied up for a long time."

"We've talked about that—a lot." If the firm didn't start pulling in some bread-and-butter cases, they would be lucky if the money from the sale of her house and paintings lasted long enough to see them through another year.

Adam picked up a paperweight from the receptionist's desk, tipped it over and watched the snow fall to the dome. "How does Clifford fit into all of this?"

Miranda could see how much the question had cost him. "Prominently, but not the way you think."

"He's not one of your new partners then?"

"As far as I know Clifford has never even seen this place." It was obvious Adam didn't want her to think he still cared. But then why had he come? "In addition to the gun and militia groups and the Trout estate, we're suing several of the partners at Coker/Standish, Clifford is one of them. The way they represented the interests of the families after the shooting was so self-serving it bordered on malfeasance."

He let out a low, soft whistle. "Discovering something like that must have been hard on you."

He understood her so well. "I was outraged. I think in the beginning it was my anger that gave purpose—a 'cause' as you so aptly put it."

"And is it that anger that sustains you now?"

"There's still a lot left, but it doesn't control me the way it once did. I've come a long way, Adam. I'm not the same woman you pulled out of the ocean."

"I can see that." He kept waiting for some sign, at least some mention of the postcard she'd sent. Her surprised reaction to his arrival made it obvious it wasn't because she'd decided she couldn't live without him. All the way there from the airport he'd told himself not to expect more, but it was impossible to keep the disappointment from nearly overwhelming him. Less than two feet separated them. All he had to do was raise his arm and . . . To keep from giving in to his need to touch her, Adam moved to the other side of the desk, pulled out the chair, and sat down.

"The suit with Coker/Standish will never reach the courts. They'll settle first." Miranda ran her hand through her hair in a futile attempt to comb it, desperately wishing he'd come an hour earlier when she'd still been wearing her blue skirt and sweater. The torn jeans and paint-stained sweatshirt she'd changed into when she went upstairs an hour ago for a bowl of soup were hand-me-downs from Keith, and they made her look like a bag lady. The Adam she'd known wouldn't have cared about such things, but she'd seen little evidence that man still existed.

He picked up a pencil and balanced it between two fingers. "Who is the 'we' you keep referring to?"

"We're an odd lot, but dedicated. There are a couple of the attorneys I worked with at Coker/Standish who decided the suits sounded interesting so they signed on. Margaret, she's the one who—"

"I remember you telling me about her," Adam said.

"Anyway, with Margaret and her assistant and four law clerks, there are nine of us working here." Their must notable victory to date had been the fund Coker/Standish had set up for Margaret's medical insurance.

Adam rocked back in the swivel chair and folded his arms across his chest. His body language spoke volumes. "Why the postcard, Miranda? Why didn't you just call me and let me know what was happening to you?"

She frowned. "What postcard?"

"The one you sent a couple of months ago with your name and address on it."

"I didn't send you anything, Adam. There's no way I'd involve you in something like this." Not that she hadn't picked up the phone a hundred times, not that she didn't put herself to sleep every night imagining a conversation between them, and not that she didn't stop at least once a day and realize that what she was doing or saying or feeling was because of him.

He stared at her with a cold fury in his eyes. "Why? Because you still think I'm some kid who needs to be protected?"

"Look around you, Adam. This isn't some game we're playing. The bars on the windows are real and so is the guard outside. It isn't as if there are other law firms lined up to take our place if something happens to us. All these people have to do is get rid of us and their troubles are over."

"And in your mind it's all right for you to assume that risk, but not me?"

She was caught off guard by the depth of his anger. This was her chance. If she told him he was right, that as far as she was concerned, nothing had changed between them, it would send him away. He would be protected, safe from the danger of being around her. But it would be a lie. Before she could answer, the private line in her office rang. "I have to get that," she said, praying he would understand. "I didn't turn on the answering machine and no one calls here this late unless it's important."

"Be my guest."

She hurried into her office but whoever it was hung up before she could answer. When she turned to go back she saw that Adam had followed her. He was staring at the painting on the wall opposite her desk, the one Jason had sent her.

"How did you get that?" It was everything he could do to keep the defeat from his voice. He knew now who had sent the postcard. God, how could he have been so stupid? The clues were obvious, the supposed forwarding to Jason's, the unreadable cancellation mark . . . His disappointment threatened to choke him.

"Jason sent it to me."

"You've been in touch with him then?"

"Almost from the beginning."

Adam felt a deep sense of betrayal. "He never said anything."

"I asked him not to." She moved the chair she'd left under the stain in the ceiling. "About the militia groups, Adam, I don't think you—"

He put a hand up to stop her. "It doesn't matter." Seeking an action that would hide what he was feeling, Adam wandered over to her desk. With seeming casualness, he picked up a photograph and studied it. "Jenny?"

"Amanda—my brother's daughter. It was taken during the week I spent with them this summer."

"You never mentioned having a brother."

"I have two sisters, too. We're getting together for Thanksgiving. We've never done that before." Miranda handed him the other photograph on her desk. "This is Jenny—and Keith."

Adam looked at the man and child that had once been the core of Miranda's life and could no longer hold on to the defensive anger he'd harbored since coming there. He'd never known these people, and that sometimes made it easy to forget what their loss had meant to Miranda—how it had effected her, how it always would. How could he sit in judgment of whatever course she chose to follow to survive and to move on with her life?

"It isn't a very good picture, she was much prettier than that. But it was a special day. I remember the good times more than the bad now." She looked at Adam, needing to give him something for all he'd given her. "You taught me that."

"I wasn't the only teacher, Miranda. I'm not the wanderer I used to be."

A sadness stole over her. She'd never known anyone like Adam. She didn't want him to be different. "I'm sorry. I never meant to change you."

A rueful smile formed. "And at the time it wasn't something I wanted either."

"Are you saying you like the settled life?"

"The transformation I went through was mental, not physical. I don't think anyone would consider the life I'm living now settled."

She didn't understand. "You have a new job?"

"I'm surprised Jason didn't tell you."

"We never talked about you—at least he didn't. In the beginning I would ask questions, but he'd always cut me off." There were times when she'd been so hungry for news of Adam she'd damned near begged Jason to tell her something, anything. He'd steadfastly refused. She'd never decided whether his reticence came from stubbornness or loyalty. Now she wondered if it wasn't something else altogether, something far more clever.

"If you wanted to know what I was doing, why didn't you call me yourself?"

"Jason used to ask me the same thing," she admitted.

"How did you answer him?"

"I didn't."

"Then tell me. I think I have a right to know, don't you?"

She hesitated. "What if I had contacted you? What would you have thought?"

He stared at her a long time. Finally, he said, "Thought . . . or hoped?"

The raw emotion in his voice was a window to the lonely months he'd spent without her. She moved to touch him but pulled back before making contact. "I never meant to hurt you."

"It's in the past."

She could see the lie in his eyes. "Not for me."

"What are you talking about?"

The reasons she'd left, the reasons she'd stayed away were as true and real now as they'd ever been, but she couldn't make them matter anymore, he was too close, her own need was too great. "I love you."

"You have a funny way of showing it, Miranda."

He didn't believe her. She tried to smile. It was either that or cry. "You gave me back my life."

"And you made it clear there was no room for me in it."

"I was wrong."

"When did this revelation take place?"

What had made her believe all she had to do was admit her feelings and everything would be as it had once been between them? She put her hand against her chest as if she could stop the pain. "Why are you doing this?"

He was quiet for a long time, his gaze fixed on the green blotter on the desk. "I'm afraid of you," he finally said.

"Why?"

"I don't know what I would do if I let you back into my life and you left a second time."

The revelation was like a physical blow. Her throat tightened with the effort to hold back tears. "I'm so sorry, Adam."

"Yeah, me, too," he said softly.

"What are we going to do?"

"Before I came here I would have said the answer was obvious. Now, I'm not so sure. You've made a new life for yourself. You've moved on without me."

Damn it, she would not let him go again. "You're just going to give up on us? You're going to let go without a fight?"

"What do you want from me, Miranda?"

"We gave being apart a try. It didn't work. At least not for me."

"You've spent the last year doing everything you could to keep us apart and now you're saying you think we should be together?"

"Yes."

Something deep inside told him not to push too hard, but he was through listening to warnings. "It has to be on my terms."

"All right."

She'd tipped his world over as easily as he had the paperweight. "You don't even want to hear what they are?"

"I don't care."

He studied her. "What if it's marriage?"

"All right."

"That's it? You aren't going to tell me what a mistake it would be and list all the reasons it would never work?"

"I will, if that's what you want, but it won't

change my mind. And there's no way I'll let it change yours."

He'd dreamed this too many times to accept it readily now. "When?"

"Tonight if you want—whatever it takes to keep you from leaving."

Finally, he believed her. He held out his hand and she came into his arms. His eyes closed and he pressed the side of his face into the softness of her hair, letting its fragrance fill his lungs. In that instant he understood what unspoken and unnamed force had driven him back to her, why he was destined to come eventually, postcard or not. After a lifetime of searching, his heart had found its home.

After a while she leaned her head back and looked into his eyes. "Realize this, Adam Kirkpatric, and never doubt it. *I love you.*"

He kissed her then, long and hard and deep, giving his need free reign. She responded with an intensity that almost stole what little reserve he had left. Before he could let that happen, he wanted to tell her that he would bring more than himself to their marriage, that from then on, her fight would be his—his money, hers. "There are some things you don't know about me."

"I don't care."

"You will."

She looked confused and then frightened.

"Good things," he reassured her.

"Then they can wait until later."

Finally there was a reason to smile. "And in the meantime?"

A seed of warmth burst inside Miranda. "You want me to spell it out for you?"

He kissed her again and then murmured against her lips, "As a matter of fact, I do."

Words she'd spoken long ago echoed in her mind. Only then she'd wanted to forget, tonight she wanted to remember. "Make love to me."

"I was beginning to think you would never ask."

"I just needed a little encouragement."

He bent and lifted her into his arms. "Where's the bedroom?"

"Upstairs."

He put her back down again.

"What's the matter?"

The mischievousness was back in his smile. "I know you haven't said anything, but I'm sure you noticed the change. I turned thirty a while back—that puts me in your decade. I'm going to have to learn to pace myself."

Her laughter echoed joyfully in the room as he picked her up once more and she wrapped her arms around his neck. Life would be good to them.

Free Book Offer

Fill out the coupon below and send it together with your store receipt, with the price of *Far From Home* circled on the receipt, to the address indicated below and receive a FREE copy of Georgia Bockoven's novel of love, music, and second chances, *Alone in a Crowd*.

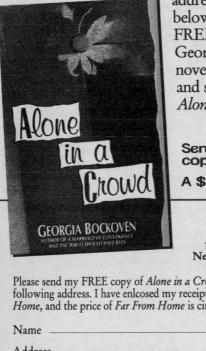

Send for your copy today.
A $4.99 value!

HarperPaperbacks
Free Book Offer
Dept. FC/AIAC
10 East 53rd Street
New York, NY 10022